The Restoration of Grace

Teresa McBride

Photo cover model: Chelsea Keeler
Old Photo Texture stock: poisondropstock.deviantart.com
Art Nouveau Border: solstock.deviantart.com

I want to thank my precious mother, my husband, my family, my children, and my sweet God-friends who have supported me and encouraged me in my passion for writing. I want to thank Brittany Comeaux, my niece, for all of her help with the editing process, and finally yet most importantly, I would like to thank my Heavenly Father for blessing me with the passion and gift for writing. Without all of you, I would not have been able to accomplish this! God bless you all!

Something happened—but what? Grace Beeson pushed her weak and trembling body into a sitting position, rubbing her throbbing head, dazed and confused. Her eyes fluttered wildly as she cautiously gazed around her. Her breath caught in her throat. She was all alone. All she could see was open prairie land with a lone cottonwood here and there, dotting the large foothills in the far distance. The night creatures echoed their evening cry from afar, causing her heart to race in fear.

As her head swam in confusion, she could not help but notice the beautiful sunset snuggling along the hazy ridge as a myriad of colors splashed against the vast horizon.

Any other time she would have gratefully lingered to view the beautiful strokes of color in the western sky, but today was different; instead of being inviting, it was eerie.

"Where am I?" she questioned aloud as her trembling hand reached up to rub the back of her neck, trying to work out the knots in her sore muscles. Her mind was a whirlwind of confusion.

Grace started to pull herself up so she could get her bearings, stopping instantly. She froze, rigid with fright, as she heard the heart-stopping hiss of a rattlesnake. A quick prayer escaped her dry lips as a gunshot echoed in the warm evening air, killing the deadly rattlesnake that was only inches from striking her.

"Sorry to startle you like that, Miss," said the tall, dark figure as he slid down off his dark stallion, silhouetted from the evening sun. "I just wasn't taking any chances on that rattler getting any closer to you than he already was."

"Th-Thank you, Sir," Grace replied with a mixture of relief and trepidation. She was thankful that the rattlesnake was no longer a threat, but silently wondered if the tall and mysterious gunman was.

Where had he come from? She raised her hand to her temple as it continued to pulsate, shooting lightening-like pains throughout her head. Her mouth was dry as cotton and she could taste gritty prairie dirt on her tongue. *What a sight she must be!*

"Howdy, Miss, let me introduce myself," he greeted as he reached out a hand to help her stand. "My name is Cole Matthews."

"Oh, ouch! I-I think something's wrong with my ankle," Grace gasped as she stumbled, instinctively reaching for her injured leg.

"Here, let me help you. Sit back down and I'll take a look at it," the stranger replied with concern edging his voice. Ever so gently he steadied her and lowered her gracefully back onto the dry, dusty ground. "Now where does it hurt, Miss?" he spoke softly, careful not to frighten her.

The young woman's gaze settled upon her rescuer, her heart beating rapidly. His broad Stetson sat low over the stranger's eyes, shadowing his face. His dark brown curls snuck out from underneath his hat as he knelt down in front of her.

Although she could not see him very well, the fear in her slowly subsided by the gentle way he spoke and the tender administration of his care.

As she modestly lifted her skirt, she noticed a small hole in her stocking. Her hands continued to tremble as she unlaced her shoe. "Here, it's my ankle; I-I must have hurt it," she winced as she allowed her shoe to slip to the ground.

He slipped off his leather gloves and placed them beside him on the ground. "May I?" he asked, reaching for her foot ever so gently.

After catching her eye for a brief moment, Cole quickly lowered his gaze and gently palpated her ankle with his fingers. "It doesn't feel broken; it's probably just a sprain, Miss. All the same, though, I'd like to see you to a doctor, just to be sure." The stranger stood to help her up. "If I may ask, what're you doing out here all alone, anyway?"

"Well, I-I don't really know. I must have blacked out. All I remember is waking up with a terrible headache, and then moments later you came to my rescue," she replied, exhaling deeply, trying to sort out her jumbled thoughts.

"Well, that does seem like a problem, Miss, but if you can tell me your name and where you're from, then I can get you to a doctor and back home in no time at all," he replied, "allow me," he said as he effortlessly lifted her up to carry her to his curious mount.

"M-my name?" Grace stammered. Her mind felt as though engulfed in a thick fog; her heart began to race once again.

"I...I don't remember what my name is...I-I can't seem to remember anything. Oh my," she cried as she felt her stomach turn. "Why can't I remember anything?"

"Don't worry, Miss," the man replied as he hoisted her up onto his large stallion. "I'll just take you back to town, and maybe Doc or some of the townsfolk will recognize you. More than likely you just took a bump to your head and have some temporary memory loss...or something like that."

"Yes, maybe so," she sighed, trying her best to arrange her dress in a lady-like manner. She willed her heart to slow to its normal rhythm. *She couldn't fall apart, not now.* Cole climbed up in front of her and took hold of the reins. "I just hope you're right. I'm sure someone is probably worried about me by now."

"I'm sure they are," he acknowledged as he kicked the anxious horse in its sides. "Let's go Jake!"

The chestnut stallion danced around eager to head for home. He obediently turned his head with the pull of the reins and began a slow trot towards town.

"Where're we going?" Grace wanted to know. Reluctantly, she grabbed hold of the stranger's old Benjamin coat as the horse broke into a light gallop.

"Garden City; does it sound familiar?"

"No, it doesn't," Grace sighed with disappointment as she struggled to hold onto the handsome stranger, bouncing from one side of the smooth saddle to the other.

"I'll take you to see Doc Miller first; he's a real nice fellow and real good at what he does. He'll fix you up in no time. Then I'll take you over to Ms. Millie's," he continued. "She runs the boarding house in town. She'll take real good care of ya. She's one of those mother-hen types, if you know what I mean," Cole commented with a chuckle.

Grace rode in quiet distress as she watched the beautiful sunset bed down behind the low hills. She fought to remember something–anything–about her life, not to mention why she was alone and so far from town.

Oh Lord, what is happening? I'm so frightened. Why can't I remember anything? What has happened to make me forget? Please help me to remember and to find my way back home, and protect me in all Thy ways.

Grace felt a sense of peace trickle into her soul after her short prayer, and knew within her heart that no matter what happened, God was in control.

Cole turned slightly in the saddle, breaking into her troubling thoughts. "It's just up here a ways, Miss, just past those hills."

"You don't need to keep calling me 'Miss,' Mr. Matthews," Grace stated pointedly, stopping short as she heard him chuckle. "And what's so funny?" she asked from behind him as her fingers started to cramp from holding on so tight.

"I'm sorry, Miss," he said with a smile in his voice, "I just don't know what else to call you since you can't tell me your name. Just struck me as funny, I guess."

"Oh, you are right at that," she sighed in resignation. "I guess 'Miss' will just have to do until I can remember my name."

A mixture of tears and dust burned her eyes as they traveled on.

Lost in their own thoughts, the two strangers rode in silence with the exception of the steady rhythm of the horse's hooves clopping over the dry prairie.

***

It was late in the evening as the sun had descended, offering only a few light brushstrokes of yellow and orange to light their way into town. Grace was grateful that most of the townsfolk had already closed up shop and headed for home. She was in no mood for questioning stares and small town gossip.

"Whoa, Jake." Cole pulled back on the reins. The weariness of the day was quickly settling over him. "Doc Miller's office is just over there next to the General Store," he nodded as he absently dismounted before her. He lifted Grace off the smooth worn saddle to carry her to Doc Miller's office, and gently kicked the door so Doc would let them in.

"Well, hello there, Cole. Now, who do we have here?" Doc asked, holding up a socket lamp to see them more clearly. Cole nodded, muttered a hello, and crossed over to lay Grace gently on the examining table.

"Well, I'm not too sure, Doc," Cole admitted as he removed his hat, wiping his brow with an already soiled handkerchief he had pulled from his back pocket. "I just happened to find this young lady outside of town. She was all alone and couldn't remember a thing; not to mention she injured her ankle and has a bad bump on her head to boot."

While the men were talking, Grace stole a few moments to study her rescuer. He had removed his Stetson as he spoke, and ran his hand through his flattened curls. In the dancing firelight, she could finally see what he looked like. He did not look as she had expected, but attractive in his own rugged way. She could see that he worked outside regularly by the evidence of his tanned skin, as well as his muscular arms and shoulders molded from obvious hard labor.

Her heart went out to him as she noticed a rough scar etched in his tanned face that hinted of either a horrible accident or possibly a dangerous fight. Nevertheless, she could sense that he was a man with a good heart. Not many men would have been so kind and treated her like a lady as he had.

Cole turned and cleared his throat as he caught Grace staring at him. "Well, I had better get out of here so you can do your thing, Doc," Cole stated as he self-consciously replaced his hat and walked toward the door. "I'll be back in about 20 minutes." With that, he touched the brim of his hat and headed for the door. Grace's eyes followed his stealth figure. *Will he be back?*

"Well, young lady, let's take a look at that ankle," Doc winked with a smile as he slipped off the already unlaced shoe. "My name's Frank Miller. Most people around here just call me Doc. Guess that just goes with the territory," he chuckled as he reached for his glasses. Doc Miller was a kind man with graying hair and a full bushy mustache that twitched when he spoke.

"Oww..." Grace scrunched up her face, bravely pushing through the pain, as he twisted and probed her ankle. She took a deep breath. "It's nice to meet you, but I'm afraid I don't have any money to pay you for your services."

"Ah, don't worry Miss. I'm sure Cole and I can work something out," he said with a twitch of his salt and pepper mustache. "Lucky for you it's just a sprain. I'll wrap it up," he said as he pulled out a roll of gauze from under the exam table, "but you'll need to stay off of it as much as possible for the next week or so."

"But..."

"No buts young lady. Ms. Millie will be more than happy to care for you until you heal."

Doc Miller finished wrapping her ankle, catching her grimace out of the corner of his eye. "I'll give you some pain medicine, but only take it when you need to," warned the kindly old doctor, turning towards his medicine cabinet.

Tears collected on her lashes. "D-do you think my memory will come back soon?"

"We can only wait and see, Miss," he replied, walking back to the exam table carrying a couple packets of medicine. "Sometimes memory can come back quickly—other times it doesn't. It's just hard to say. Everyone is different."

Grace winced as her fingers found the painful lump on her head. "I must have hit my head on something. I have a terrible headache."

"Hmm…let's see. Can you remember anything?" asked Doc, pulling the lamp closer towards them. He pushed back her dark auburn tresses to examine her scalp.

"Nothing at all, I'm afraid, except for tonight."

A shudder shimmied up her spine as she thought of how close that rattlesnake had been. If it hadn't been for Mr. Matthews…

"Well, Miss, you're definitely in good hands with Cole. He's a right nice young man," Doc was saying as he cleaned up the dried blood on the side of her head. "You sure got yourself a good goose egg there and a small abrasion. No need to worry though, it's nothing serious from what I can tell. You just need to keep it clean," Doc ordered as he tossed the bloodstained tissue in the trash.

As Doc Miller walked over towards his desk to record his findings, Grace settled back onto the exam table allowing her thoughts to wander as she waited for Cole Matthews to return…*if he returned.* She couldn't blame him if he just up and left town. What concern was she to him anyway?

Silently she prayed for strength and guidance on what to do about her troubling situation. *What am I to do, Lord? Why am I here? Please help me to remember and find my way back home.*

Cole returned just as he said he would. She sighed in relief at seeing the kind stranger once again, her heart going out to him as she could see the evidence of pure weariness resting upon his chiseled features. He nodded towards Grace, pulling his Stetson lower over his eyes, conscious of the scar she had noticed earlier. The men talked quietly. Grace knew by their hushed voices that they were discussing her condition as well as her bill as Cole dug into his front jeans pocket and handed Doc some crumpled bills before turning his attention to Grace.

"Looks like Doc got you all taken care of, Miss. Here, let me help you sit up," Cole said as he splayed his large hand out across her back. The feel of his strong arms sent a strange sensation throughout her entire being.

"Doc says that he'll give you a crutch to use while you're mending. Good thing it's only a sprain, it could've been much worse," Cole hurried on as he noticed her staring again. "Let's get you on over to Ms. Millie's. It's getting late."

Cole accepted the crutch from Doc's hand and firmly secured it under Grace's arm. "I'm not sure if I can do this," she cringed, tentatively lowering her injured foot to the floor. "I've never had to use one of these things before."

"You'll do fine, Miss. Just use the crutch in place of your injured foot, and you'll get the hang of it fast enough," Doc stated as he opened the door and stepped aside, anchoring his thumb inside his vest pocket.

"Thank you, Doctor. You've been very kind," Grace said as she hobbled to the door with a weary, although gracious smile.

Cole repressed a sigh as he noticed her beautiful smile. *What am I getting myself into?* Cole asked himself as they stepped out into the star-studded darkness. A beautiful *and* helpless woman…*Lord, give me strength.*

Chapter Two

The night air was warm and balmy with a multitude of twinkling stars up above lighting their way through town. Under different circumstances, Grace would have enjoyed the nightly stroll, but tonight she was in an unfamiliar town with unfamiliar people, and faced with an unknown future.

Even though Grace could sense a certain goodness about Cole, she was still a little uneasy about being alone with him on such a dark and desolate evening. She wondered why he was being so kind to her and why he didn't just drop her off at the doctor's office and be on his way. *He must have a family to care for,* she told herself. Many questions plagued her thoughts as Cole patiently guided her down the boardwalk. She could hear the ruckus and the lively piano playing from the saloon down the street and shivered as she thought of all the other men who could have come to her rescue, grateful that God had sent her the kind man beside her to take care of her.

There ahead of them was a large two-story clapboard house with a lamppost in the front yard. After a long and tiring day, the soft glow was a welcoming beacon to her weary soul and her body longed for a soft bed and a good night's sleep.

"Well, Miss, this is the place, Ms. Millie's Boarding House–best care in all of Kansas," he assured her. Grace reluctantly leaned heavily on Cole's arm as he helped her maneuver the crutch up the steps.

Her body was so close. He held his breath as he helped steady her footsteps, trying to shake off the feelings that were taking over his body. He did not want to admit his attraction to the young woman; he didn't think his heart could take it.

"I'll come by in the morning to check on you," he said softly as he knocked on the front door. He shifted uncomfortably as they waited; the thought of her eyeing the nasty scar on his cheek up close was unsettling.

To his relief, the growing sound of heavy footsteps echoed behind the front door. "Well, I'll be…what brings ya out this late at night, Cole?" asked a smiling, rotund woman.

Ms. Millie Ramsey, her white hair neatly twisted into a loose bun, was the perfect picture of a dear grandmother. Her eyes danced with delight as they swept over Grace with hopes of a new border to spoil.

"Howdy, Ms. Millie," Cole smiled as he tipped his hat courteously, "can you put this lovely lady up for a night or two?"

"Of course! Come in, come in," she exclaimed as she led them into the elegant, yet homey parlor. "What's your name, dear?"

"She doesn't remember, Ms. Millie," Cole spoke up. "She has amnesia and a sprained ankle," he replied as he settled his Stetson back upon his dark curls.

Cole yawned, dipping two fingers into his front shirt pocket. "Doc said she would need a teaspoon of this powder tonight, then only when needed after that. I'll come by in the morning to fill you in on the rest, but right now we both need some sleep."

"Alright, dear, that's just fine; I'll see that she gets some warm milk in her belly and a good night's rest. Go on now," she said, playfully shoving Cole towards the door. "Tell your Ma I said hello."

Cole tipped his hat and with a half-smile, he disappeared into the night.

Grace's eyelids were heavy as she surveyed the interior of the early Victorian parlor. The whitewashed walls contrasted well with the burgundy velour curtains, which set off the room with simple elegance. Upon further inspection, her eyes were drawn to a beautiful flagstone fireplace that was proudly displayed at the far end of the room, flanked by lovely rosewood bookshelves. On the adjacent wall, rosewood end tables graced both sides of a burgundy velour sofa with matching plush wingback chairs positioned across the room. To top it off, scenic Currier and Ives prints graced the open wall space.

A large sewing basket sat at the foot of one of the wingback chairs. Draped on one of the padded arms was a lovely piece of floral fabric that Ms. Millie had surely been sewing just prior to their unexpected arrival.

"Here, dear," Ms. Millie smiled as she guided Grace to the beautiful medallion-back sofa. "Sit down and I'll fetch ya a cup of warm milk and a couple apple muffins I baked earlier. Make yourself at home."

As Ms. Millie bustled toward the kitchen, a handsome young gentleman came strolling down the stairs. The sound of heavy footsteps startled Grace.

"Well, hello. I hope I didn't alarm you, Miss," said the young man with a smile. Grace quickly noted his striking appearance, his crisp white shirt and dark pinstriped suit. "My name is William Hollister II, and whom may I ask, are you lovely lady?" he asked as he laid his matching hat on his broad chest in a mock bow.

"Oh, hello, I-I…" stammered Grace, self-consciously she attempted to wipe the dust and wrinkles from her traveling dress. *I must look dreadful!*

"Good evening, Mr. Hollister." Ms. Millie boomed as she waddled back into the parlor. "I see you're getting acquainted with our newest guest," she smiled as she placed a tray of milk and muffins on a nearby table.

"Yes, Ms. Millie, I was just introducing myself, but haven't learned this lovely lady's name yet," William stated, gesturing towards Grace with a twinkle in his eye.

"Well, as a matter of fact, we don't know her name," Ms. Millie clucked with a shake of her head. "Cole brought her here just a few minutes ago. She has amnesia, don't you dear?" she asked as she sympathetically patted Grace's shoulder.

Grace sighed deeply as the clock on the mantle chimed 10 o'clock. "Yes, Ma'am. If you two would excuse me, it has been a long day, and I feel as though I could drop. If you could just show me to my room, I'd be greatly appreciative." Grace pasted on her best smile. She was tired, frustrated at what she could not remember, and hurting. She wanted to be alone, to rest, and to pray. A single tear slipped down her dusty cheek, leaving a thin smudged trail.

"Oh my, of course, dear," Ms. Millie acknowledged. "Mr. Hollister, would you help her up the stairs while I bring up her tray?"

"I'd be more than happy to oblige."

Before she knew it, the stranger scooped her up into his arms and carried her up the stairs. She started to protest, but knew that her efforts would be futile at best and resigned herself to his assistance, as barbaric as it may seem. She was just too exhausted to care.

Mr. Hollister gently laid her on the soft feather bed, said good night, and tipped his hat as he exited the door.

Grace found herself blushing as Ms. Millie rambled on about drinking her warm milk with the dissolved medicine.

Her face grew hot at the very thought of Mr. Matthews and Mr. Hollister holding her tonight. She tossed the thought aside. It could not be helped she reasoned with herself, but even as that fact surfaced, she also realized that she actually enjoyed the attention. *Oh, what has come over me?*

Forgive me, Father. I am exhausted and not myself. Help me to not let either one of these men take my mind off You. Please take away my fear and help me to remember who I am and why I am here.

She gratefully reached for the cup of milk and pursed her lips. It tasted sweet with just a hint of bitterness. *I hope the medicine will help me rest as well.*

Ms. Millie busied herself with lowering the sheets and the beautifully hand-stitched quilt. Wearily, after slipping off her dirty travel dress, Grace slipped her aching feet between the coolness of the sheets and laid her head back into the softness of the feather pillow. She closed her eyes, feeling as though she could sleep for days.

"There, now, you're all tucked in for the night. Can I get you anything else, dear?"

At the shake of Grace's head, Ms. Millie gently blew out the oil lamp and closed the door behind her.

The last thing Grace remembered was thanking God for the wonderful people in Garden City and for always watching over her. Surprisingly, a comforting verse floated through her weary mind. *'Be strong and courageous...for the Lord your God will go with you; he will never leave you nor forsake you.'* (Deuteronomy 31:6) Carefully turning on her side, slipping her hand beneath her pillow, she snuggled down into the covers and quickly fell asleep.

***

As the bright morning sunlight danced on the beamed ceiling above, Grace awoke to the enticing aroma of frying bacon and fresh bread. For a brief moment, she forgot where she was. As she rolled over, the realization hit her, feeling the pain shooting up her leg. Grace peered around the strange room. She smacked the bed in frustration as tears instantly burned her eyes. *It wasn't a dream, I'm really here. Oh, what am I to do?*

There was only one thing she knew she could do, and that was to go to her Heavenly Father in prayer. She might have lost her memory, but she could never forget her Heavenly Father and for that, she was very grateful.

A sweet peace settled upon Grace ever so gently as she spent some much-needed time talking to the Lord. Minutes slipped by quickly as she lay in sweet contentment communing with the Heavenly Father.

Liken to a shift in the wind, her thoughts suddenly turned towards the two men who came to her aid the day before. She blushed and chided herself for pondering such things. *I have to get them out of my mind and try to remember something– anything.*

A light tapping at the door interrupted her troubling thoughts. "Good morning, dear," Ms. Millie's muffled voice floated through the door. "I have your breakfast."

"C-come in." Grace spoke up as she quickly swiped at her tears.

Ms. Millie opened the door with one hand, while balancing the food-laden tray with the other. "How's your ankle this morning darlin'?" Ms. Millie asked with motherly concern, laying the tray on the bedside table.

"Good morning, Ms. Millie. Did you happen to bring up my medicine? Doc said I could take it when needed, and I believe this would be a good time," Grace admitted with a half-smile, as she carefully scooted herself up in bed. "My ankle is throbbing."

"Yes, dear, I put it in your bedside table, so you'll have it when you need it," she said as she opened the bedside drawer, pulling out the envelope. Ms. Millie stirred the medicine in a cup of hot tea and handed her the beautifully floral etched teacup. "Here dear, now drink up," Ms. Millie prodded as she turned to open the window. "I'll be up in a bit to take your tray, but no rush," she hurried on, 'maybe then we can get you into a nice warm bath. In the meantime you can enjoy the fresh morning air."

"Mmm, yes, Ma'am," Grace nodded as she slowly sipped on her hot-spiced tea. "I'd like that, thank you." Grace closed her eyes and said a silent prayer of thanksgiving for the wonderful breakfast before her, as the older woman slipped quietly out the door.

Grace's stomach growled in eager anticipation as she forked a bite of the fluffy scrambled eggs. The food smelled wonderful. She did not realize how hungry she was until that very moment. She had fallen asleep so fast last night that she had forgotten about the apple muffins, which still sat on the bedside table, cold and hard. No wonder she was so hungry. Who knows when she ate last? Grace sure didn't.

She continued to enjoy her breakfast while gazing around the freshly painted bedroom. The walls were painted white with delicate floral patterned wallpaper. On the far wall stood an old rosewood chamber set with a beautifully etched mirror hanging above it with hand-stitched floral hand towels hanging neatly on the towel rack. An old stand-up chest stood along the wall near the door, displaying beautiful hand-carved foliage along the drawers and legs. Near the window, opposite from the bed, sat a quaint old Boston rocker with beautiful matching flowers etched on the headrest.

Grace admired the homey room and inhaled deeply of the fresh dewy air. Her mind drifted, as if in a trance, watching the pale yellow curtains sway back and forth with the cool morning breeze. She forced a smile as she finished her breakfast; it was a new day with new possibilities and with God, anything was possible!

Chapter Three

"Mornin', Sanders," Cole greeted as he casually strolled into the General Store, smiling at the older man working behind the counter.

"Good morning, Cole. Nice to see ya," the tall middle-aged man replied as he wiped his dusty hands on his work apron. "I was just doing some re-stocking. My help has taken ill, so I'm pulling double duty for a few days," he smiled. "What can I get for ya?"

"Oh, I don't need anything today. I'm just tryin' to help a young lady locate her family. You haven't seen or heard of anyone with a missing relative, have you?" Cole asked as he plucked off his Stetson and ran his calloused hand through his thick dark curls.

Leaning his elbow on the smooth wooden counter, he continued, "The lady's over at Ms. Millie's. I found her last night alone on the prairie. She can't seem to remember anything, not even her name," he said as he swiped his hand over his clean-shaven chin. "I've been to the Feed Store, Tom's stable, the Town Square Restaurant, and even to Clancy's Saloon, but I can't seem to find anyone who might know of her. I tried the Sheriff, but he wasn't in his office; I thought you might have heard something."

"Nope, I can't seem to remember hearing anything of the sort," the storekeeper replied as he scratched his head in thought. "If I do, I'll be sure to let ya know. Is there anything me and the Missus can do to help?"

"Just appreciate if you would spread the word and keep your ears open," he said with a smile. "Whelp, I guess I had better get over there and see how she's doing. Maybe her memory will come back soon, so this mystery will be solved quickly," he laughed. "Oh, and if you see the Sheriff, let him know I'm lookin' for him, if ya would."

Walt nodded as Cole grabbed his hat from the old worn counter and begun to walk away when the storekeeper stopped him.

"Hey, wait a minute, Cole," Walt said, holding up a finger in thought. "I do remember a few wagons passing through here the other day. I'd just bet that she might belong to one of those families, wouldn't ya think?"

"Hmm…couldn't hurt to check it out. I'll go to the Post Office to see if there's been any telegrams or missing person's reports. Maybe Adam has heard something. Thanks, Walt. I'll let ya know."

The sun was shining brightly, and the day was beginning to heat up as Cole absently wiped the beading of perspiration from his brow. *This is going to be a hot one*, Cole thought as his long legs carried him across the dirt-packed street towards the Post Office.

As he walked, he found it difficult to keep his mind from drifting to the unknown woman who has taken residence at Ms. Millie's boarding house, not to mention his mind as well. He knew he had a lot of work to catch up on at the ranch, but he couldn't help but be drawn to helping her. He wanted to help her find her family. She seemed so helpless, so lost…and so pretty. His heart went out to her, or was it maybe a little more than that? Cole tried to shake the thought, but the look of sadness in her eyes captured the protectiveness in him. His work could wait; he would try one more place.

Cole stepped onto the boardwalk, with the sun in his eyes, and accidentally bumped into someone. "Uh, excuse me," he said turning to the tall, solid figure.

"Hello, Matthews," came the curt reply.

Cole shielded his eyes, coming face to face with his ex-business partner as he steadied himself against the wooden post. Cole's eyes turned cold. Biting his lip, he held back the harsh words that were trying to escape from deep within his throat. Without a word, Cole eyed William Hollister sharply before quietly walking away.

I am not going to let him get the best of me. I have other matters to attend to; I will deal with him later, Cole promised himself as he entered the Post Office. Just thinking about Hollister made his blood boil.

He scolded himself again, remembering that he had given the situation over to the Lord a couple years back, and he was going to let Him take care of it. At least he was going to try.

"Cole is everything all right?" came the concerned feminine greeting.

Cole shook his head, trying to forget his wayward thoughts and looked up at the sweet face sorting the morning mail.

Amelia Cornwell was about the sweetest girl he ever knew. He grew up with her in school. She had married his best friend, Adam, this past fall and they were now expecting their first child sometime in mid to late June.

Cole admired and respected them both a great deal. Adam was the one who had led him to the Lord years ago when he was going through a rough time after losing his father. Adam's father and Cole's father were good friends for many years until Adam's parents had moved away to take care of his ailing aunt.

"Oh, good morning Amelia; I'm sorry, I was just lost in my thoughts, I guess," he smiled, as the angry creases in his forehead relaxed. He removed his hat, and as habit, ran his hand though his unruly hair. "I'm fine. How're you feeling?"

Amelia's eyes lit into a smile as she gently rubbed her bulging belly. "I'm doing well; just a little more tired and more uncomfortable than yesterday. I hope that this next month goes by as quickly as the last ones have," she laughed as she rubbed the small of her back. "I don't know how much more my back can take. This child feels as big as a lumberjack already!" she said with a twinkle in her eye.

"I can't believe that harebrained husband of yours is making you do all this work," he said smiling, thrusting his thumb in the direction of the pile of mail in front of her. "Where is the task master, anyway?"

Amelia chuckled as she continued to stamp the mail. "Adam went to deliver a parcel to Widow Harvey. She's down in her back again and feeling poorly. I asked him to keep an eye on her for me."

Sweet Amelia, always thinking of others; if it was not for the jarring buggy ride, she would be out there delivering the mail and checking on the widow herself.

"Is there anything I can help you with, or did you just come over to visit?" she smiled as she continued to stamp and sort the morning mail.

"Well, it's a long story, but there's a lady over at the boarding house, who I found out on the prairie last evening, and she can't remember anything. I was wondering if you've heard of anyone looking for someone or something of the sort. A lost person's report, maybe? Walt said that a small wagon train passed through here a couple of days ago. I thought maybe she might belong to them."

"Hmmm...I haven't heard of anyone," Amelia commented, her eyes drifting up to the rafters in thought, stamp in hand, "but I'll be sure to ask Adam when he gets back. I just came down a little while ago to cover for him. He should be back pretty soon…oh my," Amelia's face crumpled as she grabbed her protruding belly.

"Amelia, what's wrong?" Cole asked with concern as he quickly stepped around the counter.

"I'm not sure," she said with a forced smile. "I believe this little one is getting quite tired of the cramped quarters. Probably more so than his mama," she laughed as another contraction quickly seized her, almost doubling her over.

Just then, Adam walked in with the mail pouch slung over his shoulder and quickly took in the scene before him. "Amelia, are you okay?" he asked, dropping the mail pouch as he hurried around the counter.

"Just had a little pain, that's all," Amelia reassured him, still holding her belly. "Nothing to be concerned about, I'm sure."

Cole interjected, "I'll run to get the Doc."

Amelia put up her hand in protest, "No, really don't fuss, it'll pass."

Adam led his wife to a nearby chair. "Just the same, I want Doc to take a look at you. You look awfully pale."

**

Cole ran across the street, quickly dodging the passing wagon's, and threw open Doc Miller's door with a thud.

"Boy, you sure do know how to make an entrance, don't ya?" Doc asked, peering over the top of his spectacles in alarm, as he was cleaning a cut on a young man's foot.

"Sorry, Doc. Amelia doesn't look so good and she's having some bad pains. We'd like for you to take a look at her," Cole reported, almost breathless.

"Just as soon as I finish up here; run over to Ms. Millie's and ask her if she would care for Amelia until I get there. This shouldn't take too long, but I still need to stitch this young man up."

"Don't worry," Doc assured him as he noticed the concern on Cole's face. "Ms. Millie knows what to do. She's delivered almost as many little ones as I have. Now get going," he urged, with needle in hand, as he leaned over to stitch up the lacerated foot before him.

Cole heard the young man moan in pain as he hastily ran out the door, almost tripping over his feet in the process.

"My goodness Cole, what's going on?" Ms. Millie asked, laying her sewing aside, startled at the urgency of his entrance.

"Amelia's having pains," he said between breaths. "Doc told me to come and get you until he can get there."

Once again, Cole removed his hat and nervously ran his hand through his hair as he impatiently waited for Ms. Millie to gather her things and inform Jed as to where she was going.

Jed is an old boarder who stays with Ms. Millie for no charge, as he helps with the chores, gardening, handiwork, and the like. There was never anyone more loyal to Ms. Millie than Jed was. Some thought he might be sweet on Ms. Millie, but he has never made it known.

Ms. Millie bustled in the room still yelling instructions over her shoulder, "…and don't forget to put the biscuits in the oven. Keep an eye on the roast and potatoes, and don't let it boil over…oh, and don't forget to check on our guest. She'll need you to go pick up her breakfast tray soon, but don't let her get up, she has a sprained ankle and needs to stay in bed." Ms. Millie swung her shawl over her shoulders and shoved Cole out the door. "Well, let's go, dear, times awastin'."

Cole and Ms. Mille hurried down the street as the midmorning sun moved further along its circuit, sending a hazy mirage over the hot boardwalk. Dust hung thick in the air as wagons and people hurried by, kicking up the fine particles in their wake.

"Whew," Ms. Millie replied as she patted at her brow with her handkerchief. "It's gonna be a scorcher today."

Ms. Millie went on, changing the subject as she picked up her pace, "I hope it isn't time for Amelia to deliver that babe just yet," she muttered anxiously, talking half to Cole and half to herself, "it's way too early."

The little town was alive with dogs barking, children playing and the normal daily activities. Oblivious to their turbulent emotions, the passersby greeted Ms. Millie and Cole warmly as they hurried to their destination.

In no time at all, Ms. Millie opened the Post Office door, with the usual tinkle of the bell, lifted her skirts and hurried up to Amelia's room.

Cole paced impatiently, wiping his brow with the back of his sleeve. Adam finally appeared, relieved that Ms. Millie was there to take over Amelia's care.

"How's she doing?" Cole asked, already guessing the answer by Adams troubled expression.

"Not good, not good at all. She's doubled over in pain. I-I don't think this is normal, Cole. Something's wrong…something's terribly wrong. It's too soon." Adam trembled as he spoke and started to pace.

The anguish in his friend's eyes tore at Cole's heart as he walked over to stop Adam from his pacing and slid his arm around his friend's shoulder. "Let's pray."

Adam nodded, numbed by the possibility of losing his baby and possibly his wife. It is incredible how one's life can turn upside down in just mere moments. Tears slipped silently down his cheeks as the two men knelt together in prayer.

Our Dear Gracious Father, we don't know what's going on, or what's going to happen, but You do. We ask for wisdom for Ms. Millie and Doc as they tend to Amelia. We ask for comfort and peace and for the safety of Amelia and the baby. Thy will be done. In your precious name we pray, Amen.

Cole helped Adam to a nearby chair and walked into the back room to fix a fresh pot of coffee.

Moments later Doc came rushing in, bag in hand. Digesting the distraught faces before him, he hurried up the stairs, praying he was not too late.

Chapter Four

From upstairs at the Boarding House, Grace heard the front door open with a thud and Ms. Millie yelling, though she could not understand what she said.

Was that Cole's voice?

Peaked with concern and curiosity, Grace pulled herself up out of bed to see what was happening and hopped toward the door, quietly turning the knob.

"What d'ya think yer doin' young lady? Doc said yer to be off yer feet," quipped a kindly old man before her, bushy brows raised in question.

Startled, Grace jumped back.

"Howdy Miss, I'm Jed Anderson, Ms. Millie's handyman," the old man smiled, showing what few yellowed teeth he had left. "She wanted me to come and check on ya. Sorry if I startled ya."

Grace held onto the open door, balancing herself on her good leg, embarrassed that Jed had caught her out of bed and in her nightgown, no less. Flustered, Grace closed the door to a crack and peered out at the old man.

"Oh, that's okay. I was wondering what all the commotion was. Is someone hurt?" Grace asked, concern edging her voice.

Jed held up a gnarled arthritic hand. "Everything's just fine, Miss. Ms. Millie had to go help deliver a young'un. When Doc's busy or needs help, they call on Ms. Millie. She's delivered more babies than I can count," assured the old man with admiration in his voice.

"I see."

"Heard ya got in last night, sorry I wasn't here to meet ya proper like. I was a little under the weather and went to bed early. Anyway, if you'll give me yer tray, I'll take it to the kitchen for ya."

"Well, Mr. Anderson..."

"Just call me Jed. Mr. Anderson's too formal fer me," he admitted with a good-natured wink.

Grace smiled. She liked Jed already. "Well, alright then Jed, if you don't mind, I'd like to get dressed first. If you could give me about 15 minutes and then come get my tray, I'd greatly appreciate it."

"Sure thing Miss," he said with a nod. "I'll be back. Holler if ya need anything."

"Thank you."

Grace hobbled to the end of the bed in search of her dress she had shed the night before. It was nowhere to be found; in its place, she found several clean dresses and nightclothes laying on the chest at the foot of the bed.

Ms. Millie had obviously laid them out for her use. *What a dear lady she is*, Grace mused as she carefully slipped into a pale blue dress. She silently chided herself as she noticed the dirt under her fingernails, reminding her of the night before. Her dirt covered hands contrasted sharply with the beautiful blue of the dress. She decided to wait as she did not want to soil the lovely garment, carefully slipping it off and laying it back upon the trunk.

She hobbled over to the etched mirror above the washbasin and surveyed her appearance. She cringed. Her hair was a disheveled and matted mess, dirt streaks were obviously visible on her face from the many tears she had shed the previous evening.

Fresh tears started to form as she studied her reflection, stirring up emotions that she was not ready to deal with just yet.

Trying to redirect her thoughts, Grace knelt gingerly beside the bed on the braided rug and bowed her head in prayer.

Dear Lord, I pray that You go with Ms. Millie and guide her with wisdom as she helps deliver this baby. Be with the parents and comfort them. Let them feel Your presence. And, please be with the little one, may it be healthy and complete. Thy will be done. In Your Holy name I pray, Amen.

***

Amelia lay softly moaning as Doc examined her and checked on the position of the baby.

"Well, Amelia," Doc announced, hiding the concern in his voice, "it looks like it's time. No stopping this young'un now; you can push when you're ready."

Amelia twisted in pain. "It's too soon!"

"Shhh, it's ok honey, just push!" Ms. Millie assured her. She held her hand as another painful contraction slowly moved the baby further down the birth canal, encouraging her softly.

With Amelia delivering early, it didn't take long to push out the tiny infant. With a muffled scream, she wretched in pain as Doc assisted in pulling out the little purplish body.

With a pained look of alarm, Ms. Millie was instantly at his side. The baby was not responding. Trying to catch her breath, Amelia realized in horror that she could not hear her baby crying.

"Doctor," Amelia gasped, "what's wrong with my baby? Why isn't he crying?"

"Now, now, dear," Ms. Millie crooned as she hurried to Amelia's bedside. "Sometimes it takes a few minutes to get a little one to respond," she advised as she gently wiped Amelia's brow with a cool cloth. Silence loomed as the doctor worked feverishly to save the small child.

"I...I don't know how to say this Amelia." Doc's husky voice cracked with emotion as he gently wrapped the infant in a soft blanket, "he...he didn't make it. I'm so sorry. He was just too small."

Amelia lay in shock as Doc handed her the tiny lifeless bundle and sadly turned away. Even though this was his job, it was never easy to see the pain and grief on his patient's face.

"Millie, I'll need to finish up here," he said, turning to wash his hands, "Could you please go down and talk with Adam?"

Ms. Millie nodded numbly, fighting the tears that clouded her vision. Woodenly, she walked out the door, stiffening as she heard Amelia's heart wrenching sobs tearing at her very soul. She knew all too well the pain of losing a child.

Downstairs, Adam and Cole impatiently paced the floor praying with each breath they took. Just as Cole was ready to go upstairs to see what was taking so long, Ms. Millie walked slowly down the last step with tears streaming down her weathered cheeks.

Sadly, she took Adam's trembling hands in hers and gazed sadly into his anxious eyes; without words, Adam knew what she was going to say.

"Amelia, is she…," he choked on the words.

"She's doing as well as can be expected, Adam. The baby…was just too tiny. He--"

"Ms. Millie," Doc yelled from up the stairs. "Come quick!"

Quickly, Ms. Millie turned on her heel, picked up her skirts, and ran up the stairs as fast as her heavy body could carry her.

"What is it?" She asked breathless as she ran into the room, fear etched on her face.

"Amelia's having more labor pains. I think we may have another one in there by the looks of it," he exclaimed, perspiration dotting his forehead. "I can't get her to push. Please talk to her."

Ms. Millie hurried over to Amelia's bedside.

"Amelia, dear, you heard Doc, you have to push! I know you're tired and hurting, but you must push!" Gently Ms. Millie shook Amelia out of her pain and grief. "Push, Amelia, push!"

With one deep breath, Amelia scrunched up her face and pushed with all her might. Out popped a tiny pink wiggly body, which instantly cried at the top of his lungs. What a beautiful sight!

"It's another boy, and he's alive…he's alive!" Doc announced with joy-filled emotion.

"Praise the Lord!" Ms. Millie exclaimed with fresh tears in her eyes.

The baby continued to cry as Doc checked him over thoroughly and handed him to Ms. Millie so she could clean and swaddle him in a warm blanket.

Doc reached down to Amelia and gently extracted the lifeless little body out of her firm grasp while Ms. Millie replaced her empty arms with her newborn son.

Still in shock, Amelia's red-rimmed eyes fell upon her new son as she burst into tears. Sobs shook her body as she lay there, holding tightly to her baby boy.

Ms. Millie knelt by her bedside and prayed a prayer of gratitude and strength while Amelia's grief mixed emotions spilled out uncontrollably.

The baby started to cry a little louder.

"Amelia, you must try to feed him," Ms. Mille urged as she nudged the baby towards her breast. Amelia absently complied as Doc Miller sneaked out of the room to inform Adam of his new son.

Doc descended the stairs with a heavy heart and found Cole holding onto Adam. At the sound of heavy footsteps on the stairs, they turned with fearful expectation. They were confused after hearing the baby cry. Was it Ameila?

"Adam, I'm real sorry about your little one, but I came to tell you that Amelia had twins, and the other boy has survived. H-he's almost perfect. A little small, but he seems to be in good health." Doc smiled a bittersweet smile as he sympathetically patted the young man's shoulder.

Shocked, Adam grabbed onto the slat-backed chair beside him as a fresh stream of tears flowed all over again. "And, Amelia, is she alright?" he questioned eagerly.

"Amelia's fine. Tired and grieving, but fine. Go to her, Adam. She needs you, and you need to meet your new son."

That was all Adam needed to hear. He bounded up the stairs two at a time.

Doc turned to Cole, wiping the perspiration from his face with a clean hankie extracted from his vest pocket. "I'm glad you were here, Cole. I know Adam would have fallen to pieces otherwise. The Almighty sure has a way of working things out."

"That He does, Doc…that he does."

***

"Miss, if you're dressed, I'll take your tray now," Jed called through the bedroom door.

"Actually Jed," Grace hollered through the door, "if it isn't too much trouble, do you mind if I take a bath first? I feel as though I have more dirt on me than the prairie."

"Oh, of course, Miss. Let me take yer tray down, and I'll be right up with the tub and some hot water."

Grace opened the door for him to retrieve her tray and smiled her thanks as she noticed the twinkle in Jed's eyes. *What a sweet man*, Grace mused. "Thank you Jed, you're very kind."

As Grace waited for Jed to return, her thoughts traveled towards Ms. Millie, wondering how the delivery was going. Grace sat perched on the edge of the bed and closed her eyes, imagining what it would be like to have a little one of her own to love.

Many troubling thoughts whirled around in her mind like dust in a windstorm. *Do I have any children? Can I have children? Do I even have a beau?*

Oh, I have to stop this; she scolded herself as she shook her head, trying to dislodge the tangled web of thoughts. *It's all in the Lord's hands anyway.*

She whispered another prayer as she overheard Jed's labored breathing as he reached the top step.

"Here ya are Miss," Jed gasped, short of breath, as he deposited the galvanized steel tub at her door with a clang. "I'll be right back with the water; it's heating on the stove."

"Jed," Grace asked in concern, rising from the bed, "Are you alright?"

Jed paused a moment. "Yes, Miss, I think so. I just get a little winded sometimes," he chuckled. "I guess this old body just ain't what it used to be."

A little while later Grace found herself relaxing in a warm bath with just enough water to wash and rinse with. She felt bad that Jed had to carry the many buckets of hot water up the stairs, and so, only accepted enough to get a decent washing. She lingered in the tub as long as possible until the water turned cool.

Still early in the day, she allowed herself extra time in getting dressed and brushing out her coppery curls. It made her feel so much better to be clean, free from the dirt and grime of the prairie. Longing to know the outcome of the delivery, she headed downstairs.

Chapter Five

Cole walked out of the Post Office emotionally drained, absently maneuvering down the busy boardwalk to Sheriff Burge's office. Townsmen were sitting and standing around, leisurely catching up on town news, as the women were rushing by to do their shopping with children in tow. Everyone was going about their daily activities, oblivious to the grief that was weighing heavy on his heart. Lost in thought, he walked into the Sheriff's office in a daze.

"Heard you were lookin' for me, Cole, what can I do for ya?" questioned the Sheriff wryly, leaning back in his chair with his feet propped upon his old wooden desk. By the looks of it, he had just finished his lunch, a rather large one at that, as its contents were scattered all over the already cluttered desk.

"Sheriff," Cole nodded in greeting as he plopped into the scuffed wooden chair the Sheriff had offered him with a silent wave of his hand.

Absently he ran his hand over his chin in thought, making a mental note to shave the next chance he got. He looked around. "I see that Sam's back in today," he said with a shake of his head, noticing the drunkard passed out in the nearby cell. "How's his wife doin'? I heard that he took a lickin' to her the other day. Is she any better?"

"Don't rightly know. Haven't seen her in awhile," Sheriff Burge stated, taking a big gulp of water as he wiped his wet mouth with the back of his dirty sleeve. "She used to come in every once in a while to do some shopping, and even a few times to bring him some food when he'd gotten 'imself arrested, but this time I haven't seen hide nor hair of her."

"Hmmm…I hope she's alright. Maybe you should ride out to check on her."

"Don't see why I should bother to do that," quipped the Sheriff, picking his yellowed teeth with a small wooden pick.

"My days are busy enough without goin' and gettin' my nose in other folks' business."

"Because you're the Sheriff," Cole grated between clenched teeth. "If he has hurt her or those kids, then we need to know so we can help them. Besides, wouldn't your wife be upset if she knew that they may be in trouble and you didn't go out to check on them?" Cole questioned, trying not to raise his voice.

Why on earth they ever elected this man as Sheriff he would never know. The man is as lazy as the day is long. Every once in a while if Sam, the town drunk, gets into a fight, the Sheriff will lock him up for a couple days, but then he lets him go with a warning until the next time it happens. If Sam was anyone else, he would probably be harder on him, but Sam is his wife's cousin, and so, he puts up with him to appease her.

Cole was jolted out of his thoughts as Sheriff Burge loudly, and crudely, cleared his throat with a loud belch.

"Yea, well…I guess I might have a little time this afternoon to ride out there 'n check on 'em," he said as he crumpled up a wad of paper and tried to shoot it into the wastebasket and missed. "Wouldn't want Myrtle gettin' all bent out of shape again; not that she was ever in any good shape to begin with," he said, laughing uproariously at his own crude joke.

Cole was not laughing. He glared at him distastefully and cringed as he heard Sam starting to stir in his jail cell, hoping to be long gone before he woke up.

"Hey, Sheriff, you gonna get me out a here 'er what?" Sam exploded with a slur and an angry rattle of the bars.

"Just settle down, Sam; you know the drill. I won't let you out until you sober up, so go back to sleep," he ordered with an amusing smirk on his face.

Sam slurred a few choice words, stumbled back over to his cot, and passed out again. Cole shook his head, turning his attention back to Sheriff Burge.

"Well, Sheriff, the reason I was looking for you is that I found a young lady on the prairie yesterday, and she has no memory of anything. I was wondering if you knew of anyone who might be looking for her."

The Sheriff eyed him a minute, deep in thought, as he scratched his whiskery chin. "Ya know, I think I recall someone saying something about a wagon train that came through here a few days back, but I don't recall anyone missing someone," he said as he leaned over to put a pinch of tobacco in his mouth. "But I'll do some checkin' around and see what I can come up with," he mumbled.

"I'll wire ahead to Holcomb to see if anyone has heard anything. That was the next town the wagon train was going through. Maybe someone will figure out that she's missin' by then," he said with a snort, spitting a stream of tobacco juice towards the spittoon. He missed, splattering Cole's boot in the process.

Cole shook his head, too tired to deal with the Sheriff any longer. He had better things to do with his day than to sit and reason with this man. He excused himself and headed out the door not much wiser than when he went in.

***

"Easy does it, Miss," Jed warned kindly as he slowly guided Grace down the narrow wooden steps. "We don't want to take a tumble."

As they neared the bottom step, Cole walked haggardly through the front door, stopping short as he spied Grace and Jed descending the steps. Just the sight of her made his heart skip a beat. She was more beautiful than he had thought. Her hair was freshly washed and combed, and glowed in the sunlight streaming through the window.

"Ms. Millie'll be here as soon as she can," he announced, pulling off his hat and absently swiping his fingers through his hair. "She's still over at the Cornwell's," he continued, twisting his hat nervously in his large, tanned hands.

Jed motioned him towards the Parlor an offered Cole a seat as he helped Grace to the sofa.

Cole sat perched on the edge of the chair, playing with his hat, head bowed. He hated to be the bearer of bad news.

Taking a deep breath, he plunged ahead as the other two took their seat. "Amelia had two little boys today, but unfortunately one didn't make it."

Both pairs of eyes lifted quickly, with a sudden intake of breath; Cole easily caught the evidence of shock and sympathy as he continued. "Miss Millie'll probably be over there awhile. Amelia and Adam need all the love 'n support they can get right now," Cole reported solemnly, accidentally knocking his hat to the floor with a sigh.

"I'm so sorry," Grace replied sincerely, her dark brown eyes pooling with unshed tears. "Is there anything I can do?"

Cole gazed up into the most beautiful sparkling brown eyes he had ever seen. "Just pray."

Grace could sense that he was struggling with his emotions. She was impressed and greatly touched at what a caring and compassionate man he was proving himself to be. Casting her sullen eyes towards Jed, she sadly shook her head as she silently lifted the grieving family in prayer.

With the evidence of unshed tears in his eyes, Jed rose awkwardly from his seat, offering his guests some refreshment. "Care for a glass of cold lemonade?"

Grace smiled through the veil of unshed tears, grateful that Jed was so thoughtful. "Actually, could I trouble you for a cup of coffee? I just feel so tired."

Jed nodded, "Of course, Miss, no trouble. I'll be right back."

The somber mood permeated the parlor, like a thick fog, as Grace dabbed at the corner of her eyes and timidly addressed Cole.

"Mr. Mathews, if you think it would be alright, c-could I go visit her? I mean...do you think she would mind? Maybe she needs someone to talk to, or maybe even some help with the little one," Grace asked shyly, watching Cole lean back into the plush chair with a sigh.

"It's Cole," he replied huskily, staring her straight in the eyes, causing her to blush.

"Oh, sorry," she replied, flitting her lashes anxiously.

Cole was unable to pull his eyes away, feeling as though he was captured within the very depths of her soul. Struggling to keep his mind on the conversation, he forced himself to look away, softening his tone as he did so.

"I think that would be a great idea," he agreed, picking up his Stetson and brushing it off. "Might do her good to meet someone new and take her mind off of things. I have some more errands to run this afternoon, but I'll stop in and ask her if she'd be up to it."

Just then, Jed came ambling back into the room with a silver serving tray containing one coffee cup and two tall tinkling glasses of ice-cold lemonade.

"Here ya are Miss." Jed carefully held out the coffee cup with a slightly wobbly hand. "Be careful, it's hot."

Grace smiled, tears still lingering on her lashes. "Thank you, Jed."

Jed walked over and handed Cole his glass. Grasping his own glass tightly in his arthritic fingers, he deposited the tray on the end table and sat down in the opposite chair to finish their visit.

Staring down into her cup, Grace pursed her lips to sip the hot brew, trying with all her might to avoid the inquisitive pearlescent blue eyes across from her.

Cole, feeling a bit uncomfortable in the young woman's presence, quickly finished his lemonade, and after a brief visit, politely excused himself, much to Grace's disappointment.

Chapter Six

"Cole! Whoo-hoo!"

Without even turning, Cole instantly recognized the sugary voice behind him. Maryanne Brewster, daughter of the town banker. Cole tried to ignore her, but the shrill kept coming closer. Not to be rude, as his mother had taught him, he stopped and turned in resignation.

"Cole," Maryanne scolded with a pout of her cherry lips, "didn't you hear me?"

"Oh, hello Maryanne, I'm sorry; I guess I was lost in thought. How are you today?" he asked with a wry smile.

Maryanne eyed him skeptically, placing her well-manicured hand upon his arm. "Why, Cole, what on earth has you so distracted today?" she asked in a tone dripping with honey.

Maryanne knew exactly what…or in this case, who was distracting him. Her defenses were up as soon as she heard that there was a new young, pretty woman in town who was stealing all of Cole's attention, and she did not like it.

Cole smiled, although the smile did not reach his eyes. He knew Maryanne well enough to know that she knew all too well, what went on in town.

Her mother has been trying to get them together for the past three years ever since he took over his father's ranching business. He was not yet well to do, as her mother would call it, but her mother knew that it was very possible and that there were not many young, attractive, and available men left to marry her daughter before she turned spinster age.

Maryanne was very attractive with raven dark hair and sapphire blue eyes, but he had found out years ago that her beauty was only skin-deep. He had escorted her to a church social a couple years back, but after the laughing spectacle she made at someone else's expense, Cole knew that it would never work out. They were just too different.

"I just have a lot to do today, if you'll excuse me," he mumbled, turning to leave.

"Nonsense," she spat as she scurried in front of him to block his departure. "You didn't seem to be in a big hurry earlier," she pouted playfully. "Why don't you come over for supper tonight? Mother's fixing a big roast. There will be plenty," Maryanne baited, batting her long eyelashes and twirling her lacey parasol.

"I'm sorry, Maryanne, I just don't have the time. I have a lot of business to attend to."

"Well, how about tomorrow night then? You have to eat sometime," she replied matter of factly, trying to disguise the irritation in her voice.

"No, I'm afraid not. Maybe another time," Cole stated a little too emphatically. "I do need to go. Good day, Maryanne."

Stunned, Maryanne turned with an angry flourish of her skirts. *Humph! I'm not giving up on you so easily, Mr. Matthews,* she fumed silently. She had to figure out a way to get Cole Matthews to notice her once and for all!

***

"Mother!" Maryanne yelled with the slam of the screen door. "Mother! Where are you?"

"I'm right in here. You don't have to yell," her mother called from the parlor.

Maryanne rushed into the parlor and angrily told her mother what had happened with Cole.

"Can you believe it, Mother? He brushed me off, just like that," she pouted as she plopped down into the plush velour sofa. A few dark curls fell haphazardly about her heart-shaped face.

Cecilia Brewster, exasperated with her daughter's immature antics, placed her teacup on the side marble-topped table and regarded her daughter sternly.

"Darling, as I told you before, you need to start acting more mature if you want to get a man like Cole to notice you. He's not the type of man who will just fall at the feet of a beautiful woman."

With an exaggerated sniff from Maryanne, her mother walked over to where she was sitting on the circular sofa and took her slender hands in hers. "Maryanne, I love you honey, and I only want the best for you, and we both agree that Cole Matthews is the one for you, but you have to act more like the kind of woman he wants," she whispered with a sly smile. "You know…sweet, demure, innocent *and* mature…that sort of thing."

With the look of disgust on Maryanne's face, her mother went on. "Now, now dear, I know that your, uh…personality is not exactly like that, but once you get Cole to fall in love with you…well… you know what they say…love is blind, and then you can give up your little *act*, if you know what I mean," her mother interjected with a lift of her well-manicured eyebrows.

Maryanne was skeptical, her face brightening slightly. "Oh, Mother, do you really think it would work?"

Cecilia patted her daughter's dainty hand with a wink. "Trust me, dear, it will work…how else do you think I got your father to marry me?"

"Mother!" Maryanne squealed, stifling a giggle.

"Shhh," she replied with her finger against her lips, "it's our little secret."

Maryanne jumped up excitedly and gave her mother a tight squeeze before racing up the stairs to plan her next move.

***

Grace tried to reposition herself on the plush sofa and lifted her coffee cup, hoping that what was left of the tepid liquid would calm her jumbled nerves.

Jed had excused himself into the kitchen to finish the dinner preparations, leaving Grace alone to sort out her thoughts. With a heavy sigh, she bowed her head, knowing that the only way she was going to get any clarity was to bring her petitions before the Lord.

After her prayer, one of her favorite verses floated through her mind as softly as a sweet melody soothing her soul, *"And we know that in all things God works for the good of those who love him, who have been called according to his purpose."* (Romans 8:28)

Grace smiled as a warm tear slipped down her cheek, feeling as though her Heavenly Father had reached down and wrapped his arms around her.

Thank You, Lord. I know You have my life planned for Your purpose and that only goodness will come to me because I love You and desire to do Your will. Help me to remember that promise. Praise You, Father!

Moments later, she heard Ms. Millie bustling through the front door. "Oh, my, I didn't realize how long I've been gone," she panted, obviously out of breath as she hurried to the kitchen.

"Jed is the roast finished?" she asked as she lifted the lid of the big iron pot. Steam spiraled out of the pot as she poked the tender chunk of beef with a fork.

"Yes'm. Everything's ready, Ma'am," he said, stepping out of the way so she could take over.

Ms. Millie placed the lid back on the cast-iron pot with a satisfied look. "I was so worried. I was afraid something would burn, but I should've known that you'd have everything under control," she said as she continued to bustle about the kitchen checking on the wonderfully prepared dinner.

"Jed, everything smells delicious. Thank you so much for all your help!" Ms. Millie squealed as she gave Jed a quick hug.

Ms. Millie hurried to spoon the food into the serving dishes, oblivious to the boyish grin on Jed's face as he carried the plate of warm golden biscuits to the dinner table.

As the bold aroma of roast and potatoes floated into the parlor and tickled Grace's nose, she reached for her crutch and slowly made her way towards the dining room. Just as she passed the front door, Mr. Hollister walked in. Pleasantly surprised at seeing Grace freshly dressed, he quickly placed his hat on the coat rack with a smile and held out his arm.

"At your service, Miss."

"Well...thank you, Mr. Hollister." Cheeks flushed, the young woman lowered her eyes shyly and accepted his assistance as he helped her to her chair and pulled it out for her.

"If I may?" he questioned, pointing to the empty seat beside her.

Grace looked up. "Uh...yes...be my guest," Grace stammered. "Sit wherever you would like."

"Oh, my dear, how are you feeling?" questioned Ms. Millie, still out of breath as she brought in the last serving dish, heaping with garden fresh green beans.

Glad for the distraction Grace smiled, averting her eyes. "I'm doing well, Ms. Millie, thank you. Jed has been most kind and helpful," she added, eyeing Jed, who had just sat down and started to smother a generous amount of churned butter on a warm flaky biscuit.

The old man looked up with a wink. "Can't say I was too helpful, Miss, with trying to finish up dinner and Cole's visit and all," he admitted, taking a bite of his buttery biscuit.

Ms. Millie nudged him with her elbow, silently reminding him they had not yet said prayer.

"Excuse me, if we could take a moment and say grace," she turned to Jed. "Would you mind?"

Ms. Millie closed her eyes and bowed her head in expectation.

Jed swallowed, cleared his throat, and blessed the food. *Dear Lord, thank Thee for Thy bounty and for this day. Amen.*

Jed took another bite of his biscuit as he passed the steaming serving bowl to Ms. Millie with a wink.

Ignoring him, Ms. Millie turned her attention to her guests. "Mr. Hollister, with all the excitement today I haven't asked how you are," Ms. Millie stated apologetically, holding the serving bowl in midair.

"I'm doing well, thank you." Mr. Hollister spread the linen napkin out over his lap. "I heard you had quite the excitement today. How is Amelia feeling?"

Ms. Millie cleared the lump in her throat and passed the steaming bowl of potatoes before she spoke. "Well, I suppose you've all heard about the Cornwell's since Cole was here earlier," she said sadly, looking around the table.

Jed and Grace nodded sorrowfully as William Hollister looked up in question, brows raised, unaware of the recent tragedy.

A shadow passed across Ms. Millie's face as she explained to William what had happened.

"How awful for Amelia and Adam to lose such a precious blessing, but how gracious the Lord is to give them another one to help ease their grief," Grace exclaimed bittersweetly, reaching for her glass of iced tea.

"Yes, it is a shame," William chimed in with his deep baritone voice. "I mean no offense, but I just don't see how anyone can praise a God who would give a life, then take it away so quickly. It just seems cruel that…"

Shocked, Grace sucked in her breath and eyed William out of the corner of her eye, trying to hold her tongue. Unfortunately, her emotions got the best of her and her blood started to boil.

"Mr. Hollister," Grace interrupted a little too emphatically in a higher than normal pitch, shifting towards him. "It is the Lord who gives life as a gift; and if and when He chooses, it is Him who can take it away. I am *sure* that He did not do this to Amelia and Adam to be cruel. Everything He does is for our good. We may not know why this has happened, but He must have had a good reason, or he wouldn't have allowed it."

Trembling from the audacity of her boldness, Grace lowered her gaze and fidgeted with her napkin.

The room was quiet with only the light sound of tinkling silverware on the porcelain plates as the others ate in silence.

Grace, embarrassed by her loud outburst, cleared her throat and took another sip of her tea. She was a stranger in town, and instead of acting like the Christian woman she knew she was, she shot off her mouth like an immature child.

She breathed a prayer for forgiveness and peered around the table discreetly, trying to hide her embarrassment.

Fighting her flesh, she turned to William to apologize. "I-I'm sorry for my outburst, Mr. Hollister. I don't know what came over me," she said quietly as she lifted her glass, swallowing her tea along with her pride. "I am not one to judge, the Lord is, and I apologize for my rude behavior."

"Not necessary, Miss," Hollister replied with a smirk, forking a large bite of the steaming roast. After swallowing his food, he continued. "Although," he goaded, pointing his raised fork in her direction, "you apologized for your outburst, but not for what you said. Does that mean that you actually believe that?" he teased with laughter in his eyes as he took another bite.

Grace could see by the glint in his eyes that he was baiting her, probably hoping for a good-natured rebuttal. Choosing to ignore his mocking attitude, she nodded her head in devout conviction. "Yes, I do Mr. Hollister…with all my heart."

Grace stubbornly attacked her potatoes, silently announcing that the conversation was finished, as she heard Ms. Millie chuckle.

"Good girl," Ms. Millie stated proudly. "I knew you were a sweet girl, and I am right proud of you for standing up for your faith." Ms. Millie was all smiles as she took a rather enthusiastic bite of her green beans.

"Oh, speaking of," Ms. Millie swallowed, trying to redirect the conversation, "since tomorrow is Sunday, would you two like to join us for church services?"

"Oh, I'd love to," Grace admitted sincerely. A smile lit her face at the thought of hearing God's Word again. "I-I may not know who I am or where I'm from," Grace confessed, "but in my heart I know the Lord, and I know that He will guide me." Grace's eyes danced as she smiled at Ms. Millie. "I will be looking forward to it!"

All eyes settled on William Hollister as he reddened under the expectant stares. "Oh," he replied as he cleared his throat and patted his napkin around his mouth uncomfortably. "I do apologize, Ms. Millie, but I have another engagement tomorrow. Maybe another time," he said, absently downing his glass of tea and reaching for another biscuit.

"Yes, maybe another time, Mr. Hollister," Ms. Millie smiled knowingly, "maybe another time."

Chapter Seven

Cole entered the Post office, with the usual welcome of the tinkling bell above the door and walked quietly upstairs to Amelia and Adam's room. Upon hearing voices, he lightly rapped on the door.

"Come in," Adam responded in a raspy, sullen voice.

Cole entered the small room and noticed Adam sitting quietly in the rocker holding his newborn son.

The atmosphere was tense. Cole shifted his feet uncomfortably and addressed Amelia. She looked tired, and he could tell that she had been crying by the puffiness around her eyes and the splotchy redness on her face.

"Amelia, how're you feeling? Is there anything I can do?"

"Hi Cole, I think we're doing all right," she sniffed, swiping at the tears that continued to fall. "Thank you for coming and for being there for Adam during all of this. I'm so glad he had you to lean on."

Cole reached out and held Amelia's hand in comfort. His voice cracking with emotion, "I'm so sorry about your loss."

Amelia squeezed his hand, her chin trembling with a fresh round of tears. "I know. Thank you, Cole, we all are, but I'm resting in the fact that God knows best, and I do thank him that we have little Nathaniel here to help ease the pain."

As Amelia spoke, her teary, red-rimmed eyes rested on her sleeping baby, held protectively in her husband's arms. She lowered her voice and looked back at Cole, eyes pleading. "Please talk to him, Cole. He's taking this so hard."

Cole nodded in understanding. Releasing Amelia's hand, he walked over to where Adam was mechanically rocking the sleeping child, his gaze fixed straight ahead on nothing in particular.

Cole placed his hand on Adam's shoulder. "Let me see that little guy," Cole said as he lifted up the edge of the soft blanket. "He's a fine lookin' boy, Adam. I see you named him after your father. He'd be proud."

"We named our first son James, a-after my father," Amelia stated sadly. "He..."

Adam's eyes shot up quickly. "I don't want to talk about him. He's gone now." His eyes challenged her to continue.

Amelia's face crumpled. She was shocked and hurt by her husband's sudden outburst.

Cole sent Amelia a sympathetic and reassuring nod, silently telling her with his eyes that he would speak with him.

"Hey brother, why don't you give the little one to Amelia so we can talk for a while," Cole asked as he tried to lift little Nathaniel out of Adam's firm grasp. Adam finally relinquished his hold, acknowledging that he did need to talk to someone; he even surprised himself with his outburst.

Shoulders slumped in grief; Adam followed Cole out of the bedroom and into the nursery room next door. Cole gazed around the room. The nursery contained an old Saratoga trunk in the far corner under the open window and a Boston rocker sitting near the wooden cradle. Colorful rag rugs graced the cool planked floor in front of the rocker and cradle, adding splashes of color to the otherwise dull room.

"Adam, have a seat," Cole insisted, pointing to the rocking chair. Adam plopped down into the rocker, feeling as though his heart was lodged in his throat, constricting his airway. His emotions were so intertwined; a deadly combination of anger and grief, a mix that was very hard to fight, and it scared him.

Cole scooted the trunk near the rocking chair and gently perched on the edge with his elbows on his knees, trying not to put his full weight on it, fearful he would fall through. "Adam, I really don't know what to say, but I know that Amelia's troubled about the remark you made in there and the way you're handling James's death."

Adam looked up at Cole, eyes blazing with pent up anger and grief. "I told you I don't want to talk about him."

"Adam, we need to. You need to come to terms with your loss. You have to deal with this so you can go on with life, life with Amelia and Nathaniel."

Cole's tone softened.

"Adam, God gave you a beautiful wife and a beautiful son. Yes, you lost a son and that is devastating, but don't let that stop you from giving yourself to the family that's still here. God wants…"

"Don't talk to me about what God wants!" Adam exploded. "What about what I want? What about what Amelia wants? It was all taken away in an instant!" Adam snapped his fingers and rose to pace the floor. "You have no idea how I'm feeling right now, but you're telling me to think of what God wants? You want me to pretend this never happened?" Adam's chest heaved in emotional agony.

Cole shook his head, praying for the right words. "No, that's not what I'm saying, but you can't let this destroy you. If you don't deal with this now, you'll let this grow deeper into your soul, and it will destroy your family…and eventually your faith."

Adam's face darkened. "This will not affect my family. I love Amelia and the baby, but right now, I'm angry with God for lettin' this happen. He could've stopped it. He could've saved James!" he cried, turning towards Cole, his face void of color.

The grief on Adam's face was almost more than Cole could bear. His life-long friend, his brother in Christ…oh, how his heart hurt for him. He couldn't blame his friend for being angry, but he didn't want that anger to grow and take root.

Cole reached over, enveloping Adam in a brotherly embrace. The loving touch made him wrench in pain, fighting the comforting arms.

Finally, succumbing to the need of comfort, as a child in its mother's arms, Adam broke down, sobs shaking his body. Cole held him until his emotions drained and slowly led him back to the rocker.

Cole kneeled beside his friend and took his trembling hand in his. "Adam, we need to pray."

Adam shook his head. "It's no use. He won't listen to me." His head fell into his hands.

Cole swallowed hard, fighting his own tears. "Then let me pray for you."

Our Dear Heavenly Father, I come to You today to ask You to take this burden from Adam and Amelia. I know that You did not cause them to lose their little one, but allowed it to happen for whatever reason we are unable to see just now. I pray that You will comfort them and lift them to You at this time. I pray that You will take away not only the grief, but also the anger that Adam is feeling. We know that we are human and that You made us this way, so You know that our flesh is weak, but in You we are made strong. Give him the strength to lean on You during this time, and don't let the

Devil get a foothold on his soul. I pray that through this You will lead him closer to You and that You will bless him and his family and that he will see how blessed he truly is. In Your Son's name we pray, Amen.

The two men sat for a long moment to collect their thoughts as they heard a loud cry echoing from the next room. Cole stood and quickly wiped his tears with the back of his sleeve.

Trying to lighten the mood, he thumped his friend on the shoulder, "I can tell already that your boy has your temper," he teased.

Adam peered into his friend's face, his eyes speaking volumes. "I guess it's time to introduce you to my son."

The edges of Cole's mouth turned up into a smile. The two men walked back into the next room where Amelia was swaying back and forth, singing softly to quiet the crying infant. As they entered the room, Amelia looked up, taking note of the half smile tugging at her husband's lips and reached out to him.

Adam walked over, grasped his wife's hand, and sat down on the edge of the bed to gaze upon his wife and new son.

Choked with emotion, Adam reached for little Nathaniel and turned towards Cole.

"Nathaniel Adam Cornwell, meet your Uncle Cole." Adam smiled through his tears as he held the squirming infant.

Cole swallowed the lump in his throat and reached down to take the offered child. He was a beautiful baby with a patch of dark hair on the top of his small head and dark blue-gray eyes that were alert, looking straight at Cole. Cole's heart melted instantly as baby Nathaniel wrapped his little finger around his.

"Hey, I think he likes me," Cole replied with a laugh.

Amelia wiped her eyes and gave a weak laugh. "Well, who wouldn't like their new uncle?" she smiled. "Even though you're not his real uncle, you certainly fit the bill with us."

Cole's eyes sought hers. "Thank you."

He gave Amelia a slight wink after she mouthed the words 'no, thank you' above Adam's head as he reached for his son.

"Well, I'd better go and let you two have some time to get acquainted with your little one. Oh, by the way," he turned, catching the couple in an embrace.

Amelia pulled away from her husband and child. "Yes?"

"That woman I was telling you about earlier; she wanted to know if she could come by to visit?" he questioned, settling his Stetson back on his head. "Maybe she could help you out a bit until you're feeling better. She needs something to do, and I think you two would get along well."

"Oh, of course," Amelia smiled. "I'd love to meet her. Tell her she's welcome anytime."

***

As the evening sun spilled its pinkish rays into the cramped jail, Sheriff Burge awoke with a start at the sound of heavily booted feet. Quickly drawing his gun, he jumped out of his chair, knocking it to the floor, gun poised and ready to shoot.

"Hey, Sheriff, it's just me…put that thing away. You're liable to kill somebody!" his Deputy shrieked, quickly darting out of his aiming direction.

The Sheriff shook his head, returned his gun to his holster and sat back down. "I told ya to never sneak up on me like that, boy," he replied tersely, leaning back in his old wooden chair, kicking his feet back upon the desk. "Did ya check on Sam's wife and young'uns like I told ya to?"

"Sure did, Sheriff. Missus is pretty banged up, but the young'uns seem to be ok. I asked her why she hasn't come to bail him out and she said that she was just plum tired of him, and he could rot in here for all she cared."

The Sheriff shook his head in dismay. "Well, I guess I should have a talk with 'im. I can't keep 'im here much longer if she isn't going to file a complaint, but maybe I can threaten some sense into him."

"Hey, Sheriff, on my way over to Sam's I came across this here book," he said, pulling it out of his leather vest pocket. "It has a name in it." He flipped open the cover to show him. "See here, it says Grace Beeson. What do ya want me to do with it?"

"Let me see it," the Sheriff ordered as the deputy stood perusing through the pages.

"Looks like it might be someone's diary. My sister used to write in one of these. I don't see no sense for 'em, but she sure liked it."

"I said give it here," the Sheriff barked, extending his hand.

Deputy Turner heaved a sigh with a shrug of his shoulders, and tossed the book to the Sheriff.

"If you're gonna throw it away, give it to me. It'll give me somethin' to occupy my time with," the Deputy chuckled. "Might be pretty interestin' readin'."

The Sheriff skimmed through a few of the pages. "Hmmm…Grace Beeson; do we know anyone by that name?" he asked, taking a moment to read one of the private entries.

"Doesn't ring a bell to me Sheriff. What'cha gonna do with it?"

Deputy Turner pulled out a piece of beef jerky and hiked his leg to sit on the edge of the Sheriffs marred desk.

"Well, I'll leave it here for now to see if anyone comes to claim it," he said, tossing the diary on a stack of papers. "We don't know how long it's been sitting out there, but we'll give it a few days."

As the men were talking, Cole sauntered in. "Howdy, Sheriff, Deputy," he greeted with a curt nod. "I was walking by and thought I'd stop in to see if you have any news about the young lady I told you about."

The Sheriff shrugged, a smirk playing about his lips. "Nope, can't say I do, but if I hear anything, I'll let ya know."

Cole rolled his eyes. *Why did he even bother?* As he was turning to leave, he noticed the small diary sitting grossly out of place on the Sheriffs cluttered desk.

"What's that, Sheriff?" he asked pointing to the book with an embossed rose on the front cover. "Sure doesn't look like anything that would interest you."

The sheriff lowered his scuffed boots back to the floor. "My Deputy found it out on the prairie while running an errand for me this morning. He brought it in so we could find the rightful owner. Probably dropped by one of the ladies from the wagon train," he stated as he picked up the book and handed it to Cole. "Have you seen it before? It has a woman's name in it by the name of Grace Beeson."

The Sheriff walked passed him to pour himself another cup of coffee as Cole flipped through the pages.

"Hmm, I wonder…hey, Sheriff, do you mind if I take this with me? I've got a few more errands to run and I can ask around; might save you some time."

"Well, I don't know." The Sheriff debated for a minute, rubbing his whiskery chin in thought. "I think we should put it up for safekeeping since it's so personal and all," he replied, catching the Deputy's eye with a wink.

"I agree, but how can I ask around if no one knows what I'm talking about? It'd be too much of an inconvenience for them to come here," Cole stated his argument. He just had a feeling about this and needed to put his mind at ease.

"Alright, but just for today," the Sheriff conceded, raising his chipped coffee cup to his thin, chapped lips. "If you don't get any response, bring it back here, and I'll lock it in my drawer, for safekeeping of course."

The Sheriff chuckled as he took a big swig of his stale coffee and settled back in his chair.

"Uh, yeah, thanks," Cole replied absently as he walked out the door, still skimming through the pages.

Feeling as though he was intruding, he quickly tucked the book under his arm and hurried to Ms. Millie's, eager to show the diary to the young lady, in hopes that she would recognize it. *Hmm...maybe this mystery will be solved quicker than we had thought.*

Chapter Eight

After supper, as Ms. Millie rose to clear the table, William Hollister assisted Grace into the parlor and helped her onto the large plush sofa.

"Thank you, Mr. Hollister." She said with a slight lilt in her voice as she rearranged her skirt about her legs.

"Please, call me William. It looks as if we will be running into each other rather frequently," he drawled with a twist of his sleek black mustache, displaying his perfectly straight teeth.

"All right, if you insist," she agreed, cheeks reddening. Nervously she tucked a lock of auburn hair behind her ear.

William sat across from her and eyed her admiringly, obviously not one for small talk. Grace squirmed under his intense stare and readjusted herself on the sofa trying to think of something to say.

Finally, she took a deep breath, and plunged in, "So, William, what do you do for a living?"

William leaned back, interlocking his hands behind his head and perched his ankle upon his knee. "Well," he said proudly, "I'm a horse trader. I buy and sell horses for ranchers." At the look of assumed interest, he went on, "I like it because it keeps me busy, but it also gives me a chance to travel."

William's mustache twitched as he spoke, his eyes sparkling in unconcealed admiration of the beautiful woman before him, oblivious to her lack of attention.

"Next week I'm off to Colorado Springs to see a man about starting my own ranch," he stated, twisting his sleek mustache once again. "He has some mares that are ready to breed so I'm going to make sure they are well-bred and worth buying. If I'm lucky, he might even offer to sell his ranch. He's thinking of moving south."

Grace sat, staring past him, lost in thought.

"Maybe you'd care to join me on a buggy ride before I leave next Saturday?"

Still no reply.

He leaned towards her to gain her attention and cleared his throat. "Miss?"

Grace's face grew red with embarrassment as she realized that she had not been listening.

"Oh, excuse me, what was that?" Grace replied, trying to compose herself, raising her eyes to meet his.

"Miss, is there something wrong?" he questioned, dark heavy brows knit in concern.

"I'm sorry William; I guess I just need to go lie down. I don't feel so well," she apologized, placing her hand to her temple, "If you would get my crutch for me, please?"

"Of course," he acknowledged, jumping up to do her bidding. "Would you like me to help you upstairs?"

"No, thank you…I can manage," she replied with a weak smile.

Just then, Ms. Millie came in from the kitchen, cheeks red from her labor, stopping short as she noticed Grace's tired, drawn features.

"Oh dear, here, let me help you up to your room," Ms. Millie exclaimed, lightly dabbing at the beads of sweat that dotted her brow. Tucking her handkerchief back into the cuff of her blouse, she rushed over with a rustle of her skirts.

Grace felt a wave of relief as Ms. Millie came to her rescue. "Thank you, Ms. Millie. I was just telling William that I was tired and needed to lie down."

William politely excused himself with a broad smile. "Well, I have things I must attend to. Good evening, Ladies." With a wink and a tip of his hat, he was gone.

Cole, having missed William by only minutes, rushed into the Boarding House anxious to speak to Grace about the mysterious diary.

Upon hearing the door open, the two women turned on the stairs. Cole could see that Grace was troubled, but hoping that he could give her some good news, he stopped them.

"Wait, Miss, I need to speak with you a moment." At the look of hesitation in her eyes, he went on, "Please, it's important. I have something I need to show you."

He quickly extended the diary.

The two women looked at Cole curiously. "What is it?" Grace asked as Ms. Millie grabbed her elbow to assist her back down the steps.

"I was hoping that you could tell me." Cole opened the book to the first page and pointed to the name. "It says that it belongs to a Grace Beeson."

He watched Grace intently, studying her reaction. "I was hoping that this might be yours. It was found out on the prairie, not far from where I found you."

Grace was in shock. It was all too much to take in. "I'm sorry. I think I need to sit down for a minute."

Could it really be mine? Grace's heart quickened. She was afraid to get her hopes up, but also afraid of what she might find hidden within its pages.

Ms. Millie assisted Grace back to the sofa as she sat next to her, holding her breath. Cole sat across from them, anxiously perched on the edge of the chair, watching Grace as she lightly ran her fingertips over the embossed rose on the front cover.

"This does look familiar, but I don't recall it being mine," she admitted, gazing pensively up at Cole and Ms. Millie. "Would you mind if I read through it a bit to see if...," Grace's voice quivered at the thought of what answers, if any, might be lying right at her fingertips.

Cole didn't take his eyes off of her. "I was hoping you would. It would certainly answer a lot of questions if it was yours," he stated, nervously twisting his hat in his hands.

"But, I hate to read something so personal if it isn't mine," Grace sighed in an almost inaudible whisper.

"C'mon, dear," Ms. Millie stood and reached for Grace's crutch, "You look plum tuckered. Let's get ya upstairs and you can look through that later, alright?"

"Yes'm."

Cole hid his disappointment as the women excused themselves.

"Excuse me, Miss," Cole stopped them halfway up the stairs. "I forgot to tell you that Doc and Amelia thought it would be a great idea if you'd like to go over for a visit."

Grace smiled her thanks, diary in hand, and turned to go up the stairs.

***

Cole, knowing he had to get away from town to think, mounted his chestnut stallion and headed towards the edge of town. He steered his mount toward his ranch knowing that everything was well under control at the hands of his twin brother Joel, but he needed to check on things just the same.

Cole gave Jake his head as he traveled the familiar road home. He found himself reminiscing about the days when they were small boys, always wanting to follow in their father's footsteps. Martin Mathews was a strict man, but very loving and devoted to his family. He raised his boys the best he could under God's law, but eventually the boys got caught up in teenage rebellion. When they turned sixteen they wanted to try their own wings, against their father's will, and had drifted away from their close-knit family circle, not caring about anyone but themselves.

Joel, his twin brother, had left one day after an argument with his father that had been mounting for some time. From then on, the relationship between Cole and his father was strained, tearing the family apart. Cole never knew exactly what the argument was about, but knew that his father was furious and that Joel had ran off. Over the course of two months, they hadn't heard from Joel until he wrote and said that he was up North helping a family with their farm. He continued to write occasionally, sending money when he could, but their father just became more stubborn and withdrawn. The whole Matthews household was in turmoil. Their mother blamed their father for forcing Joel to run away.

Months later, Joel finally returned after hearing that their father had suffered a serious, almost fatal, accident.

"I'm sorry son," his father apologized on his sick bed, eyes sullen. "I treated you, your brother, and your mother, not as God would have wanted me to, but as I wanted to. You had every right to get mad at me for not letting you take on some real responsibility on the ranch. I guess I just wasn't ready for you boys to grow up yet…or maybe I didn't think I'd be in complete control anymore," he admitted with a shake of his head. "But after you left, Hollister finally showed his true colors. We found out that he was the one who stole our brood mare and sold it to the McMurray's. He and your brother got into a horrible fight," Martin choked up as his mind's eye replayed the horrible event, "almost cost him his life. That's why he has that bandage on his cheek."

Martin shook his head in shame. "I'm sorry for not believing in you, son. I love you, and I'm glad that you're home. The Lord has been working on me a lot lately, and He's given me this chance to change. I-I just hope you will help me…and forgive me."

Joel could see the tears pooling in his father's eyes. Swallowing his pride, he leaned over to embrace him as the warm tears slipped down his face. What a joy it was to be home again!

Chapter Nine

The busy sound of the Double M Ranch interrupted Cole's thoughts. He had been so lost in his memories that he had not realized that he was already home.

Home, what a wonderful word, Cole thought.

The "Double M" was nestled in the cleft of a large foothill with a white two-story clapboard home snuggled by a wrap-around porch with a storage barn off to the left and the horse stables to the right.

Cole gazed all around him at the rolling hills and the expanse of vast acreage surrounding the ranch. Cottonwood trees graced the hills along with oak and a few pines here and there with a wide creek running along the west side of the ranch. What a beautiful sight, Cole thought. Trees were pretty scarce in this part of Kansas, but here in the hills, there were a few trees to build with. Most homes were made out of sod, due to the limit of trees, but the Double M Ranch grew in size, mainly due to the hard work of the Mathews family and the geographical location with ample steams and vegetation.

As Cole neared the house, one of the cowhands came over to greet him, offering to brush and feed his horse.

"Hey, Chuck," he greeted, as he dismounted. "How's everything going?"

"Fine Boss, just fine; had a colt born earlier today, he's a beaut," Chuck replied, taking a moment to turn and spit his tobacco juice on the ground. He reached out for Jake's harness, "Belle was a real trooper."

"Good. I knew it'd be anytime," Cole smiled, patting the horse's rump as Chuck led him to the stables. "I'd better get in and see what Ma has for supper. Thanks Chuck."

Cole bounded up the front porch steps and entered the house with a bang of the screen door announcing his arrival. He walked over to where his mother was setting the table and kissed her on the cheek.

"Hi Ma, mmm…sure smells good," he said, dipping his finger in the buttery mashed potatoes for a taste.

Sandra Matthews playfully slapped Cole on the back of the hand. "Get out of those. Supper'll be ready soon. You go wash up," she chuckled, shaking her head at the daily exchange. *Some things never change*, she mused.

Sandra was an endearment to her two loving sons. Ever since their father's death, they had all grown closer, appreciating each other even more. Sandra made it her life's mission to take care of her boys along with the ranch. The grief she felt over losing her husband had been strong, and if it had not been for her sons, she probably would have died from a broken heart.

Martin lived for almost a year after his accident, but with the help of his sons and the love of his wife, he felt as though he was the most blessed man in the entire world. Three winters ago, pneumonia swept him away to be with the Lord, and the Matthews had been healing ever since.

"Where's Joel? Isn't he back yet?" Cole asked, pouring fresh water into the washbasin.

"He should be here anytime," his mother stated as she moved around the kitchen finishing dinner.

"Chuck said Belle had her colt today. Have ya seen 'im yet?" he asked, helping his mother place the last of the serving dishes on the table.

Sandra poured three glasses of lemonade and set them on the table. "No, I haven't had the chance yet, but I hope to get out there after supper," she answered with excitement in her voice.

With everything ready, Cole and his mother sat down at the table to wait on Joel, catching up as they did so. Cole filled his mother in on all that had transpired at the Cornwell's earlier in the day. Tears of their loss running down her weathered cheeks, knowing all too well the toll of what a broken heart can do to a person.

Time drug by and still Joel did not arrive.

"Well," Sandra stated with a swipe of her tears, "I guess Joel must've gotten caught up with something. We'd better eat before it gets too cold. Would you say grace please?"

Cole nodded, bowed his head, and blessed the food, as well as an extra little prayer to bless the Cornwell's and their loss.

Helping himself to the meat platter as his mother reached for the potatoes, he eagerly pierced a large piece of beef and dropped it onto his plate.

"Knowing my brother, he probably heard about Amelia's baby and went to see 'im," he replied, scooping a spoonful of now cold potatoes into his mouth.

Just then, as if on cue, Joel came striding in with an apologetic grin. "Sorry, Ma, I lost track of time. I heard Amelia had her baby and had to go see him."

Joel plopped on the wooden chair and said a silent prayer as Cole looked over at his mother with an 'I told you so' half-smile and popped half of a biscuit into his mouth.

***

Hours later, Grace laid awake, ankles crossed, comfortably propped up in bed, engrossed in the diary. Her tummy growled, distracting her from her reading.

She had wanted to get a little rest, but after reading the first few pages of the diary, she found it hard to put down. With every turn of the page, she prayed that the next one would jar her memory, if indeed it were hers.

Something in those pages drew her. She found it comforting, but also troubling – because if this was her diary, she had a lot to deal with in the weeks to come. Grace settled her head upon the soft feather pillow with a sigh and whispered a prayer.

Dear Gracious Father, I am intrigued but also troubled by this diary. I pray that You will reveal to me through these pages if this is mine so I will know where to go from here. Am I this woman? I pray that You will be with me and guide me in wisdom and lend me Your strength. In your Son's name I pray, Amen.

Grace leaned over to light the oil lantern, as the room grew steadily darker. Taking a deep breath, she picked up the diary and re-read the page that troubled her most.

May 10, 1866

Dear Diary,

I can't believe that Clayton would leave me like this. I cannot stop crying. I miss him terribly. I pray that he will see things differently and change his mind. I know that the Bible says that we should not be unevenly yoked, but that was before we were married. Now that I know the Lord, Clayton doesn't think we should be together. Sometimes I wonder if that is just an excuse. He has been acting different ever since we were married, even before I accepted Christ. Maybe he is just scared. I know I should go to him. I will take the wagon train out West to see if I can find him. Then maybe he will know how much I love him, and realize that we are meant to be together.

May 14, 1866

Dear Diary,

My heart still aches daily for Clayton. I have had no word from him, but I do believe that he has gone west as he planned. My parents are angry with me for deciding to follow him. They say I am better off without him, but my heart tells me differently. I have found a wagon train that is going to Colorado, although it leaves tomorrow morning. I must say my goodbyes to my family so I can start one of my own. I hope that in time they will understand why I have to do this.

As Grace was reading, she heard a light tapping on the door.

"Dear?" Ms. Millie slowly opened the door and peeked inside. "Good you're still awake," she said stepping into the room balancing a food tray on her ample hip.

"I was wondering if you might be hungry. I noticed that you didn't eat much at supper, so I thought I'd bring ya up some leftovers."

Grace smiled, setting the book aside, "Oh, Ms. Millie, you must have read my mind!" she exclaimed. "You're an angel. Thank you."

"Oh, my," Grace stated as she gazed upon the overabundance of roast, potatoes, and green beans. "It smells wonderful, but I doubt if I can eat all of this."

"Well, you eat as much as you can. We have plenty dear. You need to get your strength back." Ms. Millie walked over to the window and lifted the pane to let in the cool evening air. "My lands, it's as hot as an egg in a fryin' pan up here," she said fanning herself with her hand.

Grace forked a bite of the tender roast as Ms. Millie perched on the bed beside her. "Did you get any rest dear? I tried to keep things quiet so you could get some sleep."

"Yes, Ma'am, I did rest, but I didn't get any sleep. I was reading the diary that Mr. Matthews brought over."

At the anxious look on Ms. Millie's face, Grace went on, "I'm not sure if it's mine or not. It seems familiar, but I can't remember any of it."

Ms. Millie patted her hand. "Well, dear, the Good Lord will reveal it to ya if it's yours, I'm sure. I'll be up later to check on you and get your tray before I go to bed," she said as she rose to go. "Is there anything ya need before I go back downstairs?"

"Yes, please, could you get the medicine powders out of the drawer for me?"

Ms. Millie pulled out the package of medicine and handed it to her before she left. Grace poured half the packet of medicine in her cup of tea and ate her food in thoughtful silence.

Inhaling deeply, Grace set her tray aside and watched the warm evening air dance with the light cotton curtains, bringing with it a breath of freshness, as sleep finally proclaimed its hold on her.

***

After a deliciously filling supper, Cole, Joel, and Sandra hastily tidied up the kitchen so they could go out and check on the baby colt together.

As they entered the stable, the fresh smell of hay, along with the contented nicker of the horses welcomed them. After Cole lit the lamp, they walked over to the mare's stall and peeked in.

"Isn't he beautiful," Sandra exclaimed, reaching her hand out towards Belle, who had walked toward the gate for attention. Peering between the slats, she tried to reach her hand out to the colt, but he was skittish and hid behind his mother.

"Did ya see that marking on his head, Ma? It kinda looks like a star, don't ya think?" Joel asked as he dumped a bucket full of roughage into the horse bin.

"Sure does. If ya haven't picked out a name for him yet, Star sure would be a good one."

"Then Star it is, Ma, just for you," Cole smiled, placing his arm around his mother's shoulders and giving her a tight squeeze.

"Sounds good to me," Joel piped in, as he replaced the grain bucket. "Well, I don't know about the two of you, but I'd like to get me a cup of coffee and a piece of that cherry pie Ma baked."

With the horses fed and bedded down for the night, the trio headed towards the kitchen, merrily pointing out the fireflies as their glowing bellies contrasted sharply against the blue-black sky.

As they settled at the kitchen table with their coffee and pie, they discussed the affairs of the day before their nightly Bible reading.

Cole breached his concern over Amelia and Adam's tragic plight and the mysterious woman at Ms. Millie's boarding house, as Joel spoke of the new Stallion he bought, hoping to breed one of their young mares.

Sandra enjoyed listening to their conversation and joined in by telling her sons how nice her day had been, due to a few of the hands who came over to help her weed and water the garden. "They said there's nothing better than fresh vegetables and would like to do their part since they eat a lot of them."

They all chuckled knowing how true that statement was. The men certainly had hearty appetites, but they worked hard for it, too. Their ranch was well over 100 acres consisting of 13 horses, 50 head of cattle, several milking cows, a few pigs, and a handful of hens. Life was good and the Matthews family was happy, with the exception of the empty chair at the head of the table.

After their Bible reading, Sandra tried to stifle a yawn and rose from her chair. "I guess I had better get to bed or I'll never make it to Church tomorrow." She placed her dishes in the washbasin and kissed both boys on the cheek. "Night, see you both in the morning."

As their mother closed her bedroom door, the twins continued their earlier conversation.

"So what did she say when you handed her the diary?" Joel wanted to know, leaning back in his chair.

"Well," Cole yawned, as he scooted his chair back and stood to pour himself another cup of coffee and sat back down. "She said it looked familiar, but she wanted to read through it some to see if it triggered her memory."

"Do you think it's hers?"

"Who else's would it be? I mean, it was discovered in the same area that I found her. It has to be hers. It only makes sense." Cole stretched as the old wooden chair creaked in protest.

"Well, it'll be nice to know whether it is or not so she can get on with her life."

Cole thought for a moment before he spoke. If it is hers, she will probably be leaving pretty soon to find her family. A strange sensation struck his heart. He didn't like that idea very much. He was hoping for more time to get to know her, but maybe she would at least wait until her ankle healed, which could still be a few more weeks.

"Whelp, I think I'm ready to hit the hay, 'night Joel."

"Night."

Later that night, Cole tossed in bed, unable to sleep, with curious thoughts of the mysterious woman. Is this the Grace Beeson of the diary, he wondered?

He didn't want to intrude on her privacy by reading it, but he had to admit, he was curious. A part of him wished that he had read it so he would know more about her, but he was glad that he didn't. If it is hers, they'll find out soon enough.

After crawling out of bed to raise the window for some cool night air, he plopped back down, releasing his troubling thoughts to the Lord and quickly fell into a much-needed, heavy slumber.

Chapter Ten

Just as the day before, Grace slowly awoke to a tantalizing aroma causing her belly to rumble. She was starving! If her nose guessed right, she would soon be feasting on biscuits and sausage gravy.

Awkwardly, she repositioned herself in bed so she could reach for the diary, cringing as the lightening-like pain shot through her swollen ankle.

Anxious to read more of the diary, she opened it to where she had placed the slip of paper the night before.

May 15, 1866

Dear Diary,

Well, I have done it. I joined the wagon train this morning. I cannot stop crying. My family was so upset by my leaving, but I pray that they will understand in time. My father did not say a word, and my mother just didn't want to let go. She held me until the wagon master came to assist me on to one of the wagons. I have everything I need, except my family and my husband.

The family I'm sharing the wagon with seems nice, but I feel like an intruder. Mr. Weston is a large rugged man and looks at me strangely, but Mrs. Weston is a quiet woman with kind eyes. They have two children, a boy and a girl. The boy, Jared, is about 12 and is as quiet as his mother. The little girl, Elise, is about six years old and full of questions. She looks like a fragile china doll, so small and sweet.

It is a nice day, but the heat is downright dreadful and I am afraid that it isn't going to get any better, as it is still before noon. We have been traveling for almost four hours and my body aches already. I pray that the Lord will make this trip as easy as possible. It looks like we are ready to circle for lunch, so I will stop my writing to see what I can do to help.

Grace was so engrossed in her reading that she did not hear the knock on the door.

"I'm sorry, Miss," Jed answered, embarrassed as he caught the startled look on her face. "I thought ya heard me. Would ya like me to come back?"

"Oh, no, I'm sorry, Jed. I guess I was just lost in my reading," she replied with a smile, setting the diary aside.

Jed walked over to her bedside, placing the breakfast tray upon her lap.

"Is Ms. Millie ill this morning?" Grace asked with concern at her absence.

"No, Miss, she just wanted to eat quick-like so she could take some breakfast over to Amelia and Adam. I heard they had a rough night last night," he continued. "Ms. Millie gave me strict orders that you eat."

Grace smiled at the gentle reprimand as she reached for her fork. "Thank you for bringing it up Jed. It looks delicious!"

Jed's milky blue eyes winked merrily as he watched her fork a big bite of biscuits and gravy, satisfied, he smiled and walked out the door. *What a sweet man,* she mused.

After Grace gave thanks to the Lord, she attacked the steaming pile of biscuits and gravy with renewed energy; it not only looked delicious, it was delicious!

As she lay in bed enjoying her breakfast, she smiled, remembering that today was Sunday, and she was going to Church. Her heart soared at the thought.

Grace quickly drank her coffee with the dissolved medicine and sat the tray aside. Entertained by the songbirds outside her window, she hobbled to the chest at the foot of the bed, which Jed had moved for her convenience the day before, and searched for a nice dress. She came across a beautiful robin's egg dress with a high lace collar and puffed sleeves that narrowed at the wrist. Tiny opalescent buttons scored down the front to the narrowed princess-cut waistline. The skirt was a tiny bit short, but with the lace trim on the bottom, it shouldn't be too obvious. It was more than she had hoped.

Grace shimmied out of her nightgown and gently stepped into the beautiful dress. Careful of her injured ankle, she tugged on it gently as she slipped into it. It just barely fit. It was a little snug in the waist and bodice, but it fit.

Grace hobbled over to the washbasin and washed her face and hands. Gazing up into the oval mirror, she gasped at the sight of herself. Her hair was sticking out in complete disarray, and her face was pale and drawn. She instantly felt the heat rise to her cheeks as she wondered what Jed had thought at seeing her this way.

She quickly brushed through her long wavy auburn hair and pinned it up into a fashionable upsweep. Gently pinching her cheeks and biting her lips to give her face some color, her look was complete.

Just as she was reaching for her crutch, Ms. Millie called from the other side of the door in a singsong voice. "Are you almost ready, dear? We'll be leaving in about ten minutes."

Grace stepped out of her room and leaned against the door jam as Ms. Millie knocked on Mr. Hollister's door. Turning to the sound of Grace's door opening, Ms. Mille smiled brightly as she gazed over and found Grace in her daughter's dress. Absently she yelled through the closed door in front of her. "Mr. Hollister, we'll be leaving for church in ten minutes if you happen to change your mind."

***

Sunday morning shone bright and clear as Grace, Ms. Millie, and Jed approached the steps to the small church. The Matthews family, who were entering at the same time, greeted them warmly. Cole almost stumbled over his large booted feet as he eagerly hurried to assist Grace up the steps.

Wow! Just the sight of her made his head swim and his pulse race, especially today since she was dressed so beautifully. Her smile outshined the sun. Her figure was full but not too much so, and her radiant auburn hair was neatly swept up into a fashionable style that flattered her large brown eyes and high cheekbones. She was breathtaking.

As they entered the church, Cole continued to hold onto Grace's arm, turning her towards his mother.

"Miss, I'd like to introduce you to my mother, Sandra." Cole gestured towards a lovely woman with kind eyes and a warm smile. Grace liked her immediately. "And this," Cole clapped his hand firmly upon his brother's shoulder, "is my twin, Joel."

Grace peered into the same intense blue gaze she had seen over the past few days as she compared the two brothers, glad to see that they were not identical. "I didn't know you were a twin, Cole," she replied in wonder. "Although I see you have the same eyes."

Grace extended her gloved hand. "It's very nice to meet you both," she said as she shook their hands.

The organ began to play as the congregation shuffled around, giving quick hugs and hellos as they found their seats.

Grace scooted across the small wooden pew next to Ms. Millie, with Jed on her right, as the Matthews family claimed the pew behind them.

Grace's face warmed slightly, feeling a little uncomfortable with Cole sitting almost directly behind her. His close proximity was somewhat disturbing as she turned her attention up front. As soon as the pianist's slender fingers graced the ivory keys, Grace immediately found herself lost in worship.

The songs were familiar, and Grace knew most of them. The ones she did not know she found herself humming to as she drank in the soothing words. The hymns washed over her as refreshing as a bubbling brook, relieving her soul of the fear of the unknown, reminding her that God is always in complete control.

After the singing ended, Grace sat glued to the Reverend as he approached the pulpit. Reverend Barton was an older man, and the light in his eyes intrigued her as she leaned forward, anxious to hear him speak. She humbly bowed her head as he opened the service in prayer.

Time flew quickly by as the minister spoke from Matthew 5 on the Beatitudes.

"Blessed are the poor in spirit,

> for theirs is the kingdom of heaven.
> Blessed are those who mourn,
> for they will be comforted.
> Blessed are the meek,
> for they will inherit the earth.
> Blessed are those who hunger and thirst for righteousness,
> for they will be filled.
> Blessed are the merciful,
> for they will be shown mercy.
> Blessed are the pure in heart,
> for they will see God.
> Blessed are the peacemakers,
> for they will be called sons of God.
> Blessed are those who are persecuted because of righteousness,
> for theirs is the kingdom of heaven."

All too soon, the service was over as Reverend Barton's booming voice offered the invitation for prayer and salvation. Tears pooled in Grace's eyes as the pianist began to play a familiar hymn. Her heart swelled; she had truly been blessed by the service.

From the corner of her eye, she noticed a haggard looking man walking up front, shoulders slumped. She turned in time to see Cole follow, with an obviously heavy heart as well. As they knelt at the altar in prayer, the Reverend quietly dismissed the rest of the congregation as he walked towards the door.

Grace, with her teary eyes still lingering on Cole's broad back, was gently ushered out of the church by Ms. Millie, Jed following close behind.

The Reverend stood outside by the steps to greet everyone as they exited the Church. As Grace shook the Reverend's hand, Ms. Millie introduced them. He smiled warmly and invited her to come again.

"Thank you Reverend. I will be looking forward to next Sunday's service."

As they were riding the short distance back to the Boarding House, Grace asked Ms. Millie who the man was that had gone up to the altar.

Ms. Millie shook her head sadly. "That was Adam Cornwell. He and his wife were the ones who had lost their little one a few days ago."

"Oh, my, bless his heart, he looked so sad."

"Yes, he's taking this pretty hard. Cole talked to him, but he needs to deal with this in his own time."

Grace nodded in understanding. "Ms. Millie, do you think I could go over to see Amelia today after dinner?"

Ms. Millie brightened. "Well, I don't see why not," she replied, helping Grace up the steps to the Boarding House after Jed had dropped them off front. "Why don't you sit here in the parlor while I get dinner going? We have some good books over there on that shelf if yer interested," she told her, pointing to the bookshelf next to the fireplace.

Grace smiled. "Thank you, but I was wondering if you would have some mending to do? I would like to do something constructive with my hands."

Ms. Millie's face lit up even more. "Well how nice of you to offer, dear. Actually, I do have some sewing that needs to be done, if you're sure ya don't mind." The older woman reached into her sewing basket next to the overstuffed chair and handed her a tiny quilt. "I've been working on this in my spare time, and I'm just about finished. I was planning on giving it to Amelia for her little one, but I didn't get it done in time," she admitted as she held up the beautiful pale yellow baby quilt. "If you could just finish the edging we could give it to her this afternoon."

Grace lovingly ran her fingers over the soft cotton blocks that were expertly stitched together. *Will I ever be blessed to have a child of my own?* Her heart ached for the family she could not remember.

"I'd love to," she replied softly. Grace surveyed the delicate stitch; certain she would be able to finish it in time.

Grace worked diligently until dinner was ready, and had just finished as Ms. Millie came bustling into the parlor, face beet red, frantically fanning herself with a homemade fan.

"Whew, I don't know which is hotter, my kitchen or the outdoors," Ms. Millie exclaimed, dabbing her handkerchief at her temple.

Grace smiled and held up the baby quilt for the older woman's inspection. "It's finished."

Ms. Millie perched her glasses upon her nose and nodded her head in approval as she inspected the stitching. "You do lovely work my dear. No one would ever know that someone else finished it," she beamed, holding it up for both women to inspect with pride. "Thank you!"

Ms. Millie gave Grace a grateful squeeze and carefully laid the quilt aside. "Now let's go eat so we'll have plenty of time for a visit."

Chapter Eleven

After dinner, Grace reluctantly conceded to Ms. Millie's instructions to relax and enjoy her tea, as the older woman insisted on clearing the table by herself.

Moments later, Cole walked in with a slam of the screen door, startling Grace in the process. Grace could feel the heat rise to her cheeks and quickly lowered her eyes. Hat in hand, Cole was ready to say something when Ms. Millie popped through the doorway.

"Well, hello there Cole; we were just on our way over to Amelia's so I could introduce my new friend here," Ms. Millie stated, a little out of breath, as she waddled back into the dining room to retrieve the last of the dishes.

Cole wanted so badly to be able to sit and visit with Grace, but he knew that she had wanted to meet Amelia and the baby, and so, stood awkwardly like a shy schoolboy wondering what to say.

He stood, twisting his hat in his hands, finding it difficult to pull his gaze away from the beauty before him. He had to admit that he had a hard time concentrating on the church service that morning after he caught site of Grace. His pulse raced and he felt as though his legs would go out beneath him.

Cole shook his head as he realized that he was staring. Grace's slender fingers nervously traced the rim of her glass, obviously avoiding his gaze.

"Would you like to join us, Cole?" Ms. Millie asked, eyeing Grace questioningly.

"N-no, thank you. You ladies need time to talk and get to know each other," he stuttered, stealing another glace at Grace.

"Well, if you're sure." Ms. Millie walked to the mirror and patted her dampened hair back into place. "Are you ready to go, my dear?"

Grace nodded her head and quickly finished her tea. "Yes Ma'am."

"Good, I'll go get the baby quilt."

Cole awkwardly assisted Grace to the foyer, as she managed her crutch with growing expertise, and held the door for them. "Uh, have a nice visit…see ya later."

As the two women made their way towards the Post Office, they discussed the beautiful summer day as two young boys ran swiftly past them chasing after a mangy stray cat with an old hound dog lumbering close behind.

The afternoon sun rose high in the sky as the heat glared off the boardwalk in a hazy wave. Ms. Millie, with beads of perspiration dotting her forehead, patted at her face with her handkerchief and hurried towards the cooler interior of the Post Office.

The tinkle of the bell above the door announced their arrival as usual, as they made their way up the stairs to Amelia and Adam's room and knocked lightly on the door.

After a soft "Come in," they entered. Amelia was lying in bed, with a baby cradle sitting off to her left. The curtains were open, and the afternoon sun was spilling into the room giving it an inviting glow. The room was warm, but the open window delivered a soft breeze, making it bearable at best.

"Good afternoon, Amelia," Ms. Mille greeted as she walked over to the new mother to give her a quick hug.

"This is the young lady Cole spoke to you about," she said as she put her arm around Grace's shoulders in introduction.

"Hello," Amelia replied with a warm smile. "I'm so glad you were able to come." Ms. Millie pulled the quilt from beneath her arm and presented it to Amelia. "Here dear, just a little somethin' for the baby."

Amelia smiled, holding the quilt up in front of her. "Oh, Ms. Millie, this is beautiful! Thank you so much!"

"You're welcome, dear. This sweet girl had to help me finish the edging today because I wasn't expecting you to be needin' it so soon."

Amelia's gaze swept towards Grace as she smiled her thanks, gently laying the quilt aside.

"It's nice to finally meet you, Amelia," Grace replied as she extended her hand. "I hope you're feeling well today."

Ms. Millie made her way to the baby cradle and scooped up the squirming infant who was voicing his desire to be held as Amelia offered the women a seat.

Grace's heart melted as she gazed adoringly at the tiny little life. Her heart fluttered as Ms. Millie held out the baby for her to hold.

"Oh, Amelia, he's so beautiful!" Grace exclaimed as she tenderly cradled the newborn in her arms.

Grace's heart ached as she examined the tiny form before her, wondering if she had a family somewhere. *How precious they are.* Grace gingerly touched the dark patch of downy hair on Nathaniel's head, marveling at the miracle of life.

Amelia interrupted Grace's sweet meanderings. "Maybe you could come over and keep me company sometimes," she addressed Grace.

Grace peeled her eyes from the sweet babe. "I'd like that."

"I just wish I knew what to call you," Amelia stated, darting her eyes between the two.

Grace thought of the diary and answered Amelia apprehensively. "Well, the diary Cole brought me must be mine, but I don't know for sure. So, in the meantime, why don't you call me Grace until we know different, if that's alright?" she asked as she looked from one woman to the other with questioning approval.

Ms. Millie smiled. "Hmm…maybe the Good Lord's trying to tell ya something, dear," she beamed as she patted Grace's arm. "Grace it is then."

The women continued to visit as Adam walked into the room and stopped short. "I'm sorry, I didn't realize you had company," he mumbled, as he gazed around the room, his eyes resting on Grace in question.

Amelia smiled at her husband, introducing Grace as the "mystery woman." Grace smiled a greeting and said hello as she saw the pain of loss still obviously evident in his stormy gray eyes.

The women finished their visit quickly with Amelia inviting Grace over the following day so they could have a longer visit.

"I would love to," she answered truthfully with a twinkle in her eyes. "Maybe Ms. Millie would let me pack a lunch for us and we could have a little picnic up here in your room."

"Oh, that would be lovely! Maybe," she replied, her gaze lingering on her husband, "my loving husband would let us take the baby and picnic under the flowering dogwood out back?" She had said it more as a question to her husband than as a statement to Grace.

Amelia reached for her husband's hand and smiled demurely hoping to win his approval.

Adam looked at Amelia as if she had lost her mind. Sensing a defiant refusal, Amelia went on more seriously.

"Adam, you know Doc said I should be up as soon as I feel I'm ready, and I think tomorrow would be a great opportunity. Besides, Nathaniel needs to feel the warm breeze on his face just as much as I do. We won't be out all day. Please, Adam…" she begged as she cocked her head and pouted playfully.

Adam, feeling a bit overprotective, finally gave in to his wife's pleas, consenting to a quick picnic and back up to bed.

As Grace and Ms. Millie stood to leave, Grace handed the little one to his father so she could grab her crutch, promising to return the following day with a picnic fit for a queen.

The two women made their way back to the Boarding House, enjoying the beautiful, but hot day. Grace took this time to confide to Ms. Millie what the diary had revealed and how troubling it was to her. Ms. Millie comforted her and assured her that she would be praying for her to know the truth and to accept what God has planned for her life.

As they approached the steps, they decided to sit out on the porch swing for a leisurely visit. They talked for what seemed like hours as Ms. Millie shared with Grace about her daughter, Lenore, who had passed away almost ten years prior due to a small pox epidemic.

Grace could see the tears pool in the old woman's eyes as she spoke of her deep loss. Lenore was a very kind young lady, who enjoyed teaching the children in Sunday school. She was in love with a young man from church, but after her death, he was so heartbroken that he could no longer live in a town that reminded him of her and left to go farther west to start a new life.

Grace, flushed from the heat of the late afternoon, ran a tired hand over her brow as she noticed Cole walking towards them. He was looking straight at her, which made her feel as though her heart would jump out of her chest. She could see the evidence of concern in his eyes as he approached.

"Are you alright?" asked the deep husky voice.

"Um, yes, just a little warm out here; I guess it's making me tired."

"Cole, would you mind asking Jed for a couple glasses of ice water and some fans?" Ms. Millie asked, futilely fanning herself with her hand.

Cole respectfully complied, and returned moments later, casually propping his jean-clad leg upon the porch railing to settle in for a short visit as Jed came out moments later with the refreshments.

"Oh, thank you Jed," Ms. Millie said with relief, gulping down half the glass.

Cole's eyes darted towards Grace in amusement, as he found her hiding her smile behind her own frosted glass. Their eyes met.

"H-have you had a chance to read any of the diary I gave you?" he asked, trying to appear calm as he pulled his hat off, wiped his brow, and plopped it back upon his dark curls.

"Yes, actually, I started it last night and had a hard time putting it down," Grace admitted as she slowly fanned herself, thankful for the breeze drifting over them, "and then I read some more this morning," she admitted with a smile. "It is very intriguing."

Her face reddened slightly as she remembered what she had read. She silently wished that it were not her diary, because if it was, that would mean that she was married, and these stirrings that she felt when she was around Cole were totally unacceptable.

Cole, waiting for her to continue, delighted in the way the warm breeze was softly pushing her loose tendrils in her face as she absently pushed them away, obviously deep in thought. He wanted so much to be able to brush his fingertips across her cheek and kiss her tenderly. His heart yearned for a wife, and he was silently hoping that she might be the one...until he heard her following statement.

Knowing that Grace must confess what she had read in the diary to distinguish any spark of feelings she or Cole may be entertaining, she hurried on, "I-if it is my diary," Grace breathed, catching Cole's bright blue eyes, "then I'm married."

Cole's face instantly drained of color as Grace's heart sank. She busied herself with picking invisible lint from her dress, not wanting him to see the tears pooling in her eyes.

Feeling as though his heart had been ripped completely out of his chest, Cole let out a quiet anguished sigh as he mumbled an unintelligible excuse and made a hasty retreat, leaving the two women staring after him in concern.

He had to get out of there before she realized how much he already cared for her. Cole walked blindly back to Jake, who had been tied up outside the General Store, then rode mindlessly back to the Double M Ranch. With anger and sadness all wrapped in one turbulent emotion, he cried out to the Lord.

Why, Lord? Why would You bring her here and allow me to fall in love with her so easily, then take her away? You know how I have longed for a wife and family. I truly felt that she was the one. Why, Lord? Why…?

His prayer was lost in the wind as a hot tear ran down his scared cheek. He rode in silent torment until he reached the outskirts of the ranch and angrily swiped at the despicable tears.

Knowing that his mother would be preparing supper, he wanted to wash up before anyone noticed him. Thankfully, no one was around as he tethered his horse and walked over to the well to splash some cool water on his face, hoping to dodge any questioning looks.

After washing up, he plastered a smile on his face and walked in the back door. His mother turned, face flushed, stopping in mid-slice from cutting the fresh baked bread. The yeasty aroma made his stomach rumble.

"What's wrong, Honey?" Sandra Mathews asked knowingly, knife held in mid air. Her mother's heart always knew when something was wrong.

"Nothing, Ma, I'm fine," he fibbed, placing a quick kiss on her cheek. Cole reached for a slice of warm bread and sat down in his seat as his mother watched him with questioning concern. Before she had a chance to question him further, much to Cole's relief, Joel walked in, all smiles, exclaiming over the new colt.

"Glad to hear he's doing so well," their mother said absently as she tried to lay her concern for her son aside for the moment.

After a partly tense conversation at supper, Joel and Cole, after helping their mother clear the dishes, retired to the family room where Sandra picked up the worn family Bible to read their nightly devotions. She read from Proverbs 19.

Two of the verses caught Cole's attention immediately. *Proverbs 19:11 "A man's wisdom gives him patience; it is to his glory to overlook an offense."* Instantly it made him think of his ex-partner, William Hollister. Maybe the Lord was trying to tell him something since he kept running into him. *Oh Lord, please help me to forgive him*, he prayed.

He meditated even longer on the second verse that his mother had read that struck the cords of his heart. *Proverbs 19:21, "Many are the plans in a man's heart, but it is the Lord's purpose that prevails."*

This verse made him think of the mystery woman, who is now going by the name of Grace. He didn't even know if it was her real name, but he knew he was falling in love with her and he felt that the Lord was telling him to wait upon Him to fulfill His plans, in His time.

Cole sighed deeply; patience was not one of his virtues.

Chapter Twelve

Joel lit a lamp and leisurely strolled outside, inhaling deeply of the fresh country air. It was a clear and beautiful night. The lantern, lighting his way, swung back and forth casting long shadows all around him. He could hear the ranch hands joking and hollering back and forth in their cabin, probably over their nightly game of cards, as usual. Life was good.

As he entered the stables, the smell of fresh hay and the familiar sounds of the horses swishing their tails as they chewed their grain made Joel's heart swell in pride and gratitude. Joel smiled. Chuck must have come in during supper to bed the animals down for the night. Good 'ole

Chuck, he mused, looking around in satisfaction at a job well done.

Joel walked over to where the colt lay with his mother and leaned against the stall, breathing a prayer for his brother and whatever was troubling him.

Back in the house, with a prayer on her lips, Sandra Matthews approached her despondent son. "I know something's wrong, son. It always helps to talk about it."

Cole hung his head in shame. "Ma, I'm angry at God." At the puzzled expression on his mother's face, he continued, "I know it's wrong, and that's partly why I feel so bad."

"Why?"

He looked his mother in the eye, mixed emotions playing in his. "The woman I told you about..." with the nod of her head, he went on, "well, I gave her the diary to look through, and she told me today that if it is hers," Cole stopped and raked his fingers through his hair, sighing with resignation, "then...she's married, Ma," he said in a raspy voice.

Sandra's face fell at the realization of her son's strong feelings towards the young woman. "Oh, honey," she wrapped her arms around her grown son, pulling him to her, allowing him to let out his frustrations. She knew something had changed in the past week, but she never thought that he could have fallen in love so quickly, but then again, she had done the same thing with his father. It had been love at first sight.

"Do you know for sure that it's hers?"

Cole pulled himself away and wiped his eyes, embarrassed for acting so childish. "Not for sure, Ma, but it has to be. It all makes sense."

"Well, even if it is hers, then it's a good thing that you found out now, not weeks or months from now," she said matter-of-factly, looking him straight in the eye.

"I know. I was just hoping and praying…" He hit his knee with his fist in frustration.

"I know dear, I know…," she sympathized, patting his large, tan hand. "Just remember, God has that special someone out there for ya, and if it's not her, then you need to accept that and wait upon Him to show ya. He knows how you're feelin'. Just rest in Him, and let Him lead you."

Cole forced a smile as he gave his mother an appreciative hug. "Thanks, Ma. I know your right."

"I'll be praying that He will either give ya your heart's desire or take it away until the right one comes along."

Sandra leaned over and kissed her son goodnight, and padded to her bedroom. It was going to be a long night of prayer.

***

"Here you go, dear, if you're sure you want to do this?" Ms. Millie asked as she handed Grace her sewing basket and showed her what she had been working on earlier.

"Oh, yes. I really need something to keep me busy. I feel as though my laying around and your delicious cooking is taking a toll on my waist line," she laughed as she patted her midsection.

"Oh Miss," quipped William Hollister with a raised brow and an eloquent twist of his mustache. "If I may be so bold, you do not have anything to worry about in that regard," he remarked with a smile meant only for a husband and wife.

Grace immediately reddened at such a personal comment, pretending not to have heard and concentrated on the stitching on which Ms. Millie was instructing her.

Mr. Hollister chuckled lightly as he settled back into the overstuffed chair, keeping a steady eye on the young woman across from him. He smiled wryly, well aware that his last remark had riled her; flipping open the newspaper, he casually propped one leg upon the other, preparing for an interesting evening.

William spied over the top of the newspaper as Grace spoke with Ms. Millie. *What a beautiful creature she is*, he mused. Her dark auburn hair was swept up into a simple chignon with loose tendrils hanging down on either side. Her brown eyes looked as innocent as a fawn's, and upon further inspection, her mouth appeared to be shaped like a heart when pursed in concentration.

Grace could feel his eyes upon her and dropped her head hoping he would take the hint. Unfortunately, her plan did not work.

"Would you like some more light?" he asked, dropping his paper to his lap.

"Um, no, thank you. I can see just fine."

"How is your ankle feeling tonight?"

"It's getting better, thank you. It's still sore when I'm up too much, but it's healing. Doc said I should be able to walk without the crutch in another week or so."

Grace busied herself with her sewing, once again, hoping that he would continue reading his paper. Part of her enjoyment of sewing was spending time talking to the Lord, and she could not do that if he kept interrupting. She liked Mr. Hollister, but did not like his boldness; it unnerved her.

She suddenly remembered the diary and the fact that she might be married. After a little thought, she thought it best to tell Mr. Hollister of the possibility before he started to entertain any romantic notions. Thankfully she did not have long to wait until he broached the subject.

"I heard that the deputy found a diary out on the prairie, thinking it may be yours?" he wanted to know as his gaze blatantly swept over her.

She blushed and quickly told him the story, finishing with the part that she may be married, much to his surprise.

William's intense gaze challenged her. "Married? But you don't have a ring on your finger," he admonished, eyeing her bare ring finger.

"I know, and that puzzles me too, but that's what it says." Grace shrugged her shoulders as if to dismiss the conversation and continued her sewing.

William was taken back at her statement. *Well*, he thought, *even though she may be married, she is not wearing a ring so maybe she is mistaken.* William Hollister smiled at the thought of having this lovely young lady on his arm and showing her off in his social circle and to his business acquaintances. Wanting to win Grace's affection, he laid the newspaper aside and scooted to the edge of his chair, asking if he could get her a cup of coffee or tea.

"Why, yes, thank you, a cup of tea sounds wonderful."

Hmmm…maybe he's not so bad after all, she thought. She did find him attractive, but sometimes his attitude was not to her liking. Maybe she misjudged him after all.

"Jed!" William yelled as he lit a thin cigar. "The young lady here would like a cup of tea," he stated with pompous authority as Jed poked his head into the parlor.

"Yes Sir." Jed hobbled out to do his bidding, causing Grace to squirm uncomfortably in her seat. She was appalled at the triumphant look William threw her way; especially since he knew that Jed was already busy helping Ms. Millie do the dishes.

Well, I guess I was right about him after all; she fumed as she once again concentrated on her meticulous stitches.

Acting as if nothing was amiss, he continued speaking. "So, how do you like your stay so far in Garden City?" he asked as he puffed on his cigar, filling the room with heavy smoke.

"I like it just fine, Mr. Hollister. Everyone is so kind, and it's a beautiful little town," she replied in all honesty.

William leaned back in the chair and hoisted his leg upon his thigh. "I was hoping that maybe once you were feeling better, you might join me for a ride in my buckboard?" he asked absently between smoke rings.

Grace stopped sewing, allowing the cloth to fall to her lap, perturbed at his audacity. "Mr. Hollister, as I explained earlier, I believe I am married, so that would be totally out of the question."

"Yes, you did mention that, but as you said, you have no proof, and until you do, what harm would there be in one little ride?" He drawled out smoothly with a glint in his eye, tapping off his ashes in the glass tray beside him.

Saved by the interruption, Jed walked in carrying the ordered cup of tea and graciously offered it to Grace.

"Thank you Jed, I'm so sorry to put you out. I hope it wasn't too much trouble."

"No trouble at all, Miss," Jed said with a partly toothless grin. "It's my pleasure."

Grace finished the shirt she had been mending, tidied up her mess, and quickly drank her tea. The cigar smoke was making her sick to her stomach and she knew she had to get out of there as soon as possible. With little apology she reached for her crutch and excused herself to her room.

Just as she was about ready to mount the first step, Doc Miller walked in. "Oh, sorry, Miss," he apologized as he realized that she was headed to bed. "I can come back tomorrow."

"No, Doctor, that's quite alright," she greeted him with a smile. "Are you here to take away my crutch?" she asked hopefully, noticing the cane in his hand.

"Yes, Miss. I want to check your ankle first to make sure it's strong enough, though."

Grace hobbled anxiously to the nearest chair, all too happy to get rid of the awkward crutch.

"Oh, it looks much better," he beamed, after examining her ankle and re-wrapping it. "It's healing very nicely; how's it feel?"

"It doesn't hurt too much, only when I'm on it a lot, but I think I know my limits now," she hurried on, noticing his bushy arched eyebrows as he peered over his spectacles.

"Alright, just make sure you take it easy. This cane will help you get around better and make you more dependent on your ankle so it will get its strength back."

"Thank you, Doc."

As Grace slipped on her shoe and stood to test the cane, Doc took a moment to explain some simple exercises to help strengthen her ankle as Ms. Millie looked on. Satisfied with the progression of his patient, Doc plopped his hat back upon his head and bade them goodnight.

Chapter Thirteen

Grace exhaled as she rested against her closed bedroom door. Her dark stuffy room was a welcome exchange from the smoke-filled parlor downstairs. The stench had made her sick to her stomach.

Eager for fresh air, she practiced walking with her cane as she slowly ambled over to raise the window, gratefully filling her lungs with fresh clean air. She marveled at the beauty of the clear crisp evening with bright twinkling stars reflecting off the crescent moon hanging low in the dark blue sky.

Feeling somewhat better, she carefully maneuvered herself back to the bed, lit the lamp and removed her shoes.

Oh how her ankle throbbed! She stole a few minutes to rub her swollen ankle, in hope of relieving some tension. She was glad that it was getting better, but as she admitted to the doctor, she could tell when she overdid it, and today was one of those days.

Eager for relief, Grace hobbled over to the water pitcher that Jed had filled earlier and poured a glass of the clear liquid. If she had thought ahead, she would have brought up a cup of hot tea to dissolve her medication, but eventually succumbed to quickly gulping down the chalky white clumps in the tepid water. The bitter taste made her wince as she scrunched up her face in distaste.

Hopping back over to the bed, she turned down the comforter and propped up the pillows, eager to read more of the mysterious diary.

Snuggling under the cool crisp sheets, she picked up the diary that was lying on the bedside table, and settled back as she heard a light tapping at her door.

"Come in," she sighed.

Ms. Millie poked her gray head through the door, worry casting shadows on her aged face. "Are you feeling alright, dear?"

"Yes ma'am. I just need some rest. Besides, I was getting a little nauseous with Mr. Hollister's cigar smoke," she admitted honestly. "But I'm glad Doc came over to bring me this cane," she replied, her eyes falling upon the less cumbersome device. "It will be a lot easier than that old crutch."

"I'm sure it will. Can I get you anything before I retire?"

Grace shook her head as another wave of nausea swept over her.

"Well, I guess I had better let you rest then." Ms. Millie excused herself, worry still creasing her brow. "Goodnight dear."

"Goodnight, Ms. Millie." Grace yawned, fighting off sleep as she opened the diary, anxious to read the next entry.

May 16, 1866

Dear Diary,

Last night was absolutely awful, but I'm thankful that Mr. Weston allowed me to sleep in the family wagon, as I am not use to the strange sounds of the wilderness. My heart leapt into my throat every time I heard a coyote howl. Mr. Weston said they were far into the hills, but they sounded as if they were just outside the wagon. I had a bad dream about them attacking in the middle of the night and woke with a fright, not able to sleep much after that. I praise God for this family taking me in so I do not have to travel alone.

I helped Mrs. Weston with breakfast. We had pancakes and coffee, although the children were fortunate to have milk from the dairy cow they had brought with them.

I tried to make conversation with Mrs. Weston as we prepared breakfast, but she is not much of a talker. Elise awoke not too long after we had started breakfast and scrambled down out of the wagon to help. There wasn't much for her to do, so she stayed by my side asking all kinds of questions. She sure is a chatterbox, but very sweet. I suspect that since her parents do not talk much, she has a lot to say when she finds someone who will listen.

Mr. Weston and his son left before I awoke to speak with the Wagon Master. Mrs. Weston said to stay close because the last stage west spotted an Indian reservation not too far from the trail. She told me that since the Civil war, there have been many Indian raids. They are protesting the white men who are taking over their land. Part of me can't blame them, but the other part of me think that we should also have a right to this free country. Oh, how I wish that life wasn't so complicated! I could tell by Mrs. Weston's eyes that she is a little worried, and I would have to admit that I am too. I will continually pray that God will see us safely to our destination.

On a different note, I do not think that the Weston's are God-fearing people. I have not once heard them talk about the Lord or pray. When I pray, they sit quietly and wait until I am finished. I pray that God will use me to win these people to Him before we part.

Grace stifled a yawn as she regrettably laid the diary back upon the table as sleep pursued its claim on her. With a prayer on her lips for these unknown people and her unknown future, she fell into a deep sleep.

***

The following morning, Cole awoke with a dull headache, still feeling tired and out of sorts. He had had a fitful night of tossing and turning. His mind raced with questions; questioning his feelings for Grace and what God would want him to do. The enticing smell of breakfast hurried his steps as his stomach growled in eager anticipation.

Pulling on his jeans and a clean work shirt, he quickly dressed to start his day, anxious to see the new colt. Even though Kansas was mainly known for its cattle ranches, Cole decided to follow his father's dream and keep the horse ranch up and running, as difficult as it was. Although he enjoyed cattle ranching, he loved horse ranching more. The beauty of the strong graceful creatures always amazed him and he quickly grew to love them.

As he walked into the warm kitchen, his mother looked up, fork in midair as she was carefully retrieving the sizzling bacon from the cast iron skillet. She turned with her brows raised in question as she placed them on the serving plate.

Trying to thwart his mother's concern, he threw her a playful wink and mustered the best smile he could. "Everything's fine ma."

His mother seemed somewhat relieved and returned his smile as Joel strode in carrying a pail of fresh milk. Oblivious to the silent communication between mother and son, Joel walked over to kiss his mother on the cheek, deposited the milk pail on the counter, and sat down in his chair.

"Mmm ...smells great, Ma," he exclaimed, rubbing his taut stomach. "I'm hungry enough to eat a horse," he chuckled.

Cole sparked an idea and straddled the chair in front of him. "Hey, speaking of...I was thinking of butchering one of those steers out there, what'd ya think?"

Joel and their mother looked at him in surprise as he continued, "Well, I know we're pretty busy right now, but we do need some more beef, and with three of the cows delivering calves the last couple months, we can afford it."

Cole absently forked a bite of eggs into his mouth as he ignored his brother's furrowed brows.

"Who'd be available to help now?" Joel wanted to know as he shoved a piece of bacon into his mouth. "Ya know Chuck is busy working with the horses and the other men will be goin' to the auction this afternoon." Joel looked perplexed.

"Well, I could pull Paul out for now. He and I could do it in one day. He's the strongest and would be the most help." Cole reasoned.

"I don't know," Joel still was not convinced.

Seeing that Cole needed support, Sandra spoke up. "Well I think that's a great idea!" she stated enthusiastically as Joel shot her a curious look. "I was hoping to have a baby shower for Amelia and as big as that ornery old steer is out there, we can use part for the party, give a portion of it to the Boarding House, then Cole and Paul can cure the rest for the fall 'n winter!"

Sandra hadn't really thought that far ahead, but the more she talked, the more she liked the idea. "And I can make a beautiful cake and maybe we can churn some ice cream."

"Well, looks like I'm outnumbered," Joel stated with a lopsided grin as he pushed back his chair, screeching it against the wooden floor.

"Good! It's settled then!" their mother exclaimed as she clasped her hands together in excitement.

Sandra had not hosted a party in years, and this was just the thing she needed to lift her spirits. Lately she had been feeling the loss of her husband more and more with the approaching anniversary of his death, but this would give her something to occupy her mind, as well as Cole's.

"Good, I'll talk to Paul and set it all up," Cole stated as he carried his breakfast dishes to the washbasin. "Whelp, I'd better get going. I've got a lot to do in town today."

Not wanting to miss an opportunity to tease his brother, Joel grinned, "This wouldn't have anything to do that beautiful mystery woman, would it?"

Striking a raw nerve, Cole's face constricted and his back stiffened as the emotions from the day before resurfaced. Without another word, he stomped outdoors with the bang of the screen for his answer.

Rolling his eyes, he looked at his mother, coffee cup in midair, "What'd I say?"

Sandra sighed. "He's just having a hard time dealin' with somethin' at the moment," she explained. "He'll be fine."

Sandra rose from the table, started to clear it of the now empty breakfast dishes, and turned, "But maybe it might be best if you didn't mention anything more about that woman for now."

Chapter Fourteen

Cole traveled into town as downhearted as the day before. His heart still ached at the shocking news that Grace, if indeed that was her identity, was married. He spent his traveling time talking with the Lord. He knew that if he gave this over to Him that he would have peace with whatever may happen.

Cole dismounted from his dark stallion and started towards the Post Office. All of a sudden, Maryanne Brewster bounded out of nowhere and snatched him by the arm.

"Cole," she crooned batting her long dark eyelashes. "Where are you off to?" Maryanne pursed her full lips into a pout, "Mama's making steak and potatoes tonight. Would you like to come over for supper?"

Cole hesitated, shifting his weight from one foot to the other, and looked down at Maryanne, who was playfully spinning her parasol, awaiting his answer.

Cole did not know what to say. He didn't want to lead her on, but he couldn't go over to the Boarding House and face Grace, nor did he want to go home and deal with sympathy from his mother or questions from his brother, so he reluctantly conceded.

"Sure, uh, thanks."

"Really?" she squealed in delightful surprise, her eyes dancing. "That's wonderful!"

Remembering what her mother had said about acting more mature, she lowered her gaze and smiled demurely. "Well, then I will let you get back to your business, and I'll see you tonight at 7:00?"

"That'll be fine." He touched the brim of his hat and brushed past her.

As he entered the Post Office, he greeted Adam, who was behind the counter sorting the morning mail as usual. "Mornin', didn't you get any sleep?" Cole wanted to know, noticing the haggard look on his friend's face.

"Not much." Ignoring his friend's disdainful tone, he went on, "How's Amelia feeling?"

"Fine, she's taking a bath right now while Nathaniel's sleeping," he said solemnly as he continued to sort the mail. "That lady-friend of yours is coming over to visit in a bit, and she wanted to look her best. Plus, we're going to hold the memorial service this afternoon."

A shadow crossed Cole's face. "I didn't realize that was today."

"Well, we weren't sure either," Adam stated. "We had Mr. Hammond build the…," Adam's voice broke, "…the coffin, and we weren't sure how long it would take him, but he came in this morning and said it was finished."

Cole walked over to his friend, laid his hand upon his shoulder, and lightly squeezed it in comfort. "I'm so sorry you have to go through this, Adam. I'm here if ya need anything."

Adam broke the awkward moment and changed the subject, "Was that Maryanne I saw you talking to out there?"

Cole didn't want to discuss his run-in with Maryanne, but knew he wasn't going to get around it either. At the expectant look on his friend's face, he nodded in resignation,

"Yeah, she's been asking me for weeks to join them for supper, and I finally said I would."

Adam looked up in surprise. "And, you don't want to go do you?"

Adam had his suspicions about Cole's feelings for the mystery lady, but now he wasn't so sure.

"Hey," Cole chuckled lightly, "I hear she's a good cook." He shrugged it off trying to convince himself that it wasn't such a bad idea.

Adam wasn't convinced. "Don't you think that if you accept a supper invitation Maryanne will get the wrong idea? Or is that the idea you want her to have?"

Cole pulled out a piece of beef jerky from his shirt pocket and slumped against the counter, ankles crossed, "Oh, I don't know."

"I kinda had the idea that you were sweet on the young lady at Ms. Millie's," Adam commented, searching Cole's face for any reaction.

Adam noticed Cole's eyes growing dark as he spoke. "Well, maybe I was, but last night took care of that. She told me that if that diary is hers, then she's married." Cole shrugged again, biting off another piece of jerky, trying to hide his true feelings.

"I'm sorry, Cole, I had no idea."

"Yeah, well, I guess it just wasn't meant to be. Anyway," he said trying to change the subject. "How're you feelin'? Have you and Amelia had time to talk?"

"We talked. Maybe the memorial service will help. I-I asked Doc to deliver the message today," he admitted, focusing his frustration on stamping the envelopes.

Cole stopped chewing and stared at Adam dumbfounded.

"Why Doc, isn't Reverend Barton available?" he questioned, afraid of what his answer might be.

"Um, don't know. I never asked him," Adam replied, averting his gaze.

"Why Adam? You know he handles all of the services."

"Cole, I really don't want to get into this right now," Adam replied, agitation edging his voice. "I have all of this to do before the service," he said, waving his hand over the mound of envelopes and packages, "If you'll excuse me."

Cole could sense that Adam wanted him to go so he could drop the subject, but he could not allow him to leave the Lord out of James's memorial service. He would regret it the rest of his life.

"Adam..."

"No, Cole...," Adam was interrupted by the loud wail of little Nathaniel. Taking that as his excuse to leave, Adam excused himself to check on the baby. "I'll see you at the service at 2:00." With that, he hurried up the stairs and left Cole standing there speechless.

Just as he was about to leave, the bell above the door jingled, causing Cole to turn. His breath caught in his throat at the sight of the mystery woman, who called herself Grace. She looked beautiful with her cheeks flushed from the fresh morning air and her hair lightly tousled from the slight breeze.

"Oh, Good morning," Grace was caught off guard, breathless from the walk, as well as trying to manage her cane and the cumbersome picnic basket through the door.

Cole quickly pulled himself back to earth and apologetically hurried to help her, slipping the picnic basket from her arm.

"Mornin' Miss, I-I was just leaving," he stammered with a lopsided smile as he held the door for her. The sweet scent of lavender invaded his nostrils. His senses seemed to be soaring.

"Oh?" she asked, her voice tinged with disappointment. "I was just coming to visit Amelia and help her get ready for the service this afternoon."

Cole's eyes lost their gleam. "Yeah, Adam just told me about it," he sighed as he ran his fingers through his hair. "I need to get back out to the ranch and tell Ma and Joel."

He carried the heavy picnic basket over to the counter and gently laid it down, replacing his hat back upon his thick curls.

"Thanks. I guess I'll see you later?" Grace asked as her gaze locked with his.

"Yeah, see ya," he replied, rushing out the door.

What was it about that woman that made his pulse race every time she was near? *Oh Heavenly Father, You're going to have to help me get over these feelings.*

Cole hurried to the General Store to pick up a few items for his mother, hoping to distract himself from the ache growing deeper into his heart.

As he walked in the store, Walt greeted him with his usual smile. "Howdy Cole, what can I get for you?"

"Mornin' Walt," Cole forced a smile, as he was not in the mood for pleasantries. "I came in for some sugar and flour, two pounds each should do it."

Cole leaned his tall frame against the worn counter as Walt removed the bags from the shelf behind him and measured out the requested amount. "Anything else I can get for you?" he asked.

"Nope, that'll do it," Cole replied absently, pulling out a crumpled bill from his shirt pocket.

"Did ya ever find out anything about that young lady?" the store clerk wanted to know as he pushed a button and opened the cash register.

"Not much," he mumbled as he grabbed the items from the counter and turned to leave. "Thanks, Walt."

Walt shook his head in question at Cole's aloofness, shrugged his shoulders, and turned to continue stocking the wooden shelves, whistling a tune as he did so.

As Cole walked past the Sheriff's office, Sheriff Burge called out to him.

Rolling his eyes heavenward, he sighed and turned back. "What'cha want, Sheriff? I'm in a bit of a hurry."

Sheriff Burge shot him an unconcerned look. "I was wonderin' if ya ever found out whose diary that was."

Cole shook his head and impatiently repositioned the two sacks he was holding. "Not yet. I'm still checkin' around."

Concentrating on a card game, the Sheriff scratched his stubbly chin in thought. "Well, if no one claims it, bring it back here," he ordered, as he looked up with a sly smile, winking at his partner. "I'll find out who it belongs to, don't 'cha worry yerself none."

Cole turned to leave, and then turned again. "Hey, by the way, did you ever go out and check on Sam's family?"

"Sure did, and I'm sure you'll be relieved to know that they're all fit as a fiddle," he replied as he slapped down his cards with a howl of excitement over his lucky hand.

"Hey, you can't do that!" his deputy spat sarcastically as he threw down his cards, ignoring the ongoing conversation.

"Can too, look at that sorry hand of yers…"

Cole shrugged, emitting an impatient groan and left the two men to argue alone. He didn't have time for this. He had to get home and get ready for the service. It was going to be a long day.

Chapter Fifteen

Grace quietly ascended the steps to Amelia's room as she heard the soft whimper of baby Nathaniel and lightly tapped upon the door.

"Come in," came the warm reply. As Grace entered with a smile, Adam stood from his chair and walked over to greet Grace with an outstretched hand.

"Morning, Miss," he stated with a smile that did not reach his eyes. Adam turned to his wife. "I'll leave you ladies to your picnic, but," he said, giving Amelia a gentle, but stern look, "take it easy, and don't be out too long."

"I'll make sure she doesn't stay out too long," Grace spoke up, seeing the look of concern on his face as he turned to leave.

Amelia greeted Grace with a weary smile, absently rolling her eyes, "He worries way too much. Please, have a seat."

"Thank you. It's good to see you up and smiling this morning." Grace walked over to sit in the chair Adam had just abandoned.

"It's nice to be up," she admitted as she laid the infant across her lap and buttoned her blouse. "Adam prepared a nice warm bath for me earlier, it was almost heavenly," she smiled. "I really needed that."

"That was kind of him," Grace exclaimed. "Are you hungry?" she asked with a smile, "I hope you like fried chicken."

"Mmm...now that does sound heavenly."

After bundling the baby in a light cotton blanket, Amelia grabbed the old picnic quilt as Grace grabbed her cane and headed back downstairs.

Grabbing the picnic basket, they headed out the back door into the bright beautiful day.

"Oh, it feels so good to be out in the fresh air," Amelia sighed with pleasure, tilting her face toward the warmth of the sun. The sweet tangy scent of honeysuckle tickled her nose as she deeply inhaled, reveling in the beauty of the outdoors and the intensity of her reawakening senses.

"Here, this spot looks lovely," Amelia stated as she stood under an old dogwood tree.

Grace placed the picnic basket on the ground, and flipped the old quilt into the air as the light wind caught the quilt, flipping it around. Giggling, the women grabbed at it, laid it straight, and pinned the corners down with the picnic basket and the opposite end with Grace's cane.

"Thank you," Amelia laughed, settling herself and the baby on the quilt. Her lips lifted in laughter belying the grief in her broken heart. "With that gust of wind, I don't think either one of us could get this thing to stay on the ground ourselves!"

Grace's heart went out to her as she smiled in blossoming friendship.

Time flew by quickly as the women enjoyed each other's company and leisurely ate their lunch of fried chicken, bean salad, coleslaw, and biscuits as the baby napped contently between them.

All too soon, Adam hollered from the backdoor calling to his wife to come in to prepare for the memorial service.

The joy the two women had shared had fallen away as quickly as the dying breeze. Somberly, Grace helped Amelia stand with the baby nestled securely in his mother's arms and quietly gathered up the remains of their picnic.

Grace, needing to hurry home to freshen up, hugged Amelia thoughtfully and thanked her for a wonderful afternoon. Scurrying back to the boarding house with a heavy heart, she quickly sent up a prayer for strength and comfort for her new friends.

As Grace hurried up the steps, concentrating on positioning her cane, she almost ran into William as he came bounding down them. Quickly, he reached out a hand to steady her. "Sorry about that, Miss, I didn't mean to startle you."

"Oh, I'm sorry," she sniffed, rushing past him.

"Hey," he stopped her, reaching for her arm. "Are you alright?"

"Yes, I'm fine. If you'll excuse me, I need to freshen up before the service."

Grace lowered her head and scurried past him just as Cole came walking up the stone path, fresh from home with a crisp white shirt and black suit.

Cole silently fumed at seeing William holding Grace's arm. He first saw them as he got down out of the buggy, but could not hear what they were talking about, but he knew that Grace was not happy.

"What did you say to upset her, Hollister?" Cole threw out angrily as he watched Grace's quick departure into the house.

William looked at him in surprise and grinned. "Oh, that," he replied, casually popping open his gold pocket watch. "I was just telling the lovely lady that I have business to attend to and I'll be unable to go on our ride this afternoon," he lied, tucking his watch back into his waistcoat. "I guess she was a little upset, but I told her that we can go another time."

Cole glared at William. *Why on earth would Grace even entertain the idea of going for a ride with this scoundrel?*

Cole didn't believe him. "I'm sure she would rather go to the service anyway."

William rocked back and forth on his heels, crossing his arms over his chest. "You know," he drawled, lifting a finger in thought, "maybe I'll wait until she comes out and tell her we can go after all. I'm sure I could attend to my business this evening instead. Besides, why would she want to attend the Cornwell's service anyway? She doesn't even know these people."

"And you don't know her, so don't bother," Cole gritted between his teeth. He tried with all his might to calm his erupting anger, boldly staring the taller man in the eye, fists clenched.

"Well, I'll be getting to know her pretty soon Matthews, considering she has agreed to go on a ride with me; if not this evening, then soon."

If Cole had not been in his Sunday suit, he probably would have flattened him at that very moment. How *dare he talk of Grace that way! She wasn't even here to defend herself.*

Cole gathered what little patience he had left and pushed past William to see if Ms. Millie needed his help. *This was the reason he came over here for anyway, wasn't it?*

Cole pasted on a smile as he entered the warm kitchen. "What can I help you with Ms. Millie?" he questioned as he tipped his hat in greeting.

Ms. Millie, busy covering the dishes with cheesecloth, looked up at Cole as he walked in.

"Whew-wee, look at you! Don't you look handsome," she exclaimed as she held out a couple of dishes. "I need to get all of these dishes over to the Cornwell's. I know there's quite a few. Did ya bring the buggy?"

"Sure did, Ma'am," he stated, reaching for the dishes. Both hands full, he headed towards the door and gently kicked it open.

Temper still high, he searched up and down the street to find William Hollister strolling towards the Mercantile. Willing his temper to cool, he asked God to help him forgive his ex-partner and to control his feelings whenever he saw him. He knew it would only be by the Grace of God.

As Ms. Millie and Cole carried out the last of the food, Grace came slowly down the steps, cane in hand. Concentrating on taking it slow and easy, she did not realize that Cole was watching.

"Can I help you?" he wanted to know with concern as he stepped towards her.

Grace looked up, smiling at the now well-known deep voice, and shook her head. "No thank you, Cole. I need to be doing for myself or my ankle will never heal," she admitted, landing a bit unsteady at the bottom of the stairs.

"Well, everything's in the buggy," Ms. Millie stated, as she looked around, hoping she didn't forget anything. "Jed, ya ready? We need to be goin'," she hollered as she peered into the mirror in the foyer and gently placed her dark blue bonnet on her head, tucking in the wayward gray strands.

Jed walked in from the mudroom, looking quite handsome in his two-piece suit. "I'm ready Millie."

He smiled his welcome, and hobbled towards Grace and extended his arm, "May I?"

Grace gratefully accepted his assistance, with a twinkle in her eye, as she allowed him to help her out to the buggy, much to Cole's disappointment.

The short ride to the Cornwell's was a quiet one with everyone representing the solemn mood of the afternoon. As they disembarked from the buggy, Cole, without warning, placed his hands around Grace's waist and gently lifted her to the ground.

Grace looked up at him in surprise and nervously brushed his hands away the moment she gained her balance. "I could have managed on my own," she commented shyly.

Cole smiled a half-hearted mischievous smile, "Really?" He knew as well as she did how difficult it was for her to manage the cane, especially dismounting a buggy.

Grace just shook her head and turned towards the house, but not before she noticed Ms. Millie smiling at the young couples exchange.

As everyone gathered around the tiny gravesite to say goodbye to baby James, it began to mist. Adam stood motionless, with his arm around his grieving wife, as Doc Miller performed the service.

Amelia prodded her husband to move towards the coffin. As they ceremoniously threw a handful of dirt on the coffin, Adam broke down, falling upon the tiny casket, as the emotions of the previous days erupted from the depths of his soul.

Amelia stood by, numb with grief, swaying little Nathaniel in her arms, silently praying that God would somehow make the unbearable pain a little more bearable.

Chapter Sixteen

The afternoon slipped by quickly as friends came and went offering their condolences. Grace gave Amelia a long hug and told her she would come back the following day for a visit. It was a very emotional day for everyone.

Cole tried talking with Adam and encouraged him to lean on God for strength, but Adam refused to listen. He was angry with God over the loss of his son and it was tearing him apart.

Cole's heart broke for his dear friend, but he knew that God had to work in Adams heart in His own time.

A little while later, he bade them both goodbye and reluctantly left for Maryanne's home. Cole was in no mood to dine with anyone tonight, especially Maryanne and her family. Had he known about the funeral, he would have refused the invitation, but as it was, he would have to stick to his word.

With a heavy heart, Cole knocked on the beautifully varnished wooden door to the Brewster home, wishing he were anywhere but there.

Mr. Brewster opened the door and greeted him with a firm handshake, welcoming him in.

"Good evening, Mr. Brewster," Cole replied, pasting on another artificial smile as he removed his hat. "How are you this evening?"

"Fine, fine, come in and have a seat," he answered, waving his hand in the direction of the sofa as he took his guests hat to place on the coat tree. "Maryanne will be down shortly and Mrs. Brewster is just finishing the supper preparations," he announced as he picked up his pipe that had been smoldering in the tray.

Cole fidgeted uneasily in his seat, twiddling his thumbs, hoping Maryanne would hurry so this evening would be over and he could get back home.

The longer he sat, the more impatient he became. He tried to make small talk with Mr. Brewster, but his heart just wasn't in it. His eyes scanned the extravagant room as Mr. Brewster spoke of his banking business, oblivious to Cole's mounting dismay.

Their family room walls were adorned with Currier and Ives paintings and elegant sculptures set against a backdrop of beautiful gold etched wallpaper. He noticed a grandfather clock in the corner of the room that was chiming the hour, causing Cole to become more impatient by the minute. The mahogany furniture complimented the fine fabric of blue and green with swirls of gold woven into the intricate pattern.

Cole's eyes continued to roam the room until his attention was once again on his host, who was contently puffing away on his pipe as he continued to speak. Mr. Brewster was a hefty man, with a head full of silver hair and a full silver mustache, with small wire-rimmed spectacles perched on the end of his nose. Cole found himself thinking that if he just had a full beard and a red outfit, he would make a great Santa Claus. Mrs. Brewster, on the other hand, was as skinny as a beanpole. Her long thin face gave her the impression of a stern schoolteacher, more than likely from pulling her hair back too tightly into her usual topknot.

As before, he found his thoughts drifting back to his friends and the turmoil they were going through. He wished he could have stayed and talked more with Adam, but knew that they needed time to themselves. There would be time to talk later.

Finally, a quarter after the hour, Maryanne bustled into the parlor dressed in an extravagant burgundy dress and approached Cole with a welcoming embrace as he rose to greet her. The beautiful young woman smelled of expensive perfume, which was a little too strong for his taste as he held his breath and sat back down so he could breathe a little easier. *This is going to be a long night*, he mused.

A few moments later, Mrs. Brewster came in from the kitchen, looking neat as a pin, and welcomed Cole, motioning them all towards the dining room.

Maryanne leached onto Cole's arm and led him to the ornately decorated dinner table. The delicious aroma of steak and potatoes invaded his senses, gratefully overpowering his date's potent perfume.

Cole dutifully pulled out the heavy oak chair for Maryanne and then seated himself as he placed the floral linen napkin across his lap. He was famished.

As the steaming platter, piled with thick cut steaks was passed, Mrs. Brewster started the conversation by asking Cole if he liked Maryanne's new dress. After a receiving a courteous response, she droned on in great detail to explain where she had ordered it and how much it had cost, not to mention the fact that their daughter was well deserving of such an extravagance.

Maryanne gushed from the attention. Cole woodenly smiled and nodded his head when he felt it was appropriate, once again, wishing he were anywhere but there. However, he had to admit, the meal was delicious.

Mr. Brewster sat quietly at the head of the table as his wife did most of the talking. Maryanne sat close beside Cole, touching his arm each time she wanted to get his attention, which was more often than not. By the end of supper, Cole was too tired, emotionally and physically, to stay any longer.

"I'm sorry, Maryanne, I really have to go. I've had a long day, and I've got a lot to do tomorrow morning," he said matter-of-factly, pushing in his chair. "Thank you very much for supper, though, it was delicious."

Maryanne was not ready to let Cole leave. It had taken a long time to get him to come to supper and she was not going to let him go so quickly. Even though they had spent most of supper talking about her dress and their family, she had not had any time alone with him and she craved his full-undivided attention.

"Well, alright," she pouted, lowering her gaze. "Can you at least sit on the porch swing and visit just a few minutes?

We haven't had any time to talk alone tonight," her blue eyes pleaded.

Cole felt trapped like a restless lion in a small cage as he shuffled his feet uncomfortably. He wanted to leave, but he didn't want to be rude either.

"Alright, Maryanne," he conceded, a smile instantly lighting her face. "But only for a few minutes. I do have a busy day tomorrow."

As a spider in its web, Maryanne led Cole to the porch swing where she sat down gracefully, fanning her dress out around her.

Removing his Stetson, Cole sat on the far end of the swing, lost in thought.

"What are you thinking about?" she ventured, placing her slim, manicured hand upon his tailored sleeve.

Cole shook his head trying to clear the distracting thoughts and turned towards her. Her beautiful inquisitive sapphire eyes stared up at him making his lips curve into a smile.

He sighed. "Just tired I guess." Cole ran his fingers through his hair and leaned back into the swing as Maryanne scooted next to him.

Cole jolted back to his senses, sitting up a little straighter, feeling the urge to leave. However, with the turmoil of the day and as tired as he was, his body just did not want to cooperate.

The warm night breeze drifted lazily under the veranda, accompanied by a light scent of lavender. His thoughts, like the wind, drifted again to the woman called Grace. His heart ached for a wife. *Why was he torturing himself? She's probably married anyway.*

Cole shook his head to try to detangle Grace from invading his every thought and turned to the woman beside him. Maryanne was a beautiful woman and came from a well-to-do family. *Is that so bad?*

Maryanne gazed intently into his eyes, her beautifully etched brows knit in concern. "Is something wrong?" she softly questioned as her sweet breath lightly brushed his lips.

Against his better judgment, Cole pulled her towards him, inhaling her sweet scent and lightly brushed his lips to hers. Breathless, Maryanne eagerly pulled him down for more as the hair on the back of his neck stiffened.

What was he doing, he scolded himself. He was giving in to a beautiful woman, whom he knew he did not want a future with, just because he could not be with the woman he loved.

He gently pushed her away, pulse racing. "I'm sorry, Maryanne, but I-I've got to go. Please thank your folks for me and tell them goodnight," he sputtered. Quickly he grabbed his hat and ran to his buggy.

"Cole!" Maryanne yelled after him. "Come back!" With mixed emotions, Maryanne waited until Cole drove off and ran up to her room.

Moments later, she heard a light tap on her door.

"Can I come in?" her mother asked from the other side of the white paneled door. Mrs. Brewster opened the door and walked into her daughter's room. Maryanne was lying across her canopied bed with her head nestled in her arms.

Cecilia Brewster hurried to her daughter's side. "What's wrong, Sweetheart?"

"Oh, mother," Maryanne cried as she turned and smiled up at her mother, her eyes dancing. "He kissed me!"

Cecilia's long face registered pleasant shock. "Well, my dear, I'm sure he wouldn't have done that if he didn't have future plans in mind." Her mother's thin eyebrows rose to almost her hairline as she looked at her daughter in earnest and smiled.

"I don't know mother," she drawled out as she rolled over and rested her head on her hand. "After he kissed me he ran off. Oh, mother it was wonderful…what if he didn't like it?" she wailed, hiding her face in her arms again.

"Well, of course he did dear, look at you…," she exclaimed as she turned her daughter to face her, "you are beautiful, why wouldn't he?"

Maryanne shook her head in question. "I just wish he would have stayed." She childishly smacked the bed in frustration, her dark curls bouncing in agreement.

"Well, you seem to be doing all the right things honey, or he wouldn't have come over tonight and he certainly wouldn't have kissed you," she pointed out as she pushed a fallen stray curl away from her daughters face. "You just keep doing what you're doing dear and he'll be back." With that, Cecilia Brewster bid her daughter goodnight with a kiss on her cheek. "I'll see you in the morning, dear."

Maryanne groaned and rolled over to prepare for bed. "Night Mama."

***

The next morning, Grace woke to a throbbing headache and waves of nausea. *What is wrong with me?* She laid her head back upon the pillow and closed her eyes as she said her morning prayers. She thanked the Lord for another beautiful morning as the early sunrise sneaked its brilliant streaks of color into her small room, gleaming off the mirror gracing her room with a beautiful display of miniature rainbows.

With a light tapping at the door, Grace mustered up a greeting as the older woman carried in her breakfast tray. At one look, Ms. Millie's smile slipped from her wrinkled face as she hurried to the young woman's side, laying the tray on the bedside table. "What's wrong, dear? You don't look well."

"I'm not feeling so well, Ms. Millie," Grace admitted as another wave of nausea turned her face even more pale. I've felt this way for the last couple of weeks, but it just comes and goes, and I'm really tired. I think I'm sick"

Ms. Millie shook her head as a thought hit her like a load of bricks. "Well, I'll be."

Grace stared at Ms. Millie in confusion. "What?"

"I have a sneakin' feeling that the mysterious diary really *is* yours," Ms. Millie whispered, her eyes as big as saucers.

"I don't understand," Grace still looked confused.

"Can I ask you a personal question, dear?"

"Yes, I suppose so, what is it?" Her curiosity was peaked.

"Have you had your monthly yet this month?" Ms. Millie asked quietly.

Grace thought for a long minute and replied, "I-I'm not sure. I can't remember anything before a couple weeks ago, but...," Graces voice trailed off as she caught on to what she was trying to say. "Oh, Ms. Millie," she choked out, "you don't think..." Grace's eyes pooled as the possibility took hold. "What on earth will I do?"

"There, there, dear," Ms. Millie crooned as she patted Grace's hand reassuringly. "I'm sorry I brought it up, you just seem to have all the signs." At the crumpled emotion on Grace's face, she went on. "Well, let's not count our chickens before their hatched," she said, hoping to calm Grace with the old adage. "As you said, you're not sure, so we'll wait and see. In the meantime," she stated rather sternly, wagging an arthritic finger in the air, "ya need to rest, ya hear?"

Grace nodded silently as warm tears slid down her reddened cheeks.

Ms. Millie reached out, enveloping Grace in a warm hug. "Everything will be fine, dear. Now you try to eat something. You need your strength."

As she got up to leave the room, Grace stopped her. "Ms. Millie?"

"Yes?" she turned, brows raised in question.

"Please don't mention your suspicions to anyone, until-until we're sure."

"Oh, of course not dear, and don't ya worry none, the Good Lord's in control and either way, He knows what He's doin'."

Grace laid in bed most of the morning and ate very little of her breakfast. The more she thought on it, the more she thought Ms. Millie might be right. She remembered the previous weeks that she had been feeling sick and faint, besides the obvious fact that her waistline was thickening.

Could it really be so?

As her head continued to throb, Grace closed her eyes, allowing sleep to claim her, once again, as she dreamed of a beautiful two-story house and a family all her own.

Chapter Seventeen

The next morning as Cole was sneaking out of the house to make his rounds, his mother stopped him, "Mornin' dear, did you have a nice time at Maryanne's last night?"

Cole's heart fell, struggling to forget the kiss they had shared the night before. "It was fine ma," he fibbed, reaching for his hat. "I got things to do, see ya later."

Sandra stared after her son as she tied her apron, worry creasing her brow. Absently she prepared a breakfast of oatmeal, eggs, and toast as she spent the time in prayer.

Moments later, Joel walked in and washed his hands. "Where's Cole goin' in such a hurry?" He asked, leaning down to give his mother the usual morning kiss on the cheek.

"I don't know…he said he had things to do today," his mother sighed, setting two plates on the table. "He didn't even have breakfast."

Joel was about to make a smart remark until he noticed the worry lines etched on his mother's face. "I'll try to talk with him, Ma. It'll be alright."

Sandra smiled at her son as they bowed their heads to give thanks and to place Cole into the Lord's hands.

***

As Cole walked out the door, he sized up the day by looking to the west. It looked like it could rain, as the large grayish-blue clouds hovered low, fitting his sour mood perfectly. As he neared the horse stables, he heard raised voices and rushed in to see what the trouble was.

As Cole threw open the stable doors, he saw William throw a punch at Chuck, which threw him to the ground, hitting his head on the stable door he had just opened.

"What are you doing here, Hollister?" Cole demanded, his fists balling in anger. "You're on my property. Get out of here before I bring in the law!"

Williams scathing eyes shot towards Cole, chest heaving, as he wiped the sweat from his brow. "I came over here to talk to you and he started mouthing off to me," he barked, breathless from the exertion of the fight.

"Is this true, Chuck?"

Chuck rolled over to sit up as he wiped the blood that had started to drip from the corner of his mouth.

"No! I found 'im in here snoopin' around. When I asked 'im what he was doin' he got all defensive and wouldn't tell me."

Chuck's eyes narrowed into angry slits as Cole reached down to help him stand.

"Well, Hollister, as usual, you can't tell the truth," Cole stated unapologetically, walking purposefully towards the intruder. "Tell me. Why are you here and what exactly are you looking for?"

William gave a snort. "I told you," he snapped, standing his ground with his hands on his hips. "I came here to talk to you, but your hired hand here refused to get you," he shot an accusing glance at Chuck, who was busy brushing straw from his Levi's.

"Well, I believe Chuck over you any day," he retorted, "but I'll hear ya out." Cole did not want to talk with William, but he knew that God was working in his heart, and so, he invited him into the house for a cup of coffee.

Cole spoke with Chuck quietly before walking with William into the house. At the surprised look of his mother, hands deep in dishwater, he said, "We need to talk. Ma, if you'll excuse us."

William slipped off his hat with a smug smile and said hello. Sandra eyed Cole questioningly as she wiped her sudsy hands on the dishtowel and walked out back to finish her weeding.

Cole poured two cups of coffee and straddled the chair across from William, eyeing him suspiciously, as he handed him a steaming cup. "Well…?"

William squirmed in his seat, trying to come up with a plausible excuse. In actuality, he had snuck over hoping to check out their new stock to see if he might be able to get his hands on the new stallion they had just bought. He hadn't expected to get caught.

"Well," he replied, leaning back in the chair, buying his time. "I was thinking about going to Colorado Springs in a couple weeks to see if I could start my own ranch," he drawled, taking a big gulp of the hot coffee.

"And…," Cole prodded impatiently, his eyes not missing a thing.

"Well, I was wondering if you would go check it out for me. You know, to make sure everything is legitimate and to make sure they have good stock."

Cole stared at William apprehensively. "You want *me* to check it out?" he asked in growing suspicion, "Why me?"

"Well, you have a well-run ranch business going on here, and you know what to look for," William grinned, sweeping his hand out in front of him with false admiration as a deceitful plan slithered into his mind. Maybe if he could get Cole out of town for a while he could get his hands on that stallion, not to mention the beautiful woman at Ms. Millie's.

Cole was shocked. He didn't know what to think. He certainly didn't trust William, but he did want to offer him forgiveness and have a chance to witness to him. If this was his opportunity, he didn't want to blow it.

"Well, I'll tell you, Hollister. My gut instinct is to say no, but God has placed it on my heart to forgive you," he reached up and rubbed his stubbly chin in thought before continuing, "so, that's what I intend to do."

Cole stood up to pour them both some more coffee, unaware of the deceitful gleam in the other man's eyes. "So, tell me what you need me to do, and I'll do it, but in return, I only ask that you give me a chance to tell you about Jesus."

A deep rumble sprang from Williams lips. "You've got to be kidding," he laughed. "I know about God. I grew up in church, remember?"

Cole remembered William telling him years ago about him attending church when he was young, but to his knowledge, he had not stepped foot in a church since.

"Yeah, well I've never seen you at church, so I'd like to tell you about Jesus anyway. That's my deal; take it or leave it."

William, knowing that he wasn't going to get anywhere unless he let Cole talk, sat back and pretended to listen as he helped himself to some leftover biscuits that were sitting on a tin plate in the center of the table.

"Well, let me have it," William replied impatiently, waving a biscuit in the air. "I have business to attend to."

Cole prayed silently. *I'm doing this in obedience to You, Lord, so speak through me.*

"William, God wants me to tell you that He loves you. Even with all our sins and all our faults, He loves us and will accept us into His Kingdom, if we only believe that He sent

His son to die on the cross and that He rose from the dead so that our sins may be forgiven."

"You probably remember from when you were a child, John 3:16, which says *'For God so loved the world that he gave his one and only son, that whoever believes in him shall not perish, but have eternal life.'* And the following verse states, *'For God did not send his son into the world to condemn it, but to save the world through him.'*"

Cole could see that William was obviously not interested as he absently gazed around the homey kitchen and munched on another biscuit.

Cole kept speaking as though the Holy Spirit was speaking through him, knowing that even though it looked like the man sitting across from him was not listening, a seed was being sown.

"That means, that all we have to do is accept his free gift of eternal life by believing and trusting in Jesus," Cole exclaimed. "We don't have to be perfect and we don't have to 'buy' our way into Heaven. It's all there for the taking, if we only believe in Him, ask Him into our heart, and confess our sins."

William's dark eyes refocused on Cole. "Is that all?" questioned William, sarcasm edging his voice.

"Yes, that's it," Cole smiled. "All we have to do is accept the free gift Jesus is offering us. Answer me this, if you were to die today do you know where you would spend eternity?"

"No, I meant, are you done?" William sighed impatiently as he repositioned his tall frame in the wooden chair, causing it to creak under his weight.

Cole was taken aback. How can anyone just blow off God's gift the way he is?

"No," Cole stated with growing irritation. "Answer the question."

William rolled his eyes. "This is ridiculous. All right, I guess. I don't know. There, are you happy now?"

Cole leaned closer. "No, William, that doesn't make me happy. As angry as I have been at you and how horrible you have treated me and my family, I, with the grace of God, am coming to you to forgive you and to tell you about the Lord, and—and you just blow it off as if it's nothing."

Cole shook his head in frustration and threw his hands in the air in resignation. "Well, a deal's a deal. You listened to me, so I will go to Colorado Springs for you. Nevertheless, just know that I'll be praying for you. I've found out in the past few months that it's awful hard to hate someone you're praying for."

William ignored Cole's last remark and quickly explained to him what he wanted him to do. After discussing the plans, he triumphantly placed his hat back upon his head and walked out the door with a triumphant grin and a glint in his eye.

Cole sat staring at the closed door, stunned from the conversation that had just taken place. *Did I actually agree to go to Colorado Springs for him? Why, God...what do you have planned now?*

***

As soon as William left, Sandra came back into the house, hung her dirt-laden work apron on the peg and washed her hands, wondering what had just transpired with Williams visit.

After Cole explained to his mother the deal he had made with William, she sighed with a frown furrowing her brow and leaned back into the chair.

"Why, Cole? Why would he want you, of all people, to go to Colorado Springs for 'im?" She shook her head in confusion. "It doesn't make any sense. You'd think that he'd want to check that out for himself instead of sending someone else, especially you with your history."

"I don't know, Ma," Cole replied as he absently ran his hands through his thick curls, cradling his head in thought. "I just don't know."

He caught his mother's eyes, "At least I had a chance to witness to him. I'm sure God will honor that."

Sandra shook her head with worry as she placed her hand upon her son's arm. "I'm sure He will, dear, but you had better be very careful. I still don't trust that man."

"I will, Ma," Cole assured her as he leaned over to place a kiss on his mother's cheek. "I promise."

He turned to leave. "I need to get to town. Do you need anything? I know the baby shower is only a few days away."

Sandra's face blossomed into a smile as she thought about the party and nodded her head. "Well, ya haven't butchered that steer yet," she accused lightly, "Julia's comin' over Friday to help set up. We need it soon…and some more sugar and flour, too."

Julia was Reverend Barton's wife. She loved to host parties almost as much as Sandra did. She and Sandra had been friends ever since the Barton's moved here to take over the church sixteen years prior.

"It'll be ready, Ma. I was planning on doing it this afternoon." Cole promised as he walked to the door and slapped on his old Stetson.

"Oh, Ma?" he asked with his hand lingering on the doorknob. "Don't say anything to Joel about William coming by today. I'll tell him later."

Sandra smiled knowingly, "I won't dear. You be careful."

Chapter Eighteen

As Grace stirred from her sleep, she remembered her earlier conversation with Ms. Millie, gently laying her hand upon her still-flat belly. *Could it really be so?* Her heart fluttered at just the thought of being with child.

Lord, it's me again. I know You know what You're doing, but I don't. So if I may, she pleaded heavenward, *I ask that You let me in on it soon?*

Grace had mixed emotions at such a possibility. It would be wonderful to have a child of her own, but the thought of not knowing where her husband was plagued her. Was she really the owner of this diary?

Grace's gaze swept over the dancing curtains as she inhaled the fresh morning air spilling into her room. Her eyes rested on the diary still lying open upside down on the side table, where she had left it the night before. Eagerly she scooted herself into a sitting position, ignoring the faint shooting pains in her ankle, and reached for the book. *One of these entries has to spark a memory,* she thought.

May 17, 1866

Dear Diary,

The tension is growing with the news of the Indian attacks spreading like wildfire around the camp. I pray continually that God will protect us. I had the chance to speak to Elise today about Jesus. She asked what would happen to us if the Indians attacked. I hugged her and told her that we need to ask Jesus to protect us, and that He will if we ask Him. She asked me who Jesus was and I shared with her the gospel that was simple enough for her to understand. I could sense that she wasn't sure whether to believe me or not, and said that her Ma and Pa didn't talk about Jesus. I promised her that I would talk to her ma and pa about Jesus as soon as I could.

As the morning went on, Elise looked at me occasionally and grinned as if we had a special secret. As we stopped for our noon meal, she ran up to me with a big smile and told me that she had talked to Jesus. She was eager for me to speak to her parents. As I helped Mrs. Weston clean up after lunch, I asked about church services on Sundays. She looked at me hesitantly and shook her head, telling me I would need to speak with her husband. I approached Mr. Weston as he was checking the harnesses on the horses and he said it was my decision, but not to expect them there. Oh, diary, I have a lot of praying to do.

Grace, immersed in her reading, almost didn't hear the light tapping at her door. "Come in," came her soft reply as she reluctantly laid the book upon her lap.

Ms. Mille smiled as she brought in some milk and cookies.

"Ms. Millie, I must say you are spoiling me," Grace replied, boasting a large grin.

"Well, there's nothin' wrong with that," she admitted as she patted her arm. "I know you've only been here a couple weeks, but I feel as though we've known each other for years."

Grace squeezed her hand warmly, "I do too."

"How're you feeling, dear?" Ms. Millie questioned with raised brows.

"Fine, really," she replied at the knowing look Ms. Millie was sending her.

"Good," she brightened, changing the subject. "Cole was here this morning and said that he needed to speak with ya when you're up. He said he'd be back later."

"Oh?" Grace's heart flip-flopped at the mention of his name. "Do you know what he wanted?"

"He didn't say, but he looked pretty somber." After noticing the look of concern shadow Grace's face, she added, "I'm sure it's nothing serious, dear. Well, I'll be back up in a bit to get your tray," Ms. Millie said, changing the subject, "I need to start some sewing. Can I get you anything else?"

"No Ma'am thank you," Grace replied with a half-smile.

As Ms. Millie left the room, Grace's mind traveled to Cole. *Why did he want to speak to me? Maybe he found out something from the wire I asked Adam to send to Holcomb. Maybe ...Oh, what's the point in trying to guess? He will be here soon enough,* Grace told herself. After that thought embedded itself in her mind, she pulled herself out of bed to dress and headed downstairs.

About half-an-hour later, Grace walked slowly into the parlor with the aid of her cane, finding Ms. Millie sitting in the plush wingback chair working dutifully on her sewing. The window behind her was open wide, inviting the morning sunrise to spill its golden rays upon her sweet new friend, making her gray hair sparkle in the sunlight, giving her almost a halo effect. Grace smiled at the serene scene before her.

"Well, look at you," Ms. Millie exclaimed, startled, as she laid down her sewing to assist Grace.

Grace waved her away gratefully and hobbled over to the sofa by herself. "I didn't think I could stand one more minute being stuck in that room," Grace laughed lightly as she situated her skirt around her. "I felt as though the walls were closing in on me."

"I understand, dear, but ya do need your rest."

"I promise to take it easy," Grace replied respectfully. "Can I assist you with your mending?"

Ms. Millie thought for a moment and bent over to pick some old garments from her mending basket. "Well, if you're sure, dear, I do have some mending here to do for Mr. Anderson," she replied as she handed Grace the items that needed repaired.

"I'd love to. I need something to do, or I'll go crazy."

The two women visited as they worked, discussing many topics, one of which was the new border that would be arriving in early Fall, a new schoolteacher, Miss Bradshaw.

Ms. Millie explained to her that the last schoolteacher, Miss. Newby, had married this past spring and headed farther West to start a new life with her new husband.

"She was such a blessing. I just hope we can get another one like her," Ms. Millie mused, carefully eyeing the cloth in front of her.

"I'm sure the Lord has the right one in mind," Grace replied softly as she started on another piece of clothing.

As the women continued to talk, time went by quickly as Ms. Millie happened to notice the clock and laid aside her sewing. "Oh my, look at the time; I had better get lunch on."

As Grace continued to mend in silence, she tilted her head as she heard voices in the foyer. Grace willed her pulse to slow as she heard the familiar low voice of Cole Matthews. Was her heart beating so rapidly because of the news he had to tell her or just because he was here?

Forgive me, Lord; help my thoughts to stay pure.

As Grace sensed a peace fall upon her, Cole walked in cautiously, hat in hand, "Morning, Miss," he greeted, taking the seat across from her. He nervously cleared his throat as he propped his Stetson upon his knee. "I-I heard from Holcomb this morning."

Grace studied his handsome, rugged features as he sat wringing his tanned calloused hands in his lap.

"And…," she prompted anxiously as her heart skipped a beat.

"There's a man there claiming to be Clayton Beeson…says that his wife is missing."

At the intake of Grace's breath, Cole went on. "It seems that there was an Indian attack and they took her, uh, you, and they couldn't find you, so they had to leave the area for the safety of the other people, and when they went back to look for you, that's when they found out that you were missing."

Grace was shocked, feeling as though her heart would fail her. That would explain the diary and the entries about the Indians, but the diary said that her husband had left before her, and that she had ridden west with the Weston's.

Grace told Cole what she was thinking and watched his face as it displayed his obvious confusion. "I don't know, maybe he heard you were on that wagon stage and came back to look for you, but still...," Cole sighed and stood, absently knocking his Stetson to the floor. He started to pace before her.

"We don't even know if you *are* this Grace Beeson," he argued as he walked over and picked up his hat to place it upon the nearest end table.

Ms. Millie overheard the conversation as she walked in. "Hey, there's one way to know if it's her diary or not, and I don't know why we didn't think of this before..."

Two pairs of curious eyes darted towards Ms. Millie expectantly.

"If we get you a piece of paper, and ya wrote a few sentences," she explained, glancing anxiously between the two, "then we can match it to the handwriting in the diary."

"That's a great idea," Grace stated in agreement, half-hoping it didn't match, half-hoping it did. Her whole future depended on this one moment.

Ms. Millie pulled a piece of paper from the roll top desk and handed it to Grace, along with an ink pen and ink well.

Grace peered apprehensively from Ms. Millie to Cole as she applied pen to paper. As she was penning a few sentences, Ms. Millie ran upstairs to retrieve the diary.

Cole picked up the piece of paper, along with the diary, and studied the handwriting. After a long pause, Cole dejectedly handed the paper and diary back to Ms. Millie.

"It's a match," he replied solemnly as he ran his hand through his hair and sank into the nearest chair.

The two women examined the print for themselves. "Well, it does look like yours, dear," Ms. Millie stated simply as she held up her eyeglasses, pointing out the slant of her penmanship.

"Yes, yes it does." Grace bit her lower lip as tears filled her eyes. *What now?*

"Well, it's obvious that the diary is yours...Grace." He said her name for the first time, making Grace's heart swell. "Even so, this man may or may not be your husband. We still don't have any proof."

Both women nodded in agreement. "What should we do?" Grace whispered.

"I'll wire Holcomb and tell them that this man must come here to see you."

Ms. Millie nodded in agreement. "Yes, I think that's the best way to handle this. Whoever this man is, at least you'll be here among friends if things don't work out."

Ms. Millie patted Graces trembling shoulder and handed her a handkerchief as the tears began to fall.

"Maybe he found out that ya were on that wagon train and were kidnapped by the Indians and headed back here to find you," Ms. Millie quipped encouragingly.

Grace sniffed and blew her nose.

"I don't know," Cole stated after several minutes as he sat back in his chair and propped his leg upon his knee, tapping his boot in succession with his rapid heart rate. "I was thinking the same thing, but we can't be sure and we have to think of Grace's safety."

Grace looked frightened.

Ignoring the strong urge to wrap her in his arms, Cole rose from the chair with a heavy heart, "I'll go wire Holcomb."

Chapter Nineteen

As time passed, Grace could not set her mind to concentrate on her mending. She stuck her finger more times than she could count. Frustrated, she finally gave up.

"Ms. Millie, I think I'll go for a walk and visit Amelia. I just can't seem to concentrate on anything."

Ms. Millie looked up in concern. "Are you sure you can make it on your own, dear?"

"Yes'm, I'll be fine," Grace assured her as she reached for her cane. "I won't be long."

Oh, I will hate it if I have to leave this lovely town and these lovely people, Grace cried from within as she slowly made her way to the post office, stepping gingerly over the crevices in the boardwalk.

Help me, Father, to trust and follow You wherever You may lead me.

As Grace entered the post office with the usual musty smell and tinkle of the bell, she looked around for signs of Cole, as he was supposed to be there wiring Holcomb. When she didn't find him, much to her disappointment, she headed up the stairs to Amelia's room.

As she entered, she found Amelia sitting in the rocking chair nursing little Nathaniel and humming to him softly.

Amelia's face brightened, "Come over and have a seat," she whispered as Grace settled in the chair next to her. "I was hoping you'd come by."

Amelia carefully stood and laid baby Nathaniel in his cradle, covering him with a light blanket. Grace gave her friend a quick welcoming hug.

"Well, now that we got the niceties out of the way, will you tell me what's bothering you?" Amelia wanted to know, looking tenderly at her new friend.

Grace's face reddened. "Am I that transparent?" Grace sighed as she looked down at her hands fidgeting in her lap.

"I'm sorry, Amelia, I didn't come over here to cry on your shoulder. I came over to visit and see how you're doing."

Amelia reached for her friend's hand as Grace looked back up, tears threatening to spill. "I'm sure you did, but I see sadness in your eyes, and I want to help."

Grace melted at her friend's loving concern and instantly poured out her heart. She told Amelia everything that had transpired earlier. She cried over the fear of the future and the possibility of having to leave this small town as a torrent of tears slipped down her cheeks.

Amelia held Grace as she cried and silently lifted her up in prayer.

"Well, first you need to trust in God and stop fretting about the 'what ifs.' Just remember, God knows what's happening and it's no surprise to Him."

Grace continued to cry as she confided Ms. Millie's suspicions to her friend.

"Oh my," Amelia gasped in surprise. "Are you sure?"

"Well, pretty sure, but as much as I want children, I don't know if I can handle one by myself. If this man is my husband, how will I know, and what if he doesn't want a child?" Grace spilled all of her worries, concerns, and questions in a rush of emotion as Amelia sat, taking it all in.

"Well, first, we need to get you to the doctor to see if you are with child, then we'll wait to hear from Holcomb and go from there."

Grace nodded as she wiped her eyes with her crumpled handkerchief and blew her nose. *Why did life have to be so difficult?*

"I'll go tell Adam that we're going for a walk so he'll listen for Nathaniel. Take a moment to freshen yourself up and I'll be right back."

Amelia rushed out of the room as Grace took a quick minute to splash cool water on her tear-streaked face. After she dried and patted her face with Amelia's soft hand towel, she walked over and sat next to the sleeping baby.

Lord, if I am with child, please help me to find my husband, and please keep my baby safe. Lead, guide, and direct me and tell me what to do, Father. Your will be done. Amen.

When Amelia returned, she found Grace crying softly as she was leaning over the baby's cradle and lightly stroking Nathaniel's soft dark hair.

"He's so beautiful," she whispered as her tears fell upon him.

Amelia smiled, "Yes, he is, but I'm a little prejudiced, I'm sure."

She lightly patted Nathaniel's bottom as he began to stir and ushered Grace quietly out the door. "Adam will keep an ear out for him," she whispered as they descended the stairs.

Moments later the two women entered Doc's office together arm in arm. Doc Miller peered up from his desk with a lifted brow. "I didn't expect to see two of my best patients back in so soon. Is everything ok?"

Grace looked down at her boots peeking out from under her dress, as she felt the heat rise from the back of her neck. This was going to be embarrassing.

Amelia took charge and explained to the doctor what had transpired.

"Doc, Grace has finally found out who she is, and that she is married, but she doesn't know where her husband is," Amelia took a deep breath and continued as she squeezed her friend's hand in support, "and she suspects that she may be in the family way," she added as she looked over at her blushing friend. "She'll need an exam to confirm it if ya have the time."

"Well, it's nice to hear that you know who you are now, Miss," Doc said smiling. "I'll be happy to examine you. Why don't you remove your things and cover up with one of those blankets," he said pointing to a pile on a nearby shelf. "I'll be back shortly with the missus." With that, he left the room to give Grace some privacy.

Amelia gave her friend a quick hug, explained to her what the doctor was going to do and excused herself. "I'll be right outside if ya need me."

The sky was turning dark as Amelia perched on the wooden bench outside. She was grateful for the extended overhang off Doc Miller's office, free from any upcoming downpour.

About twenty minutes later, Grace opened the door to find a very impatient Amelia pacing back and forth. As she searched Grace with questioning eyes, she could see the tears fall as Grace threw her arms around her friend.

"Well...," Amelia prodded impatiently. "Are you going to tell me, or do I have to guess?" She said it in a teasing tone and lightly pulled herself away to look into Grace's eyes.

Grace nodded, squeezing out more tears in the process.

Amelia squealed and gave her another hug. "Oh Grace, congratulations! God has blessed you with a little one of your own...how wonderful!" She could see from her eyes that she was fighting mixed emotions.

"Oh, Amelia, I have so much to worry about already, without adding a baby to the mess I'm in. What if..."

Amelia smiled and sat Grace down on the weatherworn bench. Ignoring the threatening skies, Amelia stole a moment to comfort her friend. "Grace, you have a new beautiful life growing inside you, blessed by God Himself. God does not make mistakes. He gave you this baby for a reason; try to embrace it and enjoy it!"

Grace offered her a timid smile in return. "I have always wanted to be a mother; I guess I just never thought it would be like this."

"We never know how things are going to turn out, but believe me, there are so many people in this town that love you and would love to help you until you find your husband."

"I know. It's just that I can't even support myself, what must they think if I bring another mouth in to feed?"

"Well, I know Ms. Millie and Jed would be tickled pink to have a little one around to spoil, so don't you go worrying about that! Everything else will be in the Lord's hands."

At that moment, a loud crack of thunder made the two women jump, halting their conversation. Amelia leaped up and grabbed Grace's hand, "Come on, let's get out of this weather and go tell Ms. Millie the good news."

Grace giggled at the childlike way Amelia was pulling on her as they half-hobbled and half-ran through the rain all the way to the boarding house.

Grace and Amelia slipped off their wet bonnets and hung them on the hook to dry as they rushed into the dining room in a soggy fit of giggles.

Grace stopped short at seeing Cole sitting at the table and abruptly put her hand on Amelia's arm, silently asking her not to say anything yet.

"Well, look at the two of you," Ms. Millie chuckled at the look on the girls faces. "Hello, Amelia, I wasn't expecting to see you today. Looks like you two got caught in the rain storm," she laughed. "How's that little one of yours doing, dear?"

Amelia stifled an erupting giggle as she looked over at Grace, who just like herself was wet from head to toe. "Fine, Ms. Millie, just fine," she replied as she patted her wet face with a clean handkerchief. "He doesn't like to sleep at night, just during the day, but we're adjustin' just fine."

Ms. Millie smiled at the girls' attempt to regain their composure. "That sounds normal, Honey; he should outgrow that in a few weeks," Ms. Millie assured her.

Cole sat quietly, as the women talked, listening to the exchange and drinking his tea. Grace felt the heat rise to her face as she quickly glanced his way, only to find him studying her. She made a feeble attempt at drying her face and patting at her hair, instantly self-conscious of her appearance. Grace resisted the urge to make eye contact, knowing that if she did, he would surely see the turbulent emotions she was fighting deep within her soul.

"Anyway, what brings you here Amelia?"

"Oh, Grace came over to visit, and I thought I'd walk her back," Amelia smiled shyly. It was not her nature to tell half-truths, but she didn't want to say anything without Grace's permission. "I don't get out that often anymore," she chuckled lightly as she sat down, "even days like today are a nice diversion."

Ms. Millie laughed at her last remark, knowing all too well how true that statement is. "Did you have a nice visit?" Ms. Millie asked with a twinkle in her eyes, as she suspected she already knew the answer.

"Yes, very." Grace smiled, winking at Amelia over their special secret. Grace was still unsure of her future, but she did know that she would cherish this little one growing inside her no matter what the future may hold. As she allowed her heart to realize this truth, she instantly fell in love with her unborn child.

Cole broke into her sweet meanderings with his deep masculine voice. "I wired that man at Holcomb today. We should expect an answer soon." Quickly gulping down the remainder of his tea, Cole scooted back his chair to leave.

"Oh, I was wondering, how's your ankle?" He asked, settling his old Stetson upon his unruly dark curls.

"Uh, much better, thank you. I think it's almost healed," Grace stammered, peering up from toying with the lace tablecloth in front of her.

"Good," Cole sighed in relief, "glad to hear it."

At Grace's curious expression, he thought it best to explain himself. "I saw you go into Doc Millers when I was comin' over here earlier, I thought you might be having more trouble with it."

"Oh-uh," Grace stammered, caught off-guard, looking towards Amelia for answers.

"Doc checked her out and said that she's just fine," Amelia supplied for her.

Grace smiled back as their eyes shared their little secret.

Cole caught the exchange and wondered what was so comical, but ignored the need to appease his curiosity, tipped his hat and left.

The rain had subsided, but in its wake, left many puddles, a muddy street, and a low canopy of grayish blue clouds. Garden City has been very blessed this year. Even though they have had their share of bad storms, they have only had two twisters, that he was aware of so far this year, and those, with an exception of an old abandoned farm, did no damage to any of the settlers. Cole sent a silent prayer up to Heaven to thank God for His almighty protection right before he noticed Maryanne and her mother walking towards him. This just wasn't his day.

Chapter Twenty

"Well, hello there, Cole; how nice to see you again." Cecilia Brewster's loud voice boomed as the two women sashayed towards him.

Cole respectfully tipped his hat as he continued walking, "Good afternoon, Ladies."

Maryanne eyed him closely, expecting him to stop for a quick visit.

"Humph!" Her eyes narrowed. She refused to be dismissed so easily. "Cole," Maryanne vied for his attention in a provocative tone, making him turn in question.

Maryanne smiled and patted at her curls that were coiled neatly upon her head in a stylish chignon. "We were just on our way back home. Would you care to join us for some tea and cakes?"

Cole shook his head. "Thanks, Maryanne," he said dryly, looking from mother to daughter. "But I just had some tea and cookies over at the Boarding House and couldn't eat another bite," he said as he rubbed his taut stomach.

"Oh, well, you could just come over for a visit. Maybe I could show you our slides from California."

"No, I'm sorry Maryanne; I have a few errands to run, maybe another time."

Maryanne, not so easily put off, jutted out her chin in stark determination. "How about coming over for dinner tonight, then?"

"I'm sorry," Cole replied, trying to hide the irritation in his voice. "I have to get back to the Ranch this afternoon to butcher a steer, but thanks anyway."

Maryanne pouted and scrunched up her nose in disgust. "Well, maybe another time then. Have a good day." Dismissing Cole, she pivoted on her heel, "Let's go, Mama," she ordered. Lifting her skirts, as well as her nose in the air, she scurried across the puddle-filled street with Mrs. Brewster following closely behind.

Cole shrugged, walked into the stuffy Post Office, and greeted Adam, who was busy working behind the counter.

"Hey, Cole," Adam greeted solemnly through compressed lips. "Sorry, no word yet."

"That's alright. I thought I'd come to visit while I waited."

"You really don't have to wait around. I'll send it out to the ranch as soon as it comes in." Adam replied, stamping the envelopes piled in front of him.

"Yeah, well, I'd like to stay for a while, just in case, if ya don't mind."

"Fine with me, have a seat." Adam waved his hand in the general direction of an old deacon bench sitting against the wall. "Can I get you something to drink?"

"Naw, I'm fine," Cole answered as he sat down and propped his hat upon his knee. "I just saw Amelia at the Boarding House," Cole stated for conversation.

Adam looked up in surprise, stamp in midair. "Really? She told me she was going for a little walk with Grace and she'd be right back. What was she doing there?"

Cole shook his head. "Hard to say; they looked like they got caught in the rain. They ran in giggling, looking like they were going to say something, but they saw me and stopped. Somethin's up, but I don't know what."

"Hmmm, I couldn't imagine what it could be," Adam mused, keeping his eyes on his task.

As the men visited, they heard the unmistakable tapping of the telegraph. Cole jumped up, anxiously waiting for Adam to interpret the wire.

> I WILL BE ARRIVING IN GARDEN CITY NEXT MONDAY AFTERNOON. STOP.

"That's it?" Cole wanted to know, brows raised in question. "He doesn't seem very personable, does he?"

"Well, we'll know next week." Adam shrugged and handed Cole the telegraph.

Moments later, they were disrupted by the tinkle of the bell as it welcomed another customer. "I'll see ya later."

With that, Adam turned toward his customer as Cole walked out into the dreary afternoon, to once again, play messenger for the beautiful Grace Beeson.

***

The two young women laughed at the quizzical look Cole had given them as he left.

"Alright, what's so funny, ladies?" Ms. Millie playfully demanded as she settled two large glasses of tea in front of her guests, taking the seat next to them.

"Oh, Ms. Millie," Grace smiled as she laid her slender hand upon the elderly woman's soft arm. "I wasn't sure how I felt at first, but the Lord has given me a peace about this, and I wanted to tell you that your suspicions were correct," she announced, lightly squeezing her arm with a knowing look.

Ms. Millie glanced from Grace to Amelia and back to Grace, "Oh, my dear, how wonderful for you!" Ms. Millie gave her a congratulatory hug and listened intently as Grace told her what happened.

The women continued to talk as William Hollister strolled in interrupting their conversation. Upon seeing Grace, he smiled and tipped his hat, "Good afternoon Ladies."

"Hello, Mr. Hollister," Ms. Millie greeted, "lunch will be ready in half-an-hour. Oh, that reminds me, I had better go stir the beans." Ms. Millie jumped up and hurried off to the kitchen. "Don't want 'em to burn!"

William looked towards Grace as she sat with her eyes downcast, "Miss?"

Grace looked up, "You may call me Mrs. Beeson."

William's eyebrows shot up, "So, you're sure now? Well, I guess that changes things a bit," he said as his shoulders slumped slightly. He replaced his hat and bid the women a good afternoon, mumbling about things he needed to attend too.

"What was that all about?" Amelia wanted to know, leaning closer.

"He's been asking me to go for a ride with him. I guess he's not as interested anymore," Grace smiled as Amelia gave a soft laugh.

"Poor guy," Grace replied lightly. "He looked like a rejected puppy."

Amelia laughed aloud. "That…" she said as she bent her head towards the door. "…was not a puppy. A wolf in sheep's clothing perhaps, but not a puppy."

"What do you mean?" Grace's eyes narrowed.

Amelia sipped her tea and told Grace what had happened between Cole and William a few years back and how it almost destroyed the Matthew's family.

Grace was shocked. "I can't believe William would do such a thing. He seems like such a nice man, a little conceited maybe, but nice just the same."

"Well, I'm glad you know, so he won't be able to pull the wool over your eyes, like he did the Matthews family."

"I could tell that there was tension between those two, but I would have never guessed…," Grace just shook her head in unbelief.

"Well, sweetheart, I have to run. I told Adam I'd be right back. He's probably wondering what happened to me." Amelia gave her a quick hug and replaced her damp bonnet as she walked out the door with a wave. "I'll see you later."

After Amelia had left, Ms. Millie and Grace visited as they waited for the food to cook. Time flew by and Grace enjoyed every moment, realizing with a twinge of sadness that the longer she stayed here, the harder it would be for her to leave.

Some time later, Cole sauntered in removing his wet hat and wiped his brow with his handkerchief. "Startin' to rain again, I hope it clears up soon so we can get to that steer this afternoon," he said to no one in particular as he pulled out a chair and plopped down.

Ms. Millie stood up and on her way to the kitchen asked Cole if he would like to stay for lunch.

"Yes, I think I will. Thank you," he replied as he leaned back in the chair and pulled out a piece of paper. "But, first, I have some news."

Ms. Millie stopped and turned, all eyes on Cole, as he leaned forward and handed Grace the disturbing wire. She could see by his face that it wasn't good news

Grace scanned the message as her doe-like eyes flitted up towards his, capturing his heart once again. *She looks so frightened*, he thought. His heart ached all over again with wanting to hold and comfort her.

"What does it say?" Ms. Millie asked expectantly, as Grace sat speechless.

Grace handed her the paper with trembling hands and waited for her reaction.

"Wow, he sure doesn't waste any time, does he?" Hoping not to worry Grace, Ms. Millie smiled, "well, I'm glad he's comin' here so we can make sure he's fit for our Grace."

Ms. Millie patted Grace on the hand and stood up quickly to excuse herself, but not before Grace had detected the gleam of tears pooling in her eyes.

Cole studied the expression's playing across Grace's face, "Are you all right?"

Grace looked up, catching the endearing look in Cole's dark blue eyes. "I—I'm fine, really."

Grace fidgeted with her glass, fighting the rising emotions swelling up in her chest. Her resolve finally breaking, she cradled her head in her hands and wept. *Why is life so difficult?*

Cole rushed around the table, eager to comfort her. As if it was the most natural thing in the world, he placed his arm around her trembling shoulders and pulled her to his broad chest. Grace struggled with the urge to push him away, but her turbulent emotions would not allow her. She longed for a man's arms around her. She was scared, hungering for comfort and security.

Moments later, Ms. Millie walked in as the two drew quickly apart. Ms. Millie politely ignored the comforting, but awkward exchange, placed steaming bowls of ham and beans in front of them. "Here we go; I'll be right back."

Cole stood up quickly, embarrassed, and followed her, offering to bring in the rest of the food. Ms. Millie carried in the drinks as Cole followed behind with the cornbread.

"I thought some cold lemonade would be refreshing with the hot beans."

Grace wiped her eyes with the corner of her napkin and smiled. "Hmm...sounds wonderful. Thank you."

After the meal, Grace assisted Ms. Millie with clearing the dishes as William strolled in motioning towards Cole.

"I need to speak with you in private."

After a few moments of deliberation, Cole rolled his eyes and reluctantly followed him into the parlor.

Looking around to make sure they were out of earshot, William lowered his voice. "I wired the Marshall's, and they said you could come in my place. They think you're my business partner, so don't say otherwise."

Cole's eyes narrowed. "No! I will not go there under any false pretenses, Hollister! That was not our deal," he said with growing aggravation.

William impatiently raked his hand though his greased hair and looked around. "Keep your voice down Matthews. It's not totally untrue; we were partners at one time."

Cole lowered himself to the nearest chair and sighed, keeping his voice low, "At one time, yes, but not now."

"C'mon Matthews, I need you to do this for me. They won't sell it otherwise," William paced the room impatiently. "We had a deal, remember?"

Cole sent up a quick prayer. "I'll do it on one condition."

William threw his hands in the air. "Great, here we go again. What do you want me to do now? Memorize Bible verses?" he asked with a sarcastic chuckle.

"Well, that's not a bad idea, but no. I want you to agree to go to church on Sundays, at least until you move."

William turned towards Cole with a rakish laugh, "You've got to be kidding!"

Cole sat straighter in his chair, "No, I'm not. That's the deal now. You changed your half, so I changed mine."

At that moment, Grace and Ms. Millie walked in, startled to see the two men in such a heated discussion, and turned to leave.

Chapter Twenty-One

"Come in ladies, we're finished with our discussion." William replied, boasting his best smile. "Cole was just inviting me to church, and I thought that would be a wonderful idea," he grinned, avoiding Cole's inquisitive glare.

William slid his arm around Grace's waist. "I was wondering if you would allow me to escort you this Sunday."

Grace pulled away and hesitated, glancing between Cole and Ms. Millie, and back to William. "Uh, well…I-I always go with Ms. Millie."

William sported his charming smile, once again, showing his bright white teeth. "Well, of course," he said, grinning like a Cheshire cat. "We could all go together."

Grace smiled apprehensively. "Very well," she replied, recalling her previous conversation with Amelia about how William had not been to church in years. *Can't hurt, can it?*

Cole leaned back in the plush chair, propping his ankle upon his thigh, and watched the exchange closely. *What was Hollister up to now? How was he supposed to protect Grace when he had to go to Colorado Springs?* Cole's mind tangled in frustration, realizing that his hands were tied.

"How wonderful," Ms. Millie exclaimed with a smile, oblivious to the elevated tension in the room. "I'm so glad you changed your mind, Mr. Hollister."

"Well, I'd be right proud to escort two beautiful ladies to Sunday services," he drawled, twisting his long handlebar mustache.

Cole's eyes were fierce as he stood. "Yes, we can *all* go together," he stated between clenched teeth, eyeing William evenly.

"Oh, sorry Matthews, didn't I tell you? You will be leaving Saturday, but I will be sure to take good care of these lovely ladies in your absence," he smiled, his gaze blatantly sweeping over Grace.

"What?" Cole tried once again to control his rising anger as he noted the smug look on Hollister's face.

"Ah, yes." William pulled out a piece of paper from his front coat pocket. "Here's your train ticket," he said, handing it to Cole, "It leaves Saturday at 3:30. Mr. Marshall will be expecting you. I'm sure you understand."

William opened his pocket watch, and flipped it shut. "I must be going; I have a business meeting to attend to."

After William walked out, Ms. Millie addressed Cole. "What on earth is he talkin' 'bout?"

Cole shook his head in dismay, his fists still clenched. "Hollister wants me to go to Colorado Springs to check out a ranch he wants to buy."

"Really?" Ms. Millie questioned, reaching over to pick up her mending. "I thought he was the traveling business man."

"Whelp, as long as he's planning on moving, that's all I care about."

Hmmm, she mused, *Guess he's finally ready to put down some stakes.* Ms. Millie started her mending as Cole stood, ready to leave, and hesitated.

"Grace?" Cole breathed, enjoying her name on his lips. "It looks like the rain has stopped; would you care to go for a walk?"

Grace hesitated a moment as Ms. Millie peered over her spectacles and smiled. Grace nodded as she laid her mending back in the basket beside the sofa. A walk would do her good.

"We won't be long," Cole informed Ms. Millie as he helped Grace stand. Cole offered his arm, releasing her from the need of the cane. "May I?"

Cole and Grace walked quietly side by side down the wet boardwalk until Cole steered her off towards a small wooded area behind the boarding house. As they neared the grove of trees, Grace could hear the unmistakable gurgle of a creek.

"I had no idea this was back here," Grace exclaimed, as she gazed around them, her eyes beholding their pleasure. "It's beautiful."

"I like to come here sometimes when I need time to think and pray. I have a similar place on my ranch."

Grace sat quietly upon a large flat rock, immersing her senses in the beautiful greenery and bubbling water. Cole's nearness, along with his familiar masculine scent, made her head reel. Grace scooted away trying to hide her growing feelings.

Cole shifted, cleared his throat and gazed upon the woman beside him. "Grace, I know you're upset, and I thought we needed to talk."

Grace raised her head, drinking in the deep compassion in his dark blue eyes as he lightly brushed his fingertips against her flushed cheek.

Grace turned her head away. "Please, don't do that," she whispered with a tremble in her voice.

"I'm sorry, I can't help it. I-I feel drawn to you," Cole stood up and turned, raking his fingers through his curly hair, sighing with frustration. "Forgive me."

Grace rested her face in her hands as all of the tumultuous emotions gave way once again. Her head ached. Her heart ached.

With his back still towards her and his shoulders slumped, he spoke softly. "I never meant to hurt you, Grace. I know you may be married, but we still don't know for sure. I-I can't help the feelings that I have for you. You're a wonderful, caring, and beautiful woman; I would be crazy not to feel something," Cole's voice trembled as he spun around, both eager, yet afraid to learn her reaction.

"You don't understand," she cried, tears streaming down her cheeks. "I do care for you too, but I *am* married Cole...I-I'm with child," she hurried on, wanting to get it all out in the open. "I don't remember my husband, but I'm sure that this baby was conceived out of our love, and I have to respect that and honor him." Grace peered down as she laid her trembling hands over her still-flat belly.

All was silent except for the gurgle of the creek, the chirping birds, and the scuttle of squirrels playing tree tag.

Silently Cole walked towards the creek bed and stared, shoulders slumped even more.

"Are ya sure?" came his hoarse reply.

"Yes, I went to the doctor this morning, and he confirmed it."

Cole absently picked up a small rock and tossed it into the creek, hoping to dispel some of his pent up emotions. "How far along are you?"

"He's guessing about two-and-a-half to three months. It's hard to tell since I can't remember anything." Grace replied, her teary eyes glued to his back.

"Well, I guess it's for the best that I'm going to Colorado Springs then," he said solemnly.

Grace sniffled and nodded, wishing that things could have been different.

Cole walked over and knelt in front of her, trying to hide the evidence of his tears. "This doesn't change the fact that I still care," he told her, placing his hand over hers. "I won't be here when that so-called husband of yours arrives next week, but I'll be praying that you'll have discernment and know what to do."

Cole tenderly lifted Grace's face with his fingertips, drinking in her soulful expression, "I also want you to be careful not to get too close to Hollister. He is not a man to be trusted."

"Then why are you going to Colorado Springs for him if you don't trust him?" She asked almost accusingly, pulling away from him.

"Because," he stated patiently, as if speaking to a child. "The Lord laid it on my heart to forgive him and to witness to him. The only reason I'm going to Colorado Springs is because, in our deal, Hollister promised me that he would go to Church and listen to me when I talked to him about his salvation, but *only if* I go to Colorado Springs for him."

"Oh, Cole, I-I didn't know. I'm sorry." Grace's dark lashes flitted up for a quick moment and then back down, ashamed at her accusation.

"It's alright," Cole replied softly. "I understand that you're scared. You have every right to be, but I must follow God's direction, even if it isn't what I want to do right now."

Grace searched his warm eyes, every day growing more fond of them. She desperately longed to run her fingertips lightly along the jagged scar on his cheek, but she held herself back.

"I-I just wish you could be here when he arrives," she whispered. "I won't know what to say or know how to respond…"

"I believe that when the time comes, God will give you the answers you're searching for, but not before. Remember," he said, staring into her shining eyes, "He knows all and sees all. He hasn't forgotten you, but you must wait on His leading. Listen," he drew a deep breath, "If you don't have an answer before I come back, then just wait and pray."

Cole shifted his weight and sat beside her, as his legs were starting to ache.

"I shouldn't be gone more than a month or two."

Grace dropped her face in her hands. "Oh, if only…"

"If what?"

"If everything…if I could remember, if I wasn't pregnant, if the Deputy hadn't found my diary, so many ifs…," Grace brushed angrily at the tears that continued to fall.

Cole, once again, gently and patiently raised her chin for her to look him in the eye. He wanted her to know that she could trust him. "God has it all under control. It'll be alright, I promise."

Cole reached out to help her stand and embraced her briefly until she awkwardly pushed him away, swiping at the dirty wet spot on the back of her dress.

"I had better get back. I-I promised Ms. Millie that I would help her with the mending."

Cole nodded, all too aware of her turbulent emotions, as he took her arm and led her over the soggy path to the boardwalk.

As if on cue, Maryanne sauntered up and stopped them, deliberately ignoring Grace's presence.

"Well, hello, Cole. I didn't expect to see you out this way. Mama was wondering if you could come to supper again tonight?" she purred sweetly. "She really enjoyed your visit the other night, and," she replied in a loud whisper, "so did I."

Cole cleared his throat uncomfortably. "I'm sorry, Maryanne, as I told you earlier, I have things I need to attend to tonight, but thank your mother for me anyway."

Cole noticed the hurt expression on Grace's face and hurried to usher her into the boarding house before Maryanne could say another word, "If you'll excuse us."

"But Cole," Maryanne whined with a glint in her eye. "I thought that kiss meant something to you. I mean we…" her voice trailed off as Grace broke free from Cole's grip and rushed into the house.

Cole was fuming as he tossed an aggravated look over his shoulder at Maryanne and hurried after Grace. He could hear Maryanne calling to him as he ran. He ignored the beautiful, deceitful woman and followed the one who had already captured his heart.

Cole reached the top of the steps just as Grace slammed her door. Cole knocked anxiously. "Grace, can we talk?"

He could hear her crying and it tore at his heart. He fought the need to explain the situation and profess his love for her, but reality kept him in check. It was the wrong time.

"Please go away, Cole," she cried. "I need some time alone."

"Alright, but I'll be back later," he promised. He hesitated at the door for a brief moment, hoping she would give in. With a heavy heart, he turned to leave.

As Cole plodded slowly down the stairs, Ms. Millie met him at the bottom with concern etched deeply on her face. "What happened?"

Cole shook his head in defeat. "Can we talk a minute?"

Ms. Millie followed him into the parlor.

"What is it, dear?" Ms. Millie wanted to know as his sullen silence raised her concern even more.

"I did something very foolish, Ms. Millie, and I'm afraid I've hurt her."

Ms. Millie patted his hand sympathetically.

"I wanted to warn her about Hollister and this stranger coming. I-I was just trying to protect her, but my emotions ran away from me. I ended up telling her that I care for her and embracing her."

Ms. Millie smiled sadly and waited.

"And if things weren't bad enough, Maryanne came up as we were walking back and said things that hurt Grace. I just feel so ashamed. I never meant to hurt her," Cole held his head in shame.

"There, there dear. It'll all work out," Ms. Millie smiled, holding tightly to his trembling hand. "Remember that ALL things work to the good of those that love the Lord. Hide that verse in your heart," she instructed, lightly tapping his chest. "And see that when all is said and done, it will be His will that prevails, which is *always* for our good."

Cole nodded his head in agreement. "I know you're right, but I should've kept my feelings hidden. She doesn't need an extra burden right now."

"Maybe the Lord wanted her to know yer feelings. Let Him work it out for ya, Honey."

Cole looked up with a glimmer of hope in his eyes.

Ms. Millie squeezed Cole's hand with a wink of assurance as she reached for her mending. "I had better get to my mendin' before I have to start supper. If you see Jed on your way out, ask him to bring in some wood please."

With that as his dismissal, Cole gave Ms. Millie a quick hug and left with a heart a little less heavy.

Chapter Twenty-Two

Maryanne slammed the front door and upon hearing voices in the kitchen, stomped in, ready to explode to her mother and father about Cole's dismissive attitude.

Upon entering the kitchen, she found William Hollister sitting at their kitchen table engrossed in conversation with her father. *What was he doing home this time of day?* Maryanne shrugged and gave her father a kiss on the cheek. "Hi Papa, where's mother?"

Mr. Brewster smiled. "Hello there, Kitten," he addressed his daughter with a twinkle in his eye. "I believe your mother is over at Mrs. Hoover's having tea." Mr. Brewster looked towards William, "I'm sure you remember Mr. Hollister, dear."

William smiled at the beauty before him as Maryanne's deep sapphire eyes caught his interest. "Uh, yes, hello Mr. Hollister, how are you today?"

"Fine, thank you. And you?" He asked, perusing her up and down, one eyebrow raised.

Maryanne reddened under his intense stare. "Very well, thank you. If you'll excuse me, I need to attend to an important matter." She smiled and gave her father another kiss before bounding out of the room.

William smiled at the exuberance of the attractive young woman. "It's been a while since I have seen your daughter, George. She looks as lovely as ever," William stated, raising his coffee cup to his lips.

"Yes, I suppose it has been awhile," Mr. Brewster commented. "She's growing up way too quickly. She'll be eighteen next month."

William smiled to himself. Hmmm, he thought, she's only nine years my junior, but then he thought of Grace, who was older and more mature. William was lost in thought of the two women as Mr. Brewster cleared his throat to obtain his attention.

"Oh, I apologize, George. I guess my mind was on other matters. What was it you were saying?"

Mr. Brewster smiled. "I was saying that with the collateral of the Stallion you were telling me about, I would probably be able to give you the down payment you need on the ranch. How do you plan on financing the rest?"

***

Later that afternoon, after Grace had cried herself to sleep, she awoke feeling tired, restless, and hungry.

Reluctantly, Grace pulled herself up and made her way to the mirror to re-pin her hair and splash some cool water on her splotchy red face. Her stomach churned and twisted at the anxiety of the coming weeks.

After lightly pinching her cheeks to give her face some color and smoothing out the wrinkles from her dress, Grace headed downstairs to see what she could find to eat.

As she carefully stepped off the last step, she silently thanked the Lord for healing her ankle so quickly, as she realized that it was not bothering her as much anymore. She continued to talk to the Lord as she made her way into the kitchen.

After spying some cornbread leftover from lunch, she poured herself a glass of cold milk from the icebox and sat down at the table. Still engrossed in her conversation with the Lord, she did not hear Ms. Millie's footsteps.

"Oh, you're up. How are ya feeling?"

Grace's red puffy eyes gave away the fact that she had been crying. "I-I'm all right, Ms. Millie, just feeling a little out of sorts with all that's going on."

"I'd imagine, Sweetie. Is there anything I could do fer ya to make it easier?"

Grace smiled weakly. "No, thank you. You've done so much already. Would you care to join me?"

"Oh, I wish I could, dear, but I have to get over to the Matthews'. Sandra and I still aren't done with the fixin's for Amelia's party," Ms. Millie stated as she carried Grace's empty plate and cup to the washbasin. "Hey, how 'bout joining us? Ya wouldn't have to do anything, but maybe just gettin' out would make ya feel better, hmmm?"

Grace's face lit up. "Oh, I would love to," she exclaimed as she stood up, pushing in her chair with a screech on the wooden floor. "Just let me get my bonnet."

Ms. Millie filled a plate with leftover cornbread and covered it with a cloth to take with them to the Matthews.

"I'm ready," Grace called from the hall, already sounding in better spirits.

As the two women traveled to the ranch, they talked about Amelia's party and the cute little outfits and blankets the little one was sure to get. "I can't wait to see the look on Amelia's face when she sees the party and all the decorations," Ms. Millie exclaimed. "I remember Cole saying that he was going to be butchering a steer today, so we'll have plenty of meat for our guests and some for the boarding house as well."

As Ms. Millie continued to talk about the party, Grace's mind went ahead to the Matthews Ranch as she thought of Cole working so hard in the intense heat. After the rainstorm earlier that day, the afternoon grew hot and muggy with nary a cloud in the sky. Grace closed her eyes as she pictured him earlier that afternoon under the old dogwood at the creek and said a silent prayer that God would give them a cool breeze in which to work.

Ms. Millie rambled from topic to topic. Grace laughed merrily as she told of a letter she received from her niece commenting on the antics of her 4-year-old great-niece, Lucy. Apparently, Lucy fell into their pond trying to catch a bullfrog, making her mother run in after her. When her father saw them both, soaked from head to toe, he laughed so hard that he tripped over the front step and fell flat on his face.

As the two women entered the Matthews' yard, laughing, a smiling Cole walked up to meet them.

"Good afternoon, Ladies," he called as he steadied the horses and walked over to help them down. He extended his hand to assist Grace first, holding on a little too long for her comfort as she quickly drew away. He delighted in the twinkle in her eyes and the laughter on her lips. He never heard a sound as sweet as when he heard her laughing all the way into the yard. It was music to his ears.

Cole assisted Ms. Millie down from the buggy as the older woman tried to stifle another chuckle.

"Alright, what's so funny? I heard you two laughing all the way down the road," he smiled with laughter in his eyes.

Ms. Millie locked her arm in Cole's and smiled up at him. "Just tellin' Grace about our little Lucy."

Ms. Millie grinned with delight as she re-told the story, while Cole led her towards the house with Grace following.

Sandra Matthews greeted the women at the door and ushered them in with a friendly smile.

The warm kitchen, filled with the wonderful aroma of freshly baked bread, made Grace's stomach rumble.

"I'm so glad you could make it. And you brought some extra help, I see," Sandra smiled, giving Grace a welcoming hug. "It's so good to see you again, dear."

"Thank you, Ma'am," Grace smiled in turn, removing her bonnet. "I hope I can be of some help today."

"Please, call me Sandra," she said as she took their bonnets and placed them on the wooden coat rack near the front door.

Cole excused himself with the tip of his hat, winking at Grace as she quickly averted her eyes and deposited her attention on the conversation before her. Heat rising to her face, she eagerly followed the two women to the table to discuss the party preparations over a cup of iced tea and fresh baked bread.

The women talked and laughed for hours as they prepared for the party. Sandra and Ms. Millie were in charge of the food and cake, and Grace, still not able to stand for long periods, sat at the table and decorated the cookies the women baked, and assisted in making the party decorations.

Sighing with satisfaction of a job well done, the women retired to the front porch with a glass of ice tea before they started their way home. The sun was starting to set as the red-orange hues glowed hazily in the western sky.

"Well, I guess we'd better get going," Ms. Millie smiled, weariness edging her voice as Grace tried to stifle a yawn. "Grace looks plum tuckered."

"Yes, I'm sure we'll all need a great deal of rest tonight so we'll be able to get an early start tomorrow," Sandra agreed, dabbing a cool hankie on her neck..

Reluctantly, Grace rose from her chair as her tired muscles protested to the upcoming journey back to the boarding house.

As they said their goodbye's, Grace was disappointed that she was not able to see Cole before she left, especially since he would be leaving the following day, but comforted herself with the knowledge that she would see him in the morning.

"Goodnight ladies, see ya in the morning," Sandra hollered, as they pulled out of the yard, "bright and early!"

The trip home was quite nauseating for Grace as the wagon bounced and lurched back and forth in the mucky ruts in the road. The sun was descending deeper into the western sky, displaying its brilliant array of colors to light their way. *Oh, what beautiful handiwork the Lord has*!

As they neared town, the annoying mosquitoes started to emerge to feast on the weary travelers, making their trip just that more tiresome.

Once back at the Boarding House, Grace excused herself to her bedroom to prepare for bed. Even though sleep tried to pull her within its enticing grip, she resisted the urge as she nestled down into her pillow and opened the diary to where she had left off earlier.

May 19, 1866

Dear Diary,

I have been praying daily for the Weston's as well as all of the people on the wagon train. Everyone is becoming restless and nerves are on edge about the possibility of an attack. Mr. Weston said that our scouts have spotted a few Indians not far from here. We are on constant watch. The wagon master, Jim, keeps pushing us harder and it is wearing thin on everyone, especially the elderly.

The sweltering heat and the biting flies are almost impossible to bear. I pray that the Lord would allow us some relief. There is also a young woman in the family way two wagons ahead who passed away giving birth in the middle of the night. Fortunately, the baby made it, but my heart grieves for this little one and the husband who is out scouting. He does not even know yet that his wife is gone. Life can be so cruel at times...

Grace found herself wiping away tears, as she thought of this father and child all alone. She couldn't read any further, for tears were blurring her vision. After blowing out the table lamp, she climbed out of bed, and with a heavy heart, knelt to pray. She prayed for these unknown people, for the husband she knew she had, for the growing life inside of her, for Amelia and Adam, for the Matthews family, and for Ms. Millie and Jed. After much needed time in prayer, she climbed back into bed and fell into a deep restless sleep.

***

Morning came bright and early at the Matthews Ranch as the sun peeked merrily over the distant foothills. Cole and Joel were up early to do their morning chores, so they would have time to help set up for the party. Sandra was also up early, too anxious to sleep, baking the cake and finishing the last minute cleaning.

Happy with the way things looked outside, she breathed deeply of the fresh morning air, praised the Lord for the beautiful day, and walked back into the house to decorate the cake that had been cooling. She worked meticulously, detailing little blue booties all over the white frosting as she heard a wagon pull into the yard.

Wiping her hands on her apron, she peeked out the window to find her sons assisting Ms. Millie and Grace down from the buggy. They were chuckling at the adorable stuffed puppy Grace had made for the baby.

"The little guy's gonna love that," she heard Cole chuckle as he held it up for inspection.

"Mornin'," Sandra called as she walked towards her guests in greeting, arms outstretched.

Ms. Millie retrieved her pies from the buggy and handed them to Joel as she waved her greeting. "Mornin', Sandra!"

She gave her friend a quick hug. "Everything looks lovely," she exclaimed as she walked towards the house eyeing the tables adorned with fresh daisies. "It looks like everything's already done."

"Well," Sandra confessed anxiously, "I couldn't sleep much last night with the baby shower today and Cole leavin' and all...just too much goin' on, I guess. Besides, the boys helped out a lot."

At the mention of Cole leaving, Grace's shoulders slumped and her cheery smile slipped quickly from her face.

Pretending to be busy gathering her things, she ignored the questioning look Cole threw her way. He could sense her whirling emotions, wondering what all they entailed. The questions would have to go left unanswered as Cole reluctantly led the thirsty team to the water trough.

Time passed by quickly as the women laid out the food. They were just finishing when the entourage of wagons started rolling into the yard.

Ladies called their greetings as Joel and Cole took their teams to care for them during the party. The gift table was full, and everything was ready when a late Amelia finally pulled into the yard.

Sandra hurried over to take the baby as Amelia dismounted with the help of Joel, who had come out of the barn to assist her.

"I'm sorry I'm late, I feel just awful," Amelia said breathless, as she looked around at the gathering women. "I was just leaving when this wire came in, and I knew I had to bring it with me." Amelia gazed at her friend in empathy. "It's for you."

Grace accepted the wire with shaky hands and read it silently, "Oh my."

"What is it, dear?" Ms. Millie wanted to know, standing beside her, fanning her face.

Grace handed her the wire. "It says his plans have changed and that he will be coming in on this afternoons train at 3:00."

"Wow, he sure doesn't waste any time. Well, at least Cole will be able to meet him before he leaves," Sandra said brightly. "I'm sure he'll be on his best behavior with Cole and Joel by your side, that's for sure."

The women talked all at once wanting to know what was going on, as some were not aware of Grace's situation. Ms. Millie politely told them the facts and left it at that, relieving Grace of answering all the questions herself.

Cole, overhearing the commotion, pushed through the crowd and led a numb Grace into the warm kitchen so she could compose herself.

Cole left the door ajar and led Grace over to the kitchen table.

"I believe this is a good thing, Grace," he said, taking her hands in his. "Maybe this is the way the Lord wanted it so I could see what type of man he is before I had to leave. It'll sure ease my mind to know if he's the kind of man that will treat you right."

Grace gave Cole a wobbly smile. "It's alright Cole, I know you mean well, but this is something I have to do myself."

At the hurt look on Cole's face, Grace went on. "I mean, I want you to meet him, but I have to be the one to make the final decision."

Cole nodded glumly. "I understand, and I admire your strength, but just know that I'm here for you, and that I care for you."

Oh, Lord, why does it have to be this way? Grace pleaded with God. *Why am I falling for a man I cannot be with…and above all…when I am carrying another man's child?*

Chapter Twenty-Three

The passenger train chugged and rattled mercilessly over the endless rails, bringing with it a very nervous and frustrated occupant. Luke Mitchell repositioned himself once again on the lumpy leather seat as he wiped his sweaty hands on his trousers for the umpteenth time. The air in the train compartment was stifling with the addition of a heavy cloud of cigar smoke making it almost impossible to breath. Garden City could not come soon enough for him, or so he thought.

After hearing the news of Grace Beeson's amnesia, Luke knew that this was the woman to raise his child. Only weeks earlier, Luke was devastated to return from scouting, only to find that his wife, Ruth, had died giving birth to their daughter, who he later named Ruthie. He had seen Grace previously on the wagon train and knew that she was looking for her husband, but after the Indian attack, he didn't know what had happened to her until the wire came through at their last stop to Holcomb. He remembered thinking what a wonderful woman she was and how attractive she was. She had been his "saving grace", literally. She had given tirelessly of herself the days after Ruth's death to care for baby Ruthie as Luke escaped the pain of reality and put all of his energy into his job.

His gut burned within him, ashamed of himself for deceiving her this way. He rationalized his deceit by telling himself that he was doing her a favor by taking care of her, besides the obvious fact that he needed a mother for his little Ruthie. After talking to Mr. Weston, and paying him for information regarding Grace, he wired Garden City.

In the past month, as he mourned the loss of his wife, he turned to the bottle to try to satisfy the emptiness. He wanted to stop, but lately he was finding it more difficult to go even a day without it. He promised himself that when he and

Grace were together, he would never drink again. In the attempt to squelch his cravings, he turned his attention to the couple across from him.

They were an older couple who had shared with him earlier that they were on their way to see their new grandson.

The train lurched and hissed as the conductor hollered, "Garden City ahead!"

Luke's heart pounded rapidly as he tried to compose himself, lightly patting his coat pocket, feeling the small flask that contained his slight measure of comfort. As the train rolled to a stop, Luke Mitchell congratulated the new grandparents, smoothed his hands down his suit and exited the train as Clayton Beeson.

***

Throughout the early afternoon, the women enjoyed good food and good company while taking turns holding baby Nathaniel. As Amelia opened the gifts, she dabbed at grateful tears, awed at the generosity of the women in her community.

All during the party, Grace's stomach was tied in knots as she wondered what this day might bring. She tried to keep her mind off her troubles as she doted on Amelia and helped clean up after the party. The last wagon pulled out of the yard as an exhausted Grace finished carrying the last remnants of food back into the house.

"Grace dear, you need to sit down and take a break," Ms. Millie lightly scolded, pulling out a padded chair. "Are you alright?"

Grace gratefully plopped down with a sigh.

"I'll be alright, Ms. Millie," Grace reassured her. "I'm just tired and a little uneasy about this afternoon."

"Why don't you go lie down for a while," Sandra suggested as she noticed the girl's pale face. "We can finish up here."

Grace gazed at the worried faces around her and agreed that a nap might be just the thing.

"I'll run her to the Boarding House, Ma," Cole quipped, almost too eagerly. "I-I'm sure she'll want to lie down in her own room."

Grace quickly consented, giving Amelia and Sandra a quick hug. "I'm sorry. I just need some rest," she apologized, leaning down to place a light kiss on Nathaniel's downy head. "It was a lovely shower."

"I'll be right back, Ma," Cole called as he closed the door behind them.

"It's sure gonna be a difficult afternoon for Grace," Ms. Millie stated as she placed the leftovers in smaller bowls. "She looks so worn out; I hope she'll be alright. I worry about her health."

"I know what you mean," Sandra said with a shake of her head. "I wish Cole wasn't leaving today. He needs to be here…" Sandra was interrupted by a loud wail from little Nathaniel. "I guess he doesn't like the idea either," she chuckled.

Amelia sat at the table and laughed with the women as she tried to calm the fussing infant. "He must be hungry," she exclaimed as her son's face grew a darker shade of red. "I've found out that patience is not one of his virtues."

Amelia excused herself as the women continued their duties, chuckling in empathetic understanding.

***

The hot sun was blazing high in the afternoon sky, as the heat illuminated a watery haze across the rutted dirt road in front of them. Grace sat stiff on the opposite end of the seat as she tied her bonnet more securely under her chin. She had tired of the several times she had to pull it up as the wind struggled to pull it down. The mid day breeze was a mixed blessing. It gave them some relief from the growing heat, but in turn, stirred up the dust and dirt from the road. She felt sticky, grimy, and nauseous, altogether eager to be in out of the harsh sun.

Cole could not take the silence any longer and stopped the buggy. "Are you all right?"

Grace tucked in a few stray strands of hair that escaped from her bonnet and replied, "No, I feel like I'm going to be sick."

By the stricken expression on Grace's face, Cole patted her arm then reached for the reins. "I'll get you home as quickly as I can."

Grace lightly laid her hand upon Cole's arm. "Cole, I'm scared," her voice trembled.

Cole dropped the reins to reach out to comfort her. For a few minutes, he held her in the protectiveness of his arms and felt her relax against his chest. "Just remember, I'll be back as soon as I can. If you don't have peace about this man, then don't do anything until I come home--promise?"

Grace nodded against his chest with a sniffle, "I won't, I promise."

Grace pulled away and looked intently into Cole's beautiful dark blue eyes, trying to engrave them into her mind.

Not knowing if he would ever have this chance again, Cole drew her close and lightly brushed his lips across hers. Grace wondered if she was dreaming until he kissed her again with passionate urgency. Even though she had dreamed of this moment, she knew it was wrong, and so, broke away from his embrace.

"I'm sorry, Grace; I didn't mean to..."

Grace's voice sounded strangled. "Please take me home."

Cole nodded and shook the reins, once again, regretting his actions.

It was a silent ride back to the boarding house as the two uncomfortable occupants stared straight ahead.

Grace took this time to talk to the Lord. *Father, please forgive me. I know I cannot show my feelings to Cole. Please take away these feelings if it is not Your will.*

Grace stared off to the side as the growing heat of the day made her even more nauseous. She tried to keep her mind occupied by trying to count how many animals she could spot along the way. She made a game out of it as she spotted a hawk circling high above her head, cattle dotting the farm pastures, and a jackrabbit scurrying into a nearby bush. As they neared town she spotted barking dogs, stray cats, horses pulling buggies and even some oxen. As Grace was trying hard to keep her mind occupied, Cole's was unable to stray any farther than the beautiful woman sitting beside him.

Oh Lord, I can't believe I pushed myself on her like that. She has every reason to be angry with me. Forgive me for my actions, and please let her forgive me, too. Help me to deal with my feelings for her one way or the other.

As they pulled in front of the boarding house, Cole jumped down and walked to the other side of the buggy to assist Grace, but was caught by surprise as he found William Hollister already helping her down.

"Matthews," Hollister greeted with a pretentious sneer. "Are you packed and ready to leave?"

Cole frowned. "Yes, I'm ready, so if you'll excuse us," he replied brusquely as he grabbed Grace's arm and headed for the steps.

"What's the big hurry? You still have a couple hours to spare," he remarked with a wry grin.

"I have to get Grace inside; she's not feeling well," he replied with growing irritation.

William looked concerned. "Oh, my dear Grace, I'm so sorry. Here, let me help you," Hollister drawled as he reached for Grace's opposite arm.

"Gentlemen," Grace stated angrily, glaring between the two. "I am *not* a pull toy, I can manage by myself. Good day!" With that, Grace shook both men loose from her arms, hurried inside, and ran up to her room. As she closed the door, she could hear the two men arguing. Furiously she hurried over and slammed her window shut.

Just as she was turning from the window, she noticed Maryanne sauntering towards the boarding house. Grace felt a stab of jealousy as she noticed the two men, halting their argument to greet her as she flashed them her best smile.

"I don't need him," she cried. "She can have him!" Grace turned quickly, removed her bonnet and placed it on the side table as she plopped down on the bed and relinquished her pent up tears.

A while later, Grace, somewhere lost in a thick fog of sleep, heard a knock at the door. "Grace dear, it's after 2:00, time to get up."

Grace awoke with a start and quickly jumped out of bed as she hollered her reply. She hurriedly splashed some cool water on her face, brushed and re-pinned her hair and changed into a clean fresh dress. The dress she picked was a soft green to set off her creamy skin and medium auburn hair. Noticing again that the dress was a little snug, she tried to suck in her slightly expanding belly as she examined herself in the mirror. The heat in her face rose as she noticed that her tummy was not the only thing that was expanding.

"My goodness, dear," Ms. Millie exclaimed as Grace hurried into the parlor, flushed. "His train isn't going to be here for another half-hour yet. You have time."

"I know Ms. Millie, I guess I'm just a little nervous," she admitted. Grace paced the room, wringing her hands nervously.

Ms. Millie set her mending aside and patted the chair next to her, "Sit down, dear."

Grace perched on the edge of the chair and played with the lace trim on the sleeve of her dress, her knee bouncing nervously.

"Grace, I really believe that it'll all work out, and you know as well as I do that if Cole doesn't like the man, he'll send him packin'."

Grace peered up at Ms. Millie, searching her eyes for the truth of her words. "You really think he would be able to see if he was real or not?"

Ms. Millie nodded. "I do. Cole's a very good judge of character, and he won't leave you with this man if he doesn't approve."

Grace let out a slow, nervous breath, "Will you pray with me, Ms. Millie?"

Ms. Millie's eyes pooled at the simple request, "Of course."

Ms. Millie reached out to Grace as the two women bowed their heads. Ms. Millie lifted her prayers up to the One who knew all. The peace they felt after their prayer was a confirmation that God was and still is in control.

The two women hugged, and dabbed at the corners of their eyes as Jed walked in the parlor with two tinkling glasses of iced tea.

"Thought ya might like somethin' cold to drink before ya had to go out in that heat." Jed handed them each a glass and turned to leave when Grace stopped him.

"Jed?"

Jed turned around at the mention of his name, long bushy gray brows raised.

"Yes, Miss?"

Grace smiled graciously. "Jed, I want to thank you for all you've done to make me feel welcome here," she said, and turning her gaze towards Ms. Millie. "You have both been so very kind. I-I don't know what I would've done without you, either of you…" Grace reached for her hankie as the tears of gratitude began to fall. "I love you both, and I just want to say thank you."

***

As Luke reached for his bag, he quickly scanned the crowd to see if he could spot Grace. At first, he could not find her, but upon further searching, and with his heart pounding a mile a minute, he finally saw her, sighing in relief. She was more beautiful than he had remembered. She was obviously doing rather well as she had put on some weight and had a glow about her.

Upon further inspection, Luke noticed a rather handsome man standing beside her, almost protectively, as well as two older women. As Luke walked through the throng of people, his stomach churned and he began to perspire. He almost turned to leave, but he remembered little Ruthie back home and knew he must go through with it, for her. Squaring his shoulders and placing a smile on his face, Luke walked straight towards Grace, removed his hat and extended his hands.

"Grace," he gushed, taking her gloved hands in his. "I can't believe I've finally found you," he lied. "How have you been, my dear? You look as lovely as ever."

Taken back by the forwardness of the stranger, Grace quickly glanced towards Cole, hoping to decipher his immediate reaction.

"H—Hello...Clayton?" she asked pensively, her head slightly tilted. Her heart pounded as he nodded. She did not recognize him.

Luke squirmed uncomfortably under his dark pinstriped suit. "You don't remember me," he sighed. "I-I was hoping…"

Cole cleared his throat and gazed intently into his eyes, extending his hand, "Afternoon, I'm Cole Matthews; I'm the one that found Grace on the prairie last month."

The two men shook hands and sized each other up. "Grace doesn't have her memory back yet, but her diary seems to be helping."

Ms. Millie introduced herself next, and invited Luke to the boarding house for supper. "If ya don't mind, we can take your bag to the Boarding House and you can stay with us for a few days until you and Grace get reacquainted."

Luke smiled as he returned his gaze back upon Grace. "Thank you Ms. Millie, that's very kind of you."

"Shall we go then? We can talk more after you're settled. It's rather warm out today." Ms. Millie reached out to give Cole a quick goodbye hug before she turned to leave. "If ya follow me, I'll show ya the way."

Luke peered quizzically at Grace as he picked up his bag.

"If you don't mind," Grace posed, turning toward Luke, "Cole is leaving in 15 minutes on the next train and I'd like to see him off."

Luke did not know what type of relationship she and Cole had, but as long as he was leaving, he did not see any harm in it. It might help to break the ice between them if he allowed it. "Very well Grace, I'll be waiting on you at the Boarding House, unless you would like me to stay…"

"No, no, y-you go on and get settled in. I'll be there shortly," she stammered as another wave of nausea suddenly hit. Grace wasn't sure if it was from the heat, the baby, or just the uncomfortable situation she was faced with.

Luke's inquisitive eyes shifted between Grace and Cole before he turned to follow Ms. Millie, who was patiently waiting for him in the shade.

After Luke and Ms. Millie walked off, Cole led Grace to a nearby bench in the shade of the overhang and sat down beside her. "How are you holding up, Grace? Do you remember him?"

She shook her head with a sigh. "I'm alright, but I'm afraid I have no memory of him." Grace anxiously toyed with the hankie tucked into the sleeve of her dress and looked up into his beautiful blue eyes. "What do you think?"

"It's hard to say after just a couple minutes, but he seems nice and well-mannered. Not to mention, from the way he's dressed, he must not be bad off. I just wish I had more time," Cole removed his hat and scratched at his head as he watched the man in question departing with Ms. Millie. "It just seemed odd the way he addressed you…ah," he absently plopped his hat back on his head, "maybe I'm reading too much into it." Cole's eyes pivoted back to Grace. "Promise me you'll be here when I get back?"

Grace smiled tenderly, "I'll try, but please hurry."

Cole laid his large hands over her small trembling ones and gave them a reassuring squeeze. "I'll be back as soon as I can."

Cole ached to hold her tenderly in his arms and kiss away her fears. "Grace, I'm sorry about earlier, I-I don't know what came over me. Please forgive me."

Grace smiled and shook her head. "No need. God be with you, Cole."

With that, he rose with a heavy heart, grabbed his bags, and headed for the train as he heard the attendant yell the final boarding call. It was going to be a long couple of months.

Chapter Twenty-Four

Back at the Boarding House, a somber Grace walked in with a heavy heart to find Clayton and Ms. Millie in friendly conversation drinking ice-cold lemonade.

"There she is." Ms. Millie exclaimed. "I was just telling Clayton about our little town and was asking him if he would like to stay on for the church social we're having at the end of the month." Ms. Millie winked at Grace, hoping that she would realize what she was doing.

Grace wearily smiled her thanks as her eyes caught Ms. Millie's. She appreciated what she was trying to do, but it would take more than that at that moment to make her feel better. She felt like her whole world, or at least what she has known to be her whole world in recent weeks, was falling apart at the seams.

"That would be a great idea." Grace acknowledged as she laid her reticule on the nearby stand and forced her feet towards the nearest chair. Her heels echoed on the wooden floor; sounding hollow and empty, just like her heart.

She secretly wanted to run up to her room and throw herself on the bed and cry herself to sleep, but she knew that would be rude, and so she resigned herself to sit and acquaint herself with the stranger across from her.

Luke stole a few minutes to study Grace, his new wife, as she took her seat. He inhaled in pride as his eyes admired the woman before him. She would make a good wife and mother he was sure.

He could not help but notice her dress, which emphasized her full figure and her dark auburn tresses pinned up in a mass of curls, with the exception of a few loose strands that graced her beautiful oval face. Her eyes were the deepest brown, and her lips were full and lovely. Sensing a lull in the conversation, he looked up, finding both pairs of eyes staring back at him.

Peering between the two women, he stammered an apology. "I-I'm sorry. I can't help but stare. You're just so beautiful…more beautiful than I remember, and I-I have missed you."

Shock registered on Grace's face, her eyes squinted in disbelief. "Missed me? As I have read in my diary, *you* are the one that chose to leave." Her eyes held their questions and he could see the pain of rejection harboring within them. "Why…?" Her lower lip quivered, stopping her from continuing.

Luke knew he would have questions to answer, but he was not the slightest bit prepared for the pain that he found in her eyes.

His plan was built on lies, and his own agenda. He had not even thought of how Grace would feel, nor did he know about the diary. She hurt deeply, even if she could not remember, and he began to regret his deception once again.

Grace brought him back to earth by clearing her throat.

Luke leaned over the table, resting on his elbows. "I-I'm sorry, Grace. I regret leaving you now. I was foolish and scared. Can you ever forgive me?"

Grace searched his eyes for the truth, but saw nothing. "You're sorry?" Grace squeaked with emotion as she felt another wave of nausea creep in. "Do you realize what you have put me through? Do you realize..." Grace could not stay there a moment longer. She raced out of the room with her hand over her mouth and ran out the back door in tears.

Luke's eyes shot towards Ms. Millie with concern. "I-I'm sorry. I didn't mean to upset her. I'll go after her."

Ms. Millie jumped up, almost knocking over her chair in the process, "No, let me...y-you finish your lemonade."

Ms. Millie walked out the back door and found Grace doubled over by the water barrel. "Grace! Are you alright?" she asked as she raced to her side.

Grace nodded her head and reached for her hankie she had tucked in her sleeve to wipe her mouth. "I-I'm alright...just not feeling well. I-I'm so scared Ms. Millie. I don't remember him. I-I don't know what to do or what to say..."

Ms. Millie patted Grace's shoulder, her brows knit with concern. "Shhh, it'll be alright dear...you have enough time. I'm sure he won't rush you. He seems like a very nice man. He wanted to check on you himself, but I didn't know if you wanted him to know about your condition just yet, so I hurried out instead."

Grace shrugged and wiped her tears with the clean hankie Ms. Millie held out to her. "It doesn't really matter, does it?" she sniffed. "I mean…he'll know soon enough anyway." Grace added as she looked down at her small pooch and settled her hand upon it, "I don't think it can be hidden much longer anyway."

Ms. Millie gave her a quick encouraging hug. "You're right, Honey. Let's lay it all out on the table and see what he has to say about it, huh?"

Grace sniffed, dabbing at her eyes. "Alright, I guess this will tell us what he's made of, huh?"

Ms. Millie laughed and put her arm around Grace's shoulders and gave them a squeeze as they walked back into the house, ready for whatever may lie ahead.

***

Across town, Adam was reorganizing the storeroom as he heard the tinkle of the door alerting him of a customer. As he walked out of the back room wiping the dust from his hands on his work apron, he stopped short as he saw his mother and father walk through the door, luggage in hand.

"Ma, Pa?" He could not believe his eyes.

"What are you two doing here already? We weren't expecting you until Thanksgiving." He hurried around the counter and embraced his mother. How was it that they walked through the door just when he needed them the most?

"How're you doing, son?" His father asked as he patted him on the shoulder in greeting.

"Good, Pa. When did ya get in? Amelia's going to be so excited to see you!"

At that moment, Amelia came down the stairs with little Nathaniel. "You're here!"

Amelia rushed over and joined in the happy reunion. "I wish I would've known you were coming so we could have met you at the station."

Mrs. Cornwell waved her hand in the air to dismiss the subject as she reached out for her new grandson. "Oh, Amelia, he's just beautiful. Looky here, Nate, isn't he precious?" she cooed, turning to her husband who was peering over her shoulder.

Amelia and Adam stood back and smiled in pride as their son met his grandparents for the very first time. "Please, Mom and Dad," Amelia stated, "come upstairs and make yourselves comfortable. I was just on my way to get Adam to take a break. He's been working all afternoon cleaning out that storeroom," she said, ushering them up the stairs. "I just made a fresh pot of coffee."

Adam grabbed his parents' luggage and headed towards the stairs.

"Adam," his pa stopped him, "leave those there. We'll go over and stay at Ms. Millie's. The man at the station told us she has rooms available."

"Are you sure you don't want to stay here? We have the baby's room…"

"Naw, we'll just be bumping into each other." Changing the subject, he urged his son on with a wave of his hand, "C'mon, we had better get up there before we get hollered at."

Adam was curious as to why his folks didn't want to stay with him, but dismissed the subject until later.

"It's good to see you, Pa." He hugged his father and followed him up the stairs.

The evening flew by quickly as Myra and Nate Cornwell enjoyed passing their grandson back and forth and visiting with their son and daughter-in-law. After hearing the news of the birth of the baby, and the death of James, Myra wanted desperately to come visit, but Nate, who was a large man with a heart condition, was advised by his physician not to make the long trip.

However, when Amelia wired that Adam was turning his back on God and needed his parents, the doctor reluctantly gave Nate consent to travel, but only if he took it easy. Adam and Amelia did not know the extent of Nate's illness, but Myra knew that if they were going to make the trip, they should do it before winter set in.

Just as the sun was starting to set into its brilliant splash of pink and purplish hues, Nate and Myra excused themselves to the boarding house to settle in, promising to meet Amelia, Adam, and the baby for breakfast in the hotel lobby the following morning.

Later, as Amelia gently laid little Nathaniel down in his crib after his feeding, and covered him with the baby quilt Ms. Millie had made for him, she sighed.

"Why do you suppose your Ma and Pa didn't want to stay with us?" she whispered as she walked over to the bureau, careful to not wake the baby. "I'm worried about them," she stated as she slipped off her dress and into her nightdress. "Your father doesn't look well."

Adam was getting ready for bed himself and just nodded as he unbuttoned his shirt.

Amelia walked up to her husband and wrapped her arms around his waist, gazing up into his clouded gray-blue eyes.

"I know. He didn't seem like himself." He gave her a tight squeeze and shrugged, trying not to worry. "It's probably just the long trip out here, but I'll ask Ma about it tomorrow."

***

Luke tapped his fingers in a steady rhythm as he waited for Grace and Ms. Millie to come back into the house. As he heard the creak of the back door, he stood quickly. "Is she alright?" he asked Ms. Millie, noticing Grace had been crying.

"She's fine, Mr. Beeson…"

"Please, call me L-Clayton, or Clay if that suits you." He reddened, almost giving himself away.

"Like I was saying, she's fine. She just needs some time to sort through some things. Although I do think you two need to have a long talk."

Luke nodded his head as Grace lowered hers. Her emotions were turbulent at best, and it was all she could do just to sit still.

Ms. Millie perched on the edge of the chair next to Grace for moral support. "If ya don't mind, Clayton, I'd like to stay with Grace for now."

Luke nodded his head, "That'll be fine, Ma'am."

Ms. Millie glanced over at Grace and patted her hand. "Alright, Honey, tell him what you're feelin'."

Grace swallowed hard and toyed with the lacy placemat on the table before she mustered enough courage to look at the man who called himself her husband. "I-I really don't know where to start..."

"Then allow me," Luke offered, eyeing her attentively. "I know this is all new to you, but I'll tell you what I can." Luke shifted uncomfortably in his seat and took a long sip of lemonade, trying to recall everything Mr. Weston had told him.

"First, I want to say how sorry I am for leaving you. I realize now that I was wrong, and I want to ask for your forgiveness."

Grace's head shot up as she searched his eyes. He smiled and looked back down at the table, not wanting her to see too deep into his soul, lest she see that he was lying. Grace kept silent, waiting for him to continue.

"Anyway, after I left, I traveled with a wagon train west for a while when one day an epidemic of cholera broke out in the camp and killed many people."

At the sharp intake of breath by the two women, Luke looked up to see if they were buying his story. "I was lucky to have survived." He could feel his body go cold with perspiration. "Then, after that horrible ordeal was over, the few of us that were left had to bury the dead and take care of those that were left grieving and alone."

The two women were perched on the edge of their chairs as Luke continued his story.

Ms. Millie clucked and shook her head in sympathy, "How terrible."

"Yes, it was," Luke went on. "That evening when we broke camp, a scout came by and handed us a bundle. We had no idea what it was until we opened it. It was a baby…" Luke's voice cracked as he thought of the first time he had seen his daughter and discovered that his wife had died. He swallowed the lump in his throat and went on, "Somehow, she had survived her parents and was found in one of the wagons."

Grace's delicate hand flew to her mouth as she gasped in dismay. Tears stung her eyes as he continued his story.

"Well, to make a long story short, seeing that little one made me think more of you and what we could have if we were together again, so I took her in and came to find you."

Grace's eyes grew wide in shock. "Y-you mean you kept her? Can you do that?" Grace squeaked, looking from Ms. Millie and back to Luke. "Doesn't she have any kin? Have you tried looking?"

Luke, taken aback by her pointed questions, would have thought she would be happy that he had a little one for her to love. Once again, he questioned himself and his motives. *No*, he thought, *I have to do this…*

Luke tried to remain calm as he twisted his glass nervously in his calloused hands. "I *have* wired the authorities," Luke's eyes challenged hers. "No one else wanted her, Grace. I-I couldn't just leave her."

Grace solemnly nodded; embarrassed that she would even question his kind deed. "I'm sorry, o-of course you couldn't. I'm sure that was a very hard decision for you."

Luke looked into her eyes and saw them soften. "The only difficult part was not having you there with me."

"You've done a brave and wonderful thing, Clayton," Ms. Millie acknowledged admiringly. "Not many men would have taken on the responsibility of a child by themselves, especially a baby."

Luke shrugged. "Well, I knew my Grace, and I know she would have wanted to take her if no one else could." He directed his vision towards Grace, assuming that a softhearted woman such as herself would not deny such a statement.

Grace continued to search his eyes through a veil of tears. "You're right. I would have."

Grace smiled at Ms. Millie and reached for her hand to draw more strength. "I'm happy to know that you're sensitive and caring, Clayton, because…I-I'm going to have a baby…your baby."

Now it was Luke's turn to look shocked. He drew in a deep haggard breath and exhaled. He sure hadn't expected that bit of news. This was better than he had expected. He reached across the table for her hands and smiled. "Grace, you've just made me the happiest man in the world! When?"

Grace smiled, "Doc said sometime in late January." The glow illuminating from Grace was unlike anything he had ever seen.

Luke jumped up, strode around the table, and stood in front of her. "I-I can't believe it, I'm gonna be a daddy!" He gave a loud whoop, making Grace and Ms. Millie laugh in the process. "May I?" he asked, reaching to feel the slight bulge of Grace's abdomen.

Grace's eyes held their concern as he reluctantly pulled his hands away. "Forgive my forwardness, Grace, I guess I was just too caught up in the moment."

Grace stood quietly for a moment, placing her hand almost protectively upon her growing belly. Moments later, she reached for Luke's hand and gently put his hand under hers. With her hand on his, the emotions running through his body were hard to contain. *This will happen*, he told himself, *and we will be a family.* Ruthie will have a wonderful mother and a little playmate. He was elated that everything was happening according to plan...although, he still needed to guard his heart, just in case.

Ms. Millie stood back and watched the awkward but tender scene before her. Clayton seemed like a good man, but something about him just didn't sit well with her. There was something in his eyes...darkness...secrets, she just couldn't put her finger on it.

Chapter Twenty-Five

"Next stop, Colorado Springs!"

The conductor walked through the passenger car announcing their next stop. Cole awoke from a fitful night of trying to sleep; his shoulder and neck balking at his choice of bedding. His large frame was not accustomed to such a small space, but finally giving in, he laid his head against the windowpane with his carry-on as a makeshift pillow. The train seemed to jerk with every shift and sway of the car as he fell into a restless sleep.

As he rubbed the sleep from his eyes, he noticed that the sun was coming up, and the people on the train were beginning to stir. Hoping to work the kinks out of his neck, he rolled it from side to side and shrugged his shoulders with little relief. His head throbbed from the jostling train ride and the countless noises assailing his senses. The old man sitting next to him was still sleeping, oblivious to the growing commotion, snoring away making the rattle of the train almost quiet in comparison.

His eyes fell upon the young woman in front of him who was trying to gather up her belongings along with her children to prepare for their departure from the train. The children were grumbling, as they were tired and hungry. The poor woman looked as worn out as Cole felt. He felt sorry for her. It was hard enough for an adult to endure a long tedious train ride, let alone with two small children.

Cole held his bag on his lap, ready to depart the train as soon as they opened the doors. His eyes followed the scene before him, watching the children tug on their mother's sleeve as he remembered the extra biscuits and cheese he had in his satchel, which he had purposely saved for breakfast.

He could feel the heat rise in his face as she caught him staring.

"I'm sorry. I hope they aren't disturbing you," she apologized, referring to her rowdy children, who had stopped to peek over the back of the seats. "It has been quite a long journey for them and they ate the last of the bread and cheese last night."

"Oh, not at all; actually, I was just going to offer them a biscuit…if you don't mind, that is." Cole quickly rummaged through his bag. He extracted a smaller cloth bag and pulled out two flattened biscuits and a piece of cheese as the children's hungry eyes searched their mother's for permission.

At their mother's nod of approval, both children snatched up the biscuits and cheese in one fell swoop.

"What do you say to the nice man, children?" the mother asked with a 'where are your manners' look.

The little towheaded boy had already bit into his biscuit and mumbled a "thank you" as a few crumbs escaped from his over-stuffed mouth, and his sister giggled and said thank you before she pinched off a small piece of cheese and popped it into her mouth.

As the children ate their food, Cole introduced himself and found out that his traveling companions were following her husband to Colorado Springs, who had just started a church outside of town.

As the train came to a slow chugging halt, the young woman took the time to invite Cole to their new church for Sunday services and thanked him again for the biscuits and cheese as she ushered her children down the aisle.

As Cole disembarked the train, he searched through the crowd of people, wondering who would be able to point him in the direction of the Marshall Ranch. After retrieving his luggage, he stopped at the ticket booth to see if he could hire a driver.

As soon as he asked the question, he felt a tap on his arm. "Excuse me."

He looked down at the young woman he had spoken with earlier, as her children tugged on each hand. "I just happened to overhear that you don't have a ride out to the Marshall's," she said, shooting her children an impatient look. "If you don't mind riding with a couple of impatient ruffians, you're more than welcome to ride with us." The woman pointed toward a wagon where a colored gentleman was helping another man load a rather large trunk into the

281

waiting wagon. "That's Thomas, our driver. I'm sure he'll take you wherever you need to go."

She looked at Cole expectantly, with an occasional impatient glare towards the children who were continually pulling on her arms, obviously anxious to see their pa and their new home.

Cole smiled at their impatience, lifted his Stetson and ran his hand through his hair in thought. He really didn't want to make the driver go out of his way, but with all the people around, he knew it might be some time before he could get another ride. "I-I accept, if you're sure...," he went on, throwing a wink at the little boy who finally gave up pulling on his mother's arm to listen to their exchange.

"I'm sure. We'll be waiting by the wagon, come children." With that, she made her way to the wagon with two very eager children running ahead.

Cole reached for his bags and followed, feeling somewhat like an intruder, but nonetheless grateful for the ride.

After introductions were over, Cole found himself seated in the back of the wagon with the two little ones, who had quickly lost their initial shyness and bombarded him with tons of questions.

Little tow-headed Riley asked, "Where ya headin'?"

Cole smiled, "Marshall Ranch."

Little Natalie piped in, "What for?"

"I have a temporary job there."

"What kind of job?" Riley wanted to know as he swatted at a bee buzzing around his head.

"Will you two please leave Mr. Matthews alone?" Their mother warned as she swiveled from the front seat of the wagon. "He doesn't need to answer all your questions."

"Yes'm."

The children sat, swinging their feet, on either side of Cole with their heads hanging low at the reprimand of their mother.

Cole felt sorry for the children, but knew they must obey their mother, and so, he rode the rest of the way thinking of Grace. He prayed for the Lord to give her wisdom and guidance, and for his job to be over quickly so he could get back home as soon as possible.

Some time later as the buggy pulled up to a small home, a slender man came rushing out the door. "Rebecca! Children!"

The man hurried over to embrace his family as they ran to greet him.

"Pa!"

"Grant!"

The foursome embraced, and tears flowed at the happy reunion. Cole, once again, felt like an intruder and stood by the wagon, waiting patiently, turning his hat in his hands.

Rebecca grabbed her husband's hand and pulled him over towards Cole. "Grant, this is Cole Matthews," Rebecca introduced the two men. "He offered the children some food this morning after we had run out, so I offered him a ride to his destination." Rebecca smiled and slid her arm lovingly around her husband.

Grant Reardon extended his hand to the tall stranger, "Nice to meet you, Mr. Matthews. Thank you for your kindness to my wife and children." Grant encircled his family in his arms once again and smiled his welcome.

Cole returned the smile, instantly liking his new, yet temporary neighbors. "It was my pleasure. I just hope I'm not putting your driver out by my lack of transportation to the Marshall's."

Thomas, who was busy unloading the children's luggage, exclaimed lightly. "Lands no, it ain't very far, just a mile or so east of here."

"Here, let me help you," Cole replied as he stepped over to help Thomas with the luggage.

Thomas waved him off. "Thanks, but I can get these. I might need some help with that bigger one in a bit."

Pastor Reardon invited Cole in for a cup of coffee as his wife and children excitedly went before them to survey their new home.

As they entered the small house, Grant could see from Rebecca's fallen face and quiet demeanor that she was disappointed with their new home. To thwart any detection, she quickly lifted her chin, remarking on how cute and homey it was. Their eyes locked. Grant felt blessed to have such a self-sacrificing wife.

"Have a seat Mr. Matthews," Grant offered, "I'll be right back."

Grant followed his wife into their small bedroom, encircling her in his arms, "I'm sorry it isn't what you had expected Rebecca, but I plan on making many improvements…and building another room or two."

Rebecca's eyes shone with unshed tears. "Oh, Grant its fine, really. I'm just happy to finally be together again."

"Mmmm…me too," he purred happily.

The couple embraced privately as they heard the chatter of the children in the next room. "We'd better get out there," he said as he kissed the tip of her nose. "Those two will have his ears talked off before we know it."

Rebecca managed a light chuckle and fell into step with her husband as they walked back into the kitchen arm in arm.

Thomas had set the children's luggage in the corner of the living area along with two small cots Grant had bought in town days before their anticipated arrival.

"Children, why don't you two go set up your bedding and give us a chance to visit with Mr. Matthews for a few minutes?" Grant said as he walked over to the stove and poured four cups of coffee.

"Thomas? Care to join us?" Grant asked, raising a cup in the air as the driver walked by to retrieve another load from the wagon.

Thomas sighed in grateful relief. "Sure would, thank ya, sir."

Thomas took a seat opposite Cole and tipped his cup. "Mmm...pretty good coffee there, Pastor," he replied.

Pastor Reardon held his cup in the air with a wink. "Thank you, my dear sir, but I have to admit that's about the extent of my talents in the kitchen."

Everyone laughed as Cole sat back and relaxed in comfortable conversation. He learned that Grant had been offered a position several miles from town to preach with no established church or congregation. He has been here alone for months scouting the area and making home visitations.

Their family was originally from Indiana and felt the call to venture west to start more churches for the new settlers. His family was not accustomed to such primitive accommodations, but they were happy to be back together again doing the Lord's work.

After the men finished their coffee, they carried in the large Saratoga trunk as Rebecca started to set up house.

Thomas offered to take Cole to the Marshall's as Cole said his goodbye and promised to come and visit.

***

The days dragged slowly by as Cole found himself missing his home, his family, and of course, Grace. He knew he had feelings for her, but he did not realize how much he would miss her. Her radiant smile, the shy way she would tilt her head to look up at him, and her light laugh, even though they were far and few in between. Those memories were just a few of the things that made him smile.

Cole often found himself alone in his room in the evenings thinking and praying as guilt continued to gnaw at his heart for agreeing to come here under false pretenses.

The nights were starting to get cooler, forcing him to pull his blanket further up to his chin. He was just about to turn out the lamp when he heard a heavy knock at the door.

"Cole, ya still up?" His host, Wayne Marshall asked through the thick door.

"Yes, Sir. Come in."

Wayne Marshall, a large man, entered the doorway with his head barely missing the top doorframe.

"I saw the light on and thought I'd bring ya an extra blanket," he said as he walked in, tossing him the thick blanket. "Missus warmed it by the fire first. It's gonna get downright cold out tonight. Looks like we might be in for an early fall."

Cole smiled his thanks, wrapping his cold hands in the warm cloth before he spread it out over his body. "Thank you, Sir. I was just getting ready to blow out the lamp."

"Whelp, I'll let ya get some sleep then. Oh, by the way," he added, turning in thought. "I'd like for you to meet some neighbors tomorrow. I know it's been a lot to look at, but I'm sure you and your partner will be pleased with this ranch…it has a lot of potential."

Wayne yawned, stretching his ample arms up over his head. "I guess this place is just getting to be a bit much on me at my age. I'm glad to see that it'll be going to fine folks." Wayne smiled sleepily. "Well, see ya in the morning."

"Good night, Mr. Marshall." Cole blew out the lamp and laid back against the thick goose down pillow. He closed his eyes, begging God to forgive him for his deceit and promised that he would have an honest talk with Mr. Marshall in the morning. Feeling as though a weight had finally been lifted off his chest, he rolled over on his side, tucked the pillow securely under his head, and fell into a deep sleep.

***

As the weeks went by, Grace longed to hear from Cole. The one letter she had received from him, through his mother, was resting securely under her mattress. She had read that letter so many times that she knew it by heart. *Was it wrong for her to keep a letter from another man now that her husband had returned?*

Trying to push her feelings aside, Grace quickly tied her bonnet and threw her heavy shawl over her shoulders. As she stepped out onto the porch, she gripped her shawl closer to her as the cool September wind slapped her thick cotton dress against her legs. She had an appointment to see Doc Miller today for a checkup and was anxious to see how the baby was doing.

As Grace hurried down the wooden walk, she caught site of William Hollister exiting the Town Square Restaurant with a laughing Maryanne Brewster hanging protectively on his arm.

Grace shook her head, wondering what she ever saw in that man. Grace knew now what type of man he really was. *Oh well, no matter.* Shrugging her shoulders, she spotted the Post Office and decided to steal a minute to say hello to Amelia before her appointment.

As usual, Grace was greeted with the tinkle of the bell and was surprised to find Amelia working in the storeroom with a fussy baby on her hip.

Amelia turned, her weary face breaking into a smile at the site of her friend. "Grace, it's so good to see you! What on earth are you doing out on a day like this?" Amelia lightly scolded, bouncing baby Nathaniel on her hip, "And look at you…it has only been a week or so, but I think you've definitely blossomed from the last time I saw you!" Amelia added as she reached over and pulled open Grace's heavy shawl to get the full affect.

Grace smiled and rubbed her protruding belly. "I do seem to be showing a bit more, don't I? I guess I won't be able to keep it a secret much longer."

"Please, sit." Amelia reached for another chair. "Can you stay a minute? I've missed talking with you. With the baby teething and this crazy weather, I just haven't been anywhere."

"I know what you mean." Grace reached for the baby as he continued to fuss. "Ever since Clayton came, I feel as though life is passing me by. He doesn't want me to go anywhere."

Amelia laughed as she lightly brushed her fingers over Nathaniel's chubby cheeks to wipe away his tears. "Just wait until this little one's born, then you won't want to go anywhere, you'll want to sleep!"

Grace laughed in turn. "Well, I guess I'll know what that's like all too soon," Grace said, patting her rounded belly. "I guess I had better get going, I'm on my way to see Doc Miller for a check-up; just thought I'd stop in to say hello."

"I'm glad you did, and I'm glad that you're going to see Doc, even though you're blossoming, you do seem rather pale. Are you sure you're feeling alright?"

Grace sighed, toying with the baby's light brown locks. "I'm fine, physically. I just worry about things…"

Knowing that her friend would understand, she poured out her heart, "Oh, Amelia…I feel so guilty. Cole wrote to his mother, and in the envelope was another one addressed to me. What would Clayton say if he found out I was keeping that from him?"

Amelia touched her friend's arm to soothe her worry. "Grace, you shouldn't feel guilty. So what if Clayton finds out? He knows that you two are friends. Anyway," she pushed the thought aside with a wave of her hand and grinned, "that's beside the point. What did he say?"

Grace smiled, happy she had Amelia to confide in. "He said it's taking longer than he had expected and not to worry. He's been helping his neighbor build a church and add on to their home. He stressed how worried he was about me and urged me to stay here until he returns." Grace rushed on as a surge of tears began to flow, "And Clayton's telling me that it's time to move on, but I haven't remembered anything and I don't want to leave without seeing Cole one last time."

Grace wiped her eyes with the hankie Amelia pulled from her shirtsleeve. "I know Clayton says he's my husband and all, but there's just something about him that unsettles me. I just can't put my finger on it, and Ms. Millie says she feels the same way."

Amelia reached over to hug Grace as baby Nathaniel wailed in protest. "Here, you need to attend to Nathaniel and I need to go see Doc."

Amelia reached for her son, "I'll be here after your appointment, come by for a cup of tea, will you?"

Grace dabbed at her eyes and thanked her friend as she hurried out the door.

The wind was cold and pushed at her from all angles; she almost ran Myra and Nate Cornwell on her way through Doc's door. "Oh, excuse me," she exclaimed with an embarrassed laugh, "It's pretty windy out there."

Myra and Nate Cornwell said hello and excused themselves as they pulled their coats closer for added warmth and braved the cold outdoors.

Grace sighed; just being out of the wind was a blessing.

"Good to see you Grace. I was wondering if you'd be able to make it in today with this weather."

"Hi Doc, it's getting quite nippy out, that's for sure." Grace shivered as she removed her heavy shawl and bonnet, and placed them on the peg near the door.

Doc reached for his spectacles with a smile. "Yep, unfortunately, looks like we're in for an early fall," he agreed as he hitched up his pants and walked over to the table. "Alright, young lady, hop up here and let's see how this little one's doing."

Grace complied as she climbed up onto the exam table and laid down so the doctor could take the necessary measurements. "How've you been feeling lately?" he asked, brows knit in concentration.

"Pretty good, still tired a lot, but I guess that's to be expected."

Doc pushed, prodded, and took several more measurements. "Hmm…You should be past that part of your pregnancy by now."

Grace became alarmed. "What do you mean?"

Doc grabbed her arm and helped her sit up. "You've probably just been overdoing it, I suspect. You need to get more rest."

"I do get my rest, too much sometimes because I don't feel like I'm pulling my weight at the boarding house helping Ms. Millie," she admitted ruefully.

"Hmmm…" Doc looked at her over his spectacles with raised eyebrows, listening for the baby's heartbeat with the stethoscope. Doc listened to the heartbeat once again and walked over to his desk to write down his findings of her exam.

Chapter Twenty-Six

Grace tied her bonnet and rummaged through her reticule to come up with a couple dollars to pay the doctor. "I know this isn't much, Doc," Grace said apologetically as she walked over holding out the bills. "But I'll need to speak to my husband to see if he can pay the rest next week."

"That's fine," Doc said, writing the amount in his ledger. "Please, have a seat Mrs. Beeson."

Grace took the offered seat across from his desk as he cleared his throat and toyed with his glasses as he spoke. "As far as I can tell, your exam is normal; however, there is one thing I find different this time, but I'm not sure..."

Grace became alarmed and anxiously scooted to the edge of the chair. "Doc, what are you saying?"

Doc shook his head, looking Grace square in the eye. "What I'm suspecting, remember, just suspecting, is that there *may be* two babies instead of one."

Graces eyes were as big as saucers; she was speechless.

"Like I said, I'm just suspecting. I could be wrong, but I checked a couple of times, and both times, I believe I heard two different heartbeats; one was faster than the other was, and in different locations. With my measurements…that just seems to be the only conclusion I can come up with."

Grace leaned back in her chair, stunned. "What does this mean? What will happen? Is that why I'm growing so fast?" Questions tumbled out of Grace's mouth as fast as her lips could form them.

Even though Doc spent extra time answering Grace's questions, she still felt as shocked and uninformed as she did when he first told her.

"I'd like to see you again next month. We need to keep a close eye on this."

Absently, Grace nodded as she awkwardly slipped on her shawl, her mind whirling in disbelief, and headed towards the door.

"Oh, and congratulations."

***

The wooden floor seemed colder than normal as Cole reluctantly stepped from his warm bed. The welcoming aroma of fresh-brewed coffee hurried his steps as he slipped back into his clothes and boots. Staring at his image in the mirror, he raked his fingers though his dark curls to persuade them into some sort of order; finally conceding to the stubborn locks that defied him once again, he sighed and gave in.

After a quick clean up, Cole sent up a prayer for guidance and wisdom as he walked out into the living room and slowly made his way to the warmly-lit kitchen. He hated the thought of deceiving the Marshall's, but he knew that he must face the consequences of his actions.

"Morning, Cole," Wayne greeted him, looking up from the *Farmer's Almanac* he had been reading, his glasses perched on the tip of his nose. "How'd ya sleep?"

"Much better after you gave me that extra blanket," Cole greeted, helping himself to a cup of coffee. After taking a deep whiff of the hot aromatic brew, he sat down in the fine oak chair across from his host.

"I was just sitting here wondering how different my life will be once the missus and I leave in a few months," he mused, raising the coffee cup to his lips. Wayne hesitated as if reminiscing of sweet memories. "I've lived in this area all my life. I'm gonna hate to leave, but it's time. Almanac says that California stays pretty warm almost year-round, so that's where we'll be heading. It also says that we're to have an early winter this year. It sure feels like it," he replied, rubbing his arthritic knuckles in hopes of relieving some of the pain.

"Mr. Marshall...I'd..."

Wayne let out a good natured chuckle, "It's Wayne, remember? After knowing your Pa for so many years, it's only right that we're on a first name basis, business or no business."

"Yes, Sir."

Cole swallowed the lump in his throat, took a big swig of coffee for added strength and plunged in. "Wayne...,"

Wayne could sense the seriousness of his tone, so he pulled off his reading glasses and leaned back in his chair, folding his arms across his thick chest waiting for him to go on. "I—I hate to say this, but I have a confession to make."

Wayne's eyebrows shot up in question.

"I feel as if I've come here under false pretenses, and I want to rectify that before we go any further." Cole sat his coffee cup aside and looked directly at Wayne. "Mr. Hollister told you that we were partners. Well, the truth is, we were years ago…until he stole one of my stallions and tried to destroy my father's business as well as our family."

Wayne silently took a drink of his coffee with a slight shift in his demeanor. "I see."

Cole shared everything, from what Hollister did to him and his family, to the deal they made so he could witness to him. It all came out in an uncontainable rush of emotion.

There, he had said it and his conscious was clear, the burden was lifted. He was not happy about what he had done, but he knew that even if Mr. Marshall wouldn't forgive him, God would.

The silence was almost deafening, almost tortuous, until Wayne finally spoke up. "I don't approve of your part in this matter, Cole, but I do admire you for telling me the truth."

Cole felt the color seep back into his face as he let out a pent up breath.

"After hearing what type of character this Mr. Hollister is, I will have to revoke my offer to sell him this ranch, so I guess there's not really much more to discuss." Wayne stood as the chair screeched against the wooden floor. "I just wish you wouldn't have waited so long," he said gruffly, "so much time wasted."

"I'm really sorry," Cole just shook his head in shame as he felt a chill run up his spine. "I guess I just didn't know how to handle the situation, but I finally realized that if it was God driven, it wouldn't be deceiving."

Wayne poured himself another cup of coffee. "I can't say I'm not upset, because I am, but I'd rather you tell me about this now then find out I left my men and home to a common thief. If it wasn't for your Pa, son, the way I'm feeling right now I'd probably throw you out on your ear."

"Wayne, you have every right to be mad, but I might have a solution if you're willing to listen."

Wayne narrowed his eyes, took a long sip of his coffee, and sat back down.

"Would you be willing to sell me the ranch?" Cole felt a jolt of excitement go through him as he voiced the question aloud.

"What? Why would you want the ranch? You have your father's to tend to."

"It would be a way to start fresh on my own," Cole said excitedly, sitting straighter. "My brother Joel would be happy to take over pa's ranch. Besides, I know all about ranching, I love this country, and I would give your hands and property the best of care, I guarantee it."

Wayne shook his head. "I don't know…" He rubbed his hand over his graying beard in thoughtful deliberation.

"Just think on it, Wayne. If you're not in agreement, I'll pack up and leave, but if you can forgive me and will allow me to prove myself, then I'd like a chance to show you what I can do."

Wayne stared out the kitchen window, watching the morning sun greet the dark blue sky. "I'll think about it and speak to the missus. In the meantime, you can meet our neighbors and work with the hands today."

Cole nodded, feeling as though the weight of the world had been lifted off his shoulders.

***

Grace slowly made her way through the whipping wind back towards the Post Office for her promised visit with Amelia. She really just wanted to go back to the Boarding House and climb into bed and pull the covers over her head, but she knew she couldn't. She knew she would feel better just talking with Amelia.

"Whoa there, excuse me Miss Grace, I didn't see ya comin'." Adam repositioned the large mailbag so he could see his path more clearly.

"That's alright, Adam; I wasn't watching where I was going either," Grace's tone sounded strange, though he did not feel it his place to question her.

"Is Amelia available? She asked me to come over for some tea earlier."

"Uh, yea, she's upstairs. Go on up, she's waiting for you." Adam gave her a parting half-smile and made his way out into the cold to deliver the mail.

Grace trudged up the stairs and found the door ajar. She watched Amelia lay baby Nathaniel down in his cradle as she quietly slipped through the door.

"Well, there you are," she whispered, covering the baby with a heavy handmade quilt.

Grace's face was dumb-founded as she plopped onto Grace's bed.

Amelia was quickly at her side with concern. "What's wrong Grace? Is it the baby?"

Grace shook her head and threw back an awkward laugh, rubbing her rounded belly, "Doc said I'm gonna have twins."

Amelia shrieked and quickly covered her mouth after remembering the baby was sleeping. "What? Is he sure?" Amelia peered anxiously at her friend who looked partly shocked and partly incredulous. "A-are you okay with that?"

Grace smiled a half-smile, and nodded her head. "I-I guess. I mean I really don't have a choice either way. I wasn't sure how I was going to handle one by myself, but two?"

Amelia patted her hand, "It will just be double the love."

The two women hugged as bittersweet tears slipped down their cheeks. Amelia quickly disappeared into the next room with the excuse of gathering the tea and cookies so she could pull herself together. Pouring the tea, she placed the two steaming cups and a plate of shortbread cookies on the tray, willing her heart to be happy for her friend and slipped back into the room with a smile.

"What do you think Clayton will say?" Amelia wanted to know as she sat the tray down on the nightstand by the bed.

Grace shook her head as she reached for one of teacups, "I don't know, but somehow I don't think he'll mind."

The women visited until Adam returned from his rounds, surprised to find Grace still there.

Grace immediately jumped up, "Oh my, I can't believe how late it is. Ms. Millie must be beside herself trying to get dinner on." Grace gave Amelia a quick hug as she hurried toward the door and turned, "Thanks again Amelia," she breathed. Her eyes holding the secret of their conversation.

Amelia smiled in turn. "Have a good evening and tell Ms. Millie we said hello."

With that, Grace nodded and rushed out.

"What was that all about?" Adam wanted to know as the door shut quietly, his eyes falling upon the sleeping child.

Amelia wrapped her arms around her husband in greeting. Her smile not quite reaching her eyes, "Doc said she's gonna have twins."

Adam looked shocked, sad and mad all at the same time. "Really? Well I hope she has better luck than we did." As soon as it was out of his mouth, he looked quickly at Amelia. The slight smile she had possessed slipped quickly from her beautiful face. "I'm sorry, Amelia; I didn't mean to say that."

Adam walked over and plopped down into the rocker with a sigh, scolding himself for saying such a thing.

Amelia walked over to her husband with tears in her eyes and lifted his chin so their eyes would meet. "I know how much you're still hurting Adam. So am I, but we must not let it keep us from living." She took her thumb and wiped away a tear as it slid down his wind-chaffed cheek. "We have to put that in the past, as hard as it is…for our sake, as well as for Nathaniel's."

Adam took her hand and kissed it, laying his cheek in her palm. He gazed up at his wife and took a deep breath. What a strong, loving woman she is. "I'm trying, Sweetheart, really I am."

Amelia smiled through her tears as the baby stirred. "I know…me too."

Chapter Twenty-Seven

"Ms. Millie, I'm back!" Grace yelled breathless as she shut the door and shrugged out of her heavy shawl to hang it on the coat rack. She quickly patted at her windblown hair and hurried into the dining room to find Clayton, Ms. Millie, Jed, William, Maryanne, and Mr. and Mrs. Cornwell staring up at her from the dinner table.

"Oh, I'm so sorry I'm late," Grace apologized as she quickly walked over and took her seat beside Clayton, who glowered his obvious displeasure in her tardiness.

Ms. Millie smiled as if nothing was amiss. "Adam told us that you were visiting with Amelia when he came to drop off the mail. I assumed that you two had lost track of time. I've done that a time or two, myself."

Grace spread the cloth napkin across her lap. "Yes, we did." She peered over at Clayton, "I'll not let it happen again."

"I hope not," he replied brusquely.

This had not been the first time she had seen evidence of Clayton's temper. Even though she didn't like it, she knew she should have thought of the consequences first.

"I heard you went to see Doc today," Ms. Millie stated as she took a sip of her hot tea. "What did he say?"

Grace felt her face redden under Clayton's scrutiny. "You had a doctor's appointment, and you didn't tell me?" he asked in a clipped tone.

Everyone at the table grew silent. All eyes were on Grace and Clayton.

Grace's dark eyes met Clayton's, "Can we discuss this later please?"

Grace turned her attention towards their guests as they discussed the upcoming Fall Festival. Much to Grace's relief, she learned that William was escorting Maryanne to the Fall Harvest Dance.

Her thoughts quickly turned to Cole. She missed Cole, but with him gone, he was not such an easy target for the young beautiful woman sitting across from her. William had proven himself quite the catch in Maryanne's eyes, and hopefully her mother's as well. William had escorted Grace to church a few times but quickly became less attentive each Sunday as Ms. Maryanne Brewster started becoming more attentive, to him. Grace smiled to herself. *Those two are perfect for each other.*

After dinner, Clayton asked to speak with Grace in the parlor while everyone else lingered over pie and coffee.

As Grace entered the parlor, with Clayton close on her heels, she wondered why he was so angry. What had come over him? Grace sat on the edge of the plush chair with her hands folded in her lap as Clayton paced in front of her.

"Grace," he began in a controlled voice. "I've been here for almost six weeks now, and I thought that you were beginning to trust me." His voice rose in octaves the more that he spoke. "As I've mentioned earlier, I feel that it's time to move on, and my thoughts on this are even more clear now after finding out that you purposely kept your doctor appointment from me."

Grace sat perched uncomfortably on the edge of the chair, feeling as though she was a child being scolded by her father. "I'm sorry, Clayton. I didn't tell you because I was afraid you would want to go, and I knew I would feel uncomfortable with you there. Please forgive me."

Luke immediately regretted his outburst as he noticed her trembling hands. He walked over to where Grace sat, toying with the lace on her sleeve, and knelt down in front of her. He grasped her trembling hands in his and looked into her beautiful, yet troubled eyes. "I'm sorry, Grace; I acted like a brute. I was just a little disappointed, I guess."

Staring into his dark eyes, she could see the evidence of pain deep within his soul. She was just about to question it when he looked down quickly and changed the subject.

"What did Doc say? Is everything alright with the baby?"

Grace took a deep breath. "Well, there's no beating around the bush with this," she admitted, exhaling deeply, keeping her eyes fixed on her hands, "he said we're going to have twins."

Grace held her breath waiting for his reaction.

Luke fell into the seat next to hers. "Two? Wow…" A smile spread across his tanned face. "It's gonna be quite a handful with three little ones, but we can do it."

"Yes, we can, with God's help."

Luke hugged Grace awkwardly. Eager to tell the others, he ushered her back into the dining room where everyone was finishing their dessert, to announce the exciting news.

***

After all the excitement had died down, Grace entered her room, grateful for some time alone, out from under the watchful eye of her husband.

My Dear Gracious Father, thank You for all of Your many blessings. Thank You for this extra little one, what a wonderful surprise. Please give me wisdom and guidance on what to do, on being a good mother… and wife. And, please Lord, bless Cole, wherever he is and bring him safely home…soon. Amen.

After changing into her nightdress, Grace climbed into bed and pulled the covers up to her chin. She laid there with her eyes wide open just staring at the ceiling. She could hear the murmur of voices downstairs, as the others were getting ready to retire for the night. She heard heavy footsteps walk up to the door and stop, a light glow peaked in from under her bedroom door. She waited with pent up breath as whoever it was had obviously changed their mind and moved on.

Unable to sleep, she rolled over to light the lamp, and reached for her diary that was still lying open on the bedside table. Her mind filtered through what she read and what she knows. She knows she is married, she knows she is pregnant, but she doesn't know if this man is truly her husband. *Why don't I know this too? Something has to spark my memory, and my heart...please Lord.*

May 22, 1866

Dear Diary,

Fear is the unrelenting emotion now. More Indians have been spotted dotting the foothills, making the fear of attacks more real. My heart races with fear, but I know that the Lord is in control and I am relying on Him and His promises.

We buried Mrs. Mitchell the other day. It was a very sad service. I saw the widow with his new baby, and my heart broke for their loss. He seems so hopeless...maybe I could offer a hand taking care of the little one when he's working. I'll talk to Mr. Weston about this.

Grace anxiously turned to the next page.

May 26, 1866

Dear Diary,

It has been a busy four days. I have been watching little Ruthie for Mr. Mitchell, and she is such a joy. She is such a beautiful little baby and so good-natured. My heart longs for my husband and a family of my own.

I have heard that we cannot circle for camp tonight; the wagon leader wants to get to the next town as quickly as possible as the sound of the war drums draw closer. I pray continuously that the Lord will protect us.

I worry about Mr. Mitchell. At night after supper, I see him sharing a whiskey bottle with some of the other men in camp. I don't know if he's normally a drinking man, but I do know that he's grieving, and he needs to spend more time with his baby daughter.

Lord, give me wisdom and the words I need to speak to him. Amen.

Grace stifled a yawn, feeling the weariness of the day sweep over her, but eager to read more, she quickly turned the page. It was blank. She flipped through a few more pages and realized that was the last of the entries.

What happened? Did the Indians attack? Did she lose her diary?

Frustrated with the blank pages, and unable to sleep, Grace reached in her bedside drawer and pulled out a piece of paper. She would write Cole a letter before she retired. He had been gone a lot longer than he had intended, and his last letter to his mother reported that he was thinking of buying the ranch himself. That news tore at Grace's heart. *Will I ever see him again?*

Some time later, Grace sighed as she sat staring at the unmarked envelope. *Should I send it?*

Oh, Lord, I know you know all, but why does my heart flutter every time I think of Cole? I am a married woman with two babies on the way. Help me to get past these feelings and to love my husband only. Amen.

Grace suddenly felt the babies move within her womb as she ended her prayer. Smiling with sheer pleasure, she laid her hand protectively on her belly. "Well, I know that no matter what happens, you two will be very much loved!" The last couple of weeks, Grace had been feeling her babies move more and more within her, making her heart swell with love each precious time.

Before Grace finally drifted off to sleep, she slipped the sealed envelope in her skirt pocket that was hanging across the chair. With a prayer on her lips, she repositioned an extra pillow under her growing belly and fell into a deep sleep.

***

As the days progressed into weeks, Cole was finding himself more excited about the possibility of running his own ranch. He would hate the thought of leaving Garden City and his family, but he felt the pull towards the Marshall's ranch.

The country was beautiful with mountains, lakes, and fresh bubbling brooks. The welcoming gurgle of the nearby creek reminded him of Grace.

Ah, who was he kidding…everything reminded him of Grace. He had purposely taken his time in hopes of forgetting her. *Was it even possible? Oh Lord, how am I going to get her out of my heart?*

Late one afternoon, Cole heard the sound of excited voices and horses hooves approaching the stable. Just as he made his way to the door, it burst open as one of the hands yelled.

"FIRE!"

Cole ran out and spied a dark cloud of smoke in the west. The fire was headed straight towards the ranch! Cole felt the rush of adrenaline as he helped Jackson, one of the hired hands, release all of the horses from their stables.

"Hurry, run into barn and let the cows loose!" He heard himself yelling to another hand.

Quickly, the men swatted the muscular rumps of the stallions as they raced to untie the others. The wind was blowing more than usual, causing the stench of the smoke to spook the horses, making it just that more difficult to get them all to safety.

Wayne raced in, his face dripping with sweat. He had been out in the fields trying to locate the new colt when he spotted the fire.

Jackson released the last stallion, pausing with his hands on his knees to catch his breath. "Did ya find the colt boss?" He gasped, wiping his brow with his already soiled handkerchief.

Wayne shook his head as he surveyed the empty stables, panic and desperation evident in his aging eyes.

With the rest of the stock taken care of, Cole raced out of the barn and jumped onto the nearest horse. "I'll get 'im," he yelled.

Slapping the mustang with the reins, he urged him into a full run.

"Cole, wait!" Wayne yelled, running out of the barn to stop him.

Cole was already out of earshot and ran towards the north pasture, pushing the anxious horse as fast as his legs would carry them. He kept a close eye on the quickly consuming prairie fire and prayed to God to spare them.

As he rode, searching for the colt, his prayers and thoughts drifted towards home. Oh, how he longed to be with his family. *Were they all right?* He missed them, but most of all, he missed Grace. His heart ached at the remembrance of the letter he had received earlier that day which was still tucked safely within his shirt pocket.

October 27, 1866

Dear Cole,

I pray that this letter finds you well. A lot has happened since you left. Clayton and I found out that we are to have twins. He also told me that he took on an orphaned infant along his travels west. So, needless to say, we have a lot of planning to do.

Clayton has been pushing me to move farther West with him, but due to the unexpected news of the twins, and the early cold weather setting in, he has agreed to stay until they are born. Doc says it should be sometime in late January.

I am relieved that he is willing to stay, for I want to wait until you return. Do you think you will be home for Thanksgiving? You have been gone so long.

I pray that God will keep you safe and lead you safely home very soon.

Truly,

Grace Beeson

Cole's heart plummeted even further as he re-read her letter. She was obviously growing close to her husband. *I have to let her go.* That thought pained him more than he had realized.

The young mustang stopped suddenly at the intensity of the heat and reared his head. Absently, Cole swiped the sweat from his brow. He was running out of time.

Lord, please let me find him!

At that moment, he heard a faint cry. His eyes darted across the field and came to rest on the small colt who was trying to wrestle his way out of a thicket. Thanking God for allowing him to find the colt so quickly, Cole leaped down and ran to him.

Lord, I need your help again.

As if the briars had just magically fallen away, the colt jumped towards Cole who quickly caught him and shoved him upon the saddle, climbing up behind him. Holding tightly onto the struggling colt, he dug his heels into the mustang's flanks, "C'mon, boy, let's get out of here!"

Cole with a prayer on his lips as he raced back to the ranch, sadly watching the hungry flames consume the dry prairie. Riding into the yard, he came upon a brigade of hands, throwing buckets of water onto the stables. The heat was almost unbearable.

Depositing the colt with his mother across the creek, Cole quickly assisted the few hands that were trekking the animals to that area just east of the pasture where they would be safe.

After what seemed like hours, the trenches were finally dug and the stables were soaked with water. They did all they could. The men were worn out, covered in soot, and greatly discouraged.

Then it happened…it began to rain.

A whoop of joy and laughter burst through the heavens as the Good Lord sent down the heaviest rain Cole had seen in years.

"Woo-hoo! Thank you God!" he yelled, tossing his hat into the air. God was still in the miracle business!

Later that evening, after the men were cleaned up and the dishes were washed, Wayne and Maggie Marshall invited Cole to join them at the table for a cup of coffee.

Wayne cleared his throat as he began. "Well, I wasn't sure what to expect from you, Cole," he smiled, reaching for his wife's hand, "But after these past weeks I can see that you are a fine man, just like your father."

Cole smiled sincerely as a lump formed in his throat. "Thank you, Sir."

"Well, to get to the point, the missus and I would like to offer you the ranch."

Cole's heart pounded in excitement.

"After today, I can see that you are not only trustworthy, but able to handle the worst of adversities. I like that," the older man smiled.

Cole was speechless. He had dreamed and prayed about this for weeks, so why wasn't he jumping up and down with joy?

Cole sighed, "I-I greatly appreciate the offer, but I need more time to make this decision."

Wayne's brows knit in confusion. "More time? I don't understand. I thought you were eager to start fresh."

Cole thought for a moment, choosing his words carefully. "I am…I mean…I just need to go back home and tie up some loose ends."

He leaned forward, studying the older couple before him. They were still, after all these years, so much in love. You could see it by the way they looked at each other and by the way they still held hands. Cole's heart ached for that kind of love…if only….

He shook his head. He had to be honest with them. "Actually, I need to see if the lady I care about needs me. If she doesn't, then I will accept your offer. If she does, then I will have to discuss this with her."

Wayne and Maggie eyed each other knowingly. "I see, when will you be leaving?"

Cole's heart flipped at the thought, as he raked his fingers through his unruly hair, his mind darting a million different directions. "I-I guess on tomorrow's train. I'll wire you as soon as I have an answer."

Wayne stood, offering his hand. "Sounds good to me; we can't leave until spring now anyway."

Cole grasped his hand firmly. "Thank you…for everything."

Chapter Twenty-Eight

The week prior to Thanksgiving was a frenzied blur, as Grace grew more uncomfortable by the day; her tummy stretching more than she had thought possible. To add to her discomfiture, Clayton had become increasingly temperamental and withdrawn.

Forcing a smile, she assisted Ms. Millie with the holiday preparations of cleaning and decorating the boarding house. She was exhausted.

Early Thanksgiving morning Grace sensed, more than heard, someone in her bedroom. As her sleep-filled eyes fluttered open, taking a moment before they focused, she spied someone rummaging through her dresser.

"Clayton, what on earth are you doing?" Frightened and confused, she pulled the quilt closer around her.

He stopped and turned. "I-I was hoping you'd have a little cash stashed up here. I-I need to go to the store," he lied.

"Go to the store at this hour, on Thanksgiving?"

He shut the dresser drawer. "I-I guess you're right, guess I wasn't thinking."

Luke laughed it off and sidled over to sit on the edge of her bed. His glassy eyes drank in her beauty as his hand automatically slid up to touch her dark curls that had fallen haphazardly around her shoulders.

She held her breath, feeling trapped. Even after all these weeks, she was still not comfortable around him.

"You are so beautiful Grace," he whispered huskily, leaning down to steal a kiss. Grace felt the hair on the back of her neck rise as she smelled liquor on his breath and felt the fierceness of his kiss.

"Clayton, please don't," she pleaded, pulling away.

He ignored her, pulling her towards him.

"Clayton! I said stop!"

Grace shoved him with all her might and scooted against the wall, drawing the covers closer around her for some semblance of protection.

Luke became furious. "I've been here for quite some time now, and I'm still not allowed to kiss my wife? I think I've been more than patient with you, Grace!"

Grace crouched in the corner cowering in fear. "You've been drinking, Clayton. I can smell it on your breath, and it disgusts me!" she shrieked, hoping to draw attention.

"So what?" he hissed. "What else do you expect me to do with my time since I can't be with you? It's going to get much colder and I need something to keep me warm!" His face reddened even more as he advanced towards her. "You're my wife, Grace, and you will do as I say!"

"I told you, Clayton…I-I need time, please. I don't feel well."

In a flash, the door bolted open, knocking a picture to the floor. Cole's large figure shadowed the doorframe.

A rumble escaped from deep within his throat, fists clenched. "I believe the lady asked you to leave."

Two shocked pairs of eyes shot questioningly towards Cole.

"What are you doing here?" Luke hissed with a slur.

Cole ignored the man's question as his eyes frantically searched the darkness. His heart skipped a beat as he found Grace cowering in the corner. His love for her grew even more.

"Cole," she breathed, unable to believe her eyes.

"Is this the way you were raised to treat your wife?" He yelled at the man as she rushed to her side.

Luke's eyes followed Cole, chest heaving. He stopped short as his eyes finally focused on Grace, his anger quickly deflating. "No, no it's not. I don't know what has come over me. Please forgive me, Grace."

Grace's tear-filled eyes darted from Cole to Luke. She knew what she must say. "I-I forgive you," she whispered through the darkness.

Cole could feel her trembling. Something was wrong, something was terribly wrong.

***

Cole was uneasy the rest of the day as he continued to watch Claytons every move. He was angry. That man had no right treating Grace that way. Even though he could not have her as his wife, he was her friend, and he was not going to allow Clayton to treat her like that again.

After dinner, as Ms. Millie invited everyone into the parlor to enjoy their coffee, she could not help but notice the pallor of Grace's face and politely ordered her to go sit with her feet up.

With a grateful heart, Grace made her way slowly into the parlor as Cole hurried to her side, offering his assistance. Grace looked up with a smile lighting her face as Luke charged up behind them.

"I believe this is *MY* wife," Luke challenged him.

Cole reluctantly released Grace's arm after a slight comforting squeeze and waved his hand to Clayton in friendly surrender.

After the others had joined them and with many feeble attempts at conversation, Grace excused herself to her room as Luke jumped up to help her.

"No, please, stay and enjoy your coffee."

"I would enjoy seeing you to your room instead, my dear," he stated a little too sweetly.

Cole's inquisitive eyes studied Clayton. *Who is this man?* He leaned back into the chair in thought, propping his ankle upon his knee.

He still was not convinced that this was Grace's husband. One would think that if he were her husband she would have felt *something* for him by now. Cole watched a myriad of emotions play across Grace's delicate features, and not one of them was love, only fear and uncertainty.

Silence stretched as Grace fought to control her emotions. *She just wanted to be alone. Why couldn't he understand that?*

"Clayton, please. I am an adult, and I believe I can find my own room," she replied in a strangled voice. Tears threatened to fall as her eyes shifted towards Cole's, silently pleading for understanding the situation she had found herself in, and with that, she turned and ascended the steps without another word.

Luke just stood there, red-faced, as if she had slapped him. *How dare she disrespect me, especially in front of him!* After a few moments, he regained his composure, grabbed his hat, and angrily marched out the door.

Ms. Millie let out a pent up breath and shook her head in dismay. "I don't know about y' all," she said eyeing Cole and

Jed in particular, "But I'm wonderin' if that man's good enough for our Grace. She just doesn't seem happy when he's around…"

"I know what you mean, Ms. Millie," Cole cut in. "I walked in on them earlier and he was trying to force himself on her." Cole's blood pressure rose as the scene replayed menacingly in his mind.

"Oh my," Ms. Millie and Myra exclaimed in unison.

"I saw 'im comin' out of the saloon earlier this afternoon," Jed spoke up. "I knew that wasn't a good sign. He's a bad one, that's fer sure."

Ms. Millie shook her head. "We shouldn't talk like that, Jed. The boy's been through a lot…we just need to pray that God reaches him before they leave in the spring."

Cole didn't feel like praying for him, but knew in his heart that Ms. Millie was right. He committed to doing just that, for Grace's sake if nothing else.

***

Luke stood on the edge of the porch, staring up at the stars in the cool night sky. He sighed in frustration. Things were not going as planned.

He allowed the coolness of the air to soothe his troubled spirit, drinking in the beauty around him. He loved the outdoors and missed it greatly. He thought about the times he would lie awake at night and play dot-to-dot with the constellations as the night creatures sang their sweet lullaby.

Lullaby…his mind drifted to his baby girl. Is she crawling yet? He could only guess. His thoughts quickly changed course and traveled to the woman upstairs. He never realized he could love someone as much as he loved his wife, but after meeting Grace, he thought it might be possible to find love a second time.

The cool night air pierced his denim shirt almost as sharply as Grace's rejection had pierced his heart. Fighting the urge to escape to the Saloon, he blew in his hands and rubbed them for warmth in thought. His anger got the best of him as he thought of the way she had humiliated him in front of the others. Giving in, he quickly made his way down the street to the one place where he could find a little warmth on such a cold evening.

Hours later, Luke stumbled out of Clancy's Saloon, enraged over the loss of a card game. He flirted with the idea of going back in until he spotted the boarding house and instantly thought of Grace. *She's probably sleeping by now,* he mused. *Maybe I could sneak in and take a peek…*

Luke winced as the front door creaked behind him. He stood still for a brief moment, waiting and listening. Satisfied that no one was awake, he half tiptoed and half stumbled up the stairs, carefully avoiding the creaky step near the top. His head began to swim, almost causing him to lose his balance. Liquor was a heartless enemy.

Trying to regain his bearings, he carefully turned the doorknob and opened the door. He gasped at the sight of her. Grace was sleeping so peacefully with her hair fanned out across her pillow as the moonlight spilled in around her. Luke stood staring, as if in a trance, hoping she would not awaken and catch him in her room.

As if switching personalities, his anger sparked again as he remembered the way Grace had spoken to him earlier and the look she had given Cole-just like another slap in the face. Luke burned with jealousy at the thought of their friendship…or was it more? Could *he* be the father of her babies? Luke rubbed his throbbing head…he had to think…

Grace turned in her sleep and startled Luke back to reality. In an instant, Luke knew what he had to do. Pulse racing, he quickly grabbed all of Grace's clothes and shoved them into the travel bag that was peeking out from under her bed.

With mounting exhilaration, he slipped quietly to his room, packed his bag, and carried them both down the stairs. Even in his drunken state, he knew what he was doing was wrong, but told himself he had no choice. They had to leave and get back to Ruthie and if he didn't leave now, he may never get the chance.

Silently he slipped into the kitchen to grab as much leftover food as he could find and stashed it in his bag. In another frenzied thought, he ran down the street to the livery stable and saddled up the best-looking horse he could find. His heart was pounding erratically as the realization of what he was doing burned in his soul.

After packing the horse, he hurried up the steps and rushed into Grace's room. Grace awoke with a jolting start as he stuffed a clean rag in her mouth and hoisted her into his arms.

Instinctively she tried to scream, kicking and flailing her arms against her assailant. He held her tightly, grabbing her hands in his vice-like grip.

Lord, help me, please…she pleaded silently. Her screams muffled by the rag he had shoved in her mouth.

As they neared the bottoms of the steps, she gave one last swift kick that landed with a loud thump on the wall, knocking a picture frame off the wall and down the stairs.

Surprisingly, Jed rushed around the corner with a glass of water in hand. "What's goin' on?" he hollered, coming to a sudden stop. "Put 'er down!"

Luke, annoyed with the disruption, quickly kicked the old man out of his way as Jed fell backwards. Luke shook his head in frustration and stepped over him as Grace continued to kick and squirm.

"Stop it," he hissed. "I don't want to hurt you."

Luke was sweating by the time he wrestled Grace upon the horse, his adrenaline running high. Grateful for the full moon, he kicked the horse into a full gallop and made his way hastily out of town.

With all the commotion, William hurried down the stairs and found Jed on the ground, blood flowing out of his nose and mouth. Bending down to make sure he was still breathing, he rushed down the hall yelling for Ms. Mille.

Quickly, tying her robe as she ran, Ms. Millie rushed to Jed's side. "Jed, what happened?"

He groggily pointed to the front door. "Miss Grace...Clayton..."

Ms. Millie helped him sit up and wiped his bloody nose with the hankie she had tucked into her robe pocket. "Shhh…don't try to talk…"

Jed grabbed her hand, looking her square in the eye. "She's gone…he took 'er." His somber eyes showed their urgency.

Ms. Millie's hand froze in midair. "What'cha mean she's gone?"

Moments later William flew down the stairs already dressed. "I'll get the doctor."

"Get the Sheriff. Clayton just kidnapped Grace!" Jed announced in a raspy voice.

***

Early the following morning, unable to sleep, Cole pulled himself out of bed and padded down to the kitchen. Raking his hand through his hair, he hoped that after a cup of coffee he would feel more like himself.

As he was placing the galvanized pitcher upon the fire, he heard horse's hooves quickly approaching and hurried to the door.

"Grace has been kidnapped!" Adam quickly explained as he bolted through the door. He quickly explained what had happened as Cole burned with anger.

"I knew something like this was going to happen," he hissed, reaching for his rifle.

"What're you going to do?" Adam wanted to know.

"I don't know, but I have to do something. Does the Sheriff know?" Cole pulled on his coat and shoved the casing with the extra bullets into his pocket.

"Yeah, but he said they're married and it's their business."

Cole shook his head with disgust at the Sheriff's careless attitude. "Does anyone know which way they went?"

"Yeah, Hollister said he saw them heading south," Adam informed him. "H-he also said that he kicked Jed in the face."

Cole's fury raged even deeper, his eyes darting towards his friend. "Is he alright?"

"Yeah, just a bloody nose and a little shaken up, but Doc said he was going to be alright."

Cole's face relaxed some as he gathered what food he could and shoved it in a bag, and then marched towards the door. "Thank God!"

"Cole...wait!" Adam demanded, quickly blocking the doorway. "You can't just rush out there. You don't know where they're going or what you might run into."

Cole did not have time to waste as he pushed Adam aside. "I'll find her."

Focused and ready to go, he ran to the stables to get Lucky, the fastest and strongest horse they owned. By the time he saddled Lucky, Joel and Sandra came running out to the stables with Adam lagging behind. Cole looked over their shoulders and threw Adam an 'I can't believe you told them' stare.

The eastern sky delivered just a hint of brilliant orange beyond the horizon. It was a cold morning. Cole prayed that it would be a clear day for travel.

Sandra ran up, her face etched with worry. "Cole, ya can't just take off like this...." Her breath spiraled in white wisps as she pulled her robe closer around her.

He looked squarely at his mother and brother before they could say another word. "I *have* to do this. I'll be back as soon as I can." With that, he kicked the stallion's flanks and was gone.

Sandra stood shivering and staring, her arms wrapped tightly around her, her graying hair still loose about her shoulders blowing in the wind.

Joel mumbled angrily under his breath and shook his head. "Go in where it's warm ma, I'll get to the chores."

Joel walked over to the horses' stalls and angrily scooped the grain into the feed troughs. Even though it was cold, Joel kept warm with the exertion of his work. With every bucket of water and every forkful of dirty straw, he found himself seething. Cole always seemed to get away with leaving Joel to do most of the work...especially since he met that woman.

Frustrated with the whole situation, Joel angrily threw the pitchfork into the haystack a few feet away, just barely missing a tabby cat as he sprang out from behind the haystack with an aggravated meow.

Shaking his head with frustration, he took a moment to rest and leaned over the nearest stall with his forearms resting on the smooth worn wood. *Lord, I know these thoughts are wrong and selfish. Help me to put this anger behind me and do what needs to be done, whatever it may be.* With just a hint of hesitation, he added, *and be with Cole.*

Even though it was a short quick prayer, he felt his anger lift as he felt a soft nuzzling on his hand. Gently, he reached out, stroking Star's soft velvety nose. The colt was not as skittish as he used to be and ventured forth for a little attention, "Hey boy, how ya doing?" The colt nibbled at his cuff as Joel rubbed his head, and with a quick pat to the head, he turned to finish the chores with a lighter heart.

Chapter Twenty-Nine

Cole flipped the reins against the horses hide as he raced south of town, the cold wind biting his face. His emotions went haywire with fear, anger, and stark determination. He didn't know exactly where he was going, but he knew to head south, praying with all his might that God would lead his steps, and keep Grace safe.

Cole's pulse raced as rapidly as the horse's hooves hitting the hard-packed earth. He exhaled deeply sending spirals of white vapor into the air as the dropping temperature burned his lungs.

He was hoping for a clear day for travel as the sun spread its golden fingers up towards the heavens lighting his way, but to his dismay, after just a couple of hours, it started to snow, lightly at first, then heavier as time went on. Cole shivered in the cold, hard saddle, discouraged. *Lord, you know how cold I am already. Please make it quit snowing.*

Frustrated and shivering, Cole finally came upon an old trappers shack and slipped cautiously from the saddle. After tying Lucky to a nearby tree, he reluctantly made his way inside. It was warm, but it was dirty and it smelled like spoiled meat, hides, and cigar smoke. After surveying the small dark cabin, he was relieved to find a small cook stove, but quickly disheartened to find that there was no wood to burn.

As he started to open the stove door, he quickly felt the heat radiate, as the embers were smoldering brightly inside.

Pulse racing once again, he took a few minutes to warm himself as he thanked God. Not only was he able to get warm, but he knew he had to be going the right way. There was a reason this stove was still warm and he was sure it was due to Grace and her captor taking refuge here from the cold. Grateful for what he believed to be confirmation and with renewed energy, he quickly devoured a few biscuits and a piece of cheese and bundled himself up once again, anxious to capture their trail.

***

As Luke continued to push the stolen mount harder against the swirling snow, he struggled to hold on to Grace, as she continued to fight against him. He had her encircled in front of him with her hands tied and mouth gagged. It had been a long ride from Garden City with a half-crazed, hormonal woman kicking, screaming, and crying most of the way, his temper was just about shot.

The effects of the alcohol had long worn off as a splitting headache gradually snuck in to invade his dulled senses. Now that he was, to some extent, back within his regular state of mind, minus the throbbing headache, he questioned his judgment on his rash decision. After stopping off at the old shack to eat and warm up, Grace had tried to escape as he left her alone for a few minutes to use the outhouse. Lucky for him he was quick and did not have far to run to catch up to her. He grabbed her by her thick shawl and pulled her towards him, as she kicked and screamed in protest. He hated to raise a hand to her, but she was out of control, so he had slapped her into silent submission. The look on her face almost broke his heart but he had to do what he had to do; there was no stopping this now.

He had headed south to throw off his trail, but with the snow coming down so quickly, he decided to go ahead and ride west as planned. The weather was getting worse by the minute and he needed to get to his next destination as soon as possible. Besides, he thought to himself, no one in their right mind would try to track them in this weather, not at night anyway; or so he thought.

As they traveled on, Luke sighed in relief as Grace finally fell asleep in the cove of his arms. He watched her head bob slightly with the sway of the saddle. Her hair was tussled and falling out of the loose bun that she had styled it in earlier that day. His heart skipped a beat just thinking about a future with her, Ruthie and the babies. He promised himself that once they were home, he would do all he could to win her love, but right now he just had to get her there. *Would she ever be able to forgive him?*

***

Cole continued his weary travel south, praying for a clue to let him know that he was still on their trail. He spent the time watching and surveying his surroundings and talking to God. He knew it would help him keep his mind off the bitter cold as he concentrated on his conversation with his

Heavenly Father, something he had not done in quite a while. He told God he was sorry for not spending more time with him and asked for forgiveness for his sins. He went on to ask God to bless Grace and to keep her safe. He even ventured farther to share with him his dreams for the future, and if Grace was part of his future, than he would be very grateful, but of course, only if it is His will.

Almost an hour later, he came upon a broke tree branch and tracks in the snow heading west. His heart rate quickened. *It had to be them!* Cole sent up a prayer of thanksgiving and pulled the reins to the right, kicking Lucky in his sides with renewed energy. "C'mon, let's go get her, boy!"

***

Back in Garden City, the whole town was abuzz about Grace's kidnapping. Wires were sent to nearby towns to alert the local authorities. Ms. Millie, Sandra, Amelia, and Myra kept a steady prayer vigil on Grace and Cole's behalf.

Thanksgiving came and went without much fanfare as all were too saddened by the loss of Grace and Cole to do much celebrating. With the onset of the early snowstorm, Mr. and Mrs. Cornwell stayed on at the Boarding House longer than they had originally planned. Mrs. Cornwell became fast friends with Ms. Millie and assisted her around the boarding house in Grace's absence, while Mr. Cornwell helped Jed as he recovered from a broken nose and a bruised tailbone.

A few days later, Adam stopped over at the boarding house on his usual rounds to visit his folks. "Hi pa," he greeted as he shook the snow off his heavy coat and stomped his boots at the door. "I just wanted to see how ya'all were doing."

Nate Cornwell, resting in an overstuffed chair by the fireplace, rested the paper he had been reading on his lap and waved his son toward the chair next to him. "Doing pretty well, son, how about you? I know how worried you are, any news?"

Adam shook his head as he sat down and got comfortable. "'Fraid not."

"Hey, how about you and Amelia come over for supper? I'll mention it to Ms. Millie, I'm sure she would love to have ya. You know how she is with that young'un," he smiled as he reached for his cigar and inhaled, puffing out the smoke into a perfect circle.

Adam had always hated it when his pa smoked his pipe. He didn't like the smell and he knew it wasn't good for his health, but he had learned to keep his mouth shut and so went on, "Ok, sure. Amelia wanted to come and join Ma and Ms.

Millie in prayer tonight anyway. She prays at home, but I think she feels it is more powerful if they are all praying together," he chuckled.

The two men spent some time visiting as the clock-chimed three o'clock, making Adam jump in surprise. Oh, I had better get out there and finish my rounds so I can be back by dinnertime. I'll see ya later, pa."

Nate nodded and placed his cigar back in the ashtray and picked up the paper. "Stay warm, see ya tonight," he hollered over the paper.

As Adam was walking out after bundling back up, he could hear his father coughing from the other room. It sounded worse than usual. He made a mental note to speak with him later that evening; man to man.

***

Grace awoke with a start, as tiny ice pellets pelted her face. "W-what's going on?" She tried to reposition herself on the hard, cold saddle, quickly remembering her perilous situation.

Luke held on to her more tightly, anticipating another struggle. "Hold on, I'm just trying to find us some shelter," he yelled through the increasing wind. "It seems we're in the middle of a blizzard."

Panic seized her. *Lord, please help someone find me!*

"What d'ya make of that?" he yelled, pointing to a dark spot in the distance.

"I don't know, maybe it's some type of shelter." Grace could only hope. She was losing feeling in her fingers and toes and her body shook from the frigid temperatures.

As they rode towards the growing form, they gratefully recognized it as a small cabin with a welcoming spiral of smoke drifting lazily from the chimney. Flooded with relief, Grace thanked God for a much-needed and timely blessing.

The howling winter wind prevented the owners from hearing them as they walked upon the crumbling front porch. Upon closer inspection, Grace was leery if this was going to be a blessing after all. With the rundown appearance of the home, and the small barn across the yard, it certainly did not appear that a woman lived here as she had hoped.

As Luke rapped on the front door, they could hear chairs scooting against the wooden floor followed by a few expletives. As Grace had feared, the person that opened the door was not a woman, but a middle-aged man who looked like he hadn't bathed in months. His dark graying beard was matted with what looked to be tobacco juice and bits of food.

To make matters worse, he was holding a bottle in his right hand as the other hand held onto the doorknob for support.

"What'cha want?" he barked with a belch as he slowly lifted the bottle and took another swig.

Grace felt faint.

Luke cleared his throat and introduced themselves as he held tightly onto Grace's arm, offering his support. "Hello Sir, I'm Clayton Beeson, and this is my wife, Grace. We've been traveling for some time and have gotten lost in the snowstorm. We'd be most obliged if you'd let us come in to warm ourselves until this blows over."

The man just stood there, scratching his head as if they were an apparition and then finally came to his senses, what little was left anyway. "Guess ya can fer a while, yer missus a good cook?"

"As a matter of fact, she is." Luke grinned, pulling Grace closer. He wanted to befriend the drunk right away, as he did not seem like the friendliest of sorts.

The gruff man stepped aside eyeing them curiously, "Come on in then."

As they entered the small stench-filled cabin, they noticed another man sitting at the table, grinning from ear to ear; displaying his yellowish rotting teeth as he hungrily leered at Grace.

Luke became unnerved as he took in the scene before him. What had he gotten them into?

Grace felt her stomach roll as the stench from the cabin hit her full force. The pungent odor of tobacco, liquor, spoiled food, hides, and their unwashed host was more than she could bear.

The freezing cold is better than this, she thought. Grace used her hankie to cover her mouth and nose as she rushed back out the door. She raced behind an evergreen beside the run down cabin and vomited.

Luke raced after her; partly afraid she might try to escape and out of concern. As he found her bent over and sick, a flood of relief filled his bruised heart. He walked over to help her back into the cabin.

Angrily, Grace shook off his hands and wiped her mouth with the back of her sleeve, eyes glaring. "I'm not going back in there. I won't!"

Luke felt his pressure rise. He did not like their present situation any more than she did, but it was the best he could do for now. They had no other choice.

Luke tried to regain his composure as he grabbed her arm, a little more lightly this time. "You *are* going back in there. We don't have much of a choice, now do we?"

"You can take me back home, where I belong!" she yelled in defiance, pulling her coat more tightly around her, eyes lit in anger.

Luke squirmed with impatience and tightened his grip on her arm. "I *am* taking you home…where you *belong*…with me and Ruthie."

Grace jerked away from his clutch and marched off towards the horse they had tied up in the dilapidated barn.

"Where do you think you're going?" he demanded with a shake of his head.

She ignored him and kept walking.

Luke quickly hurried after Grace as the snow was diminishing her from his view.

"Grace, come back here!" Catching up to her, he pulled her away from mounting the horse as hot tears spilled down her cold, chapped cheeks. "We *are* going back in there!"

"Over my dead body!" She hissed, squirming angrily under his tight grasp.

Hoisting her up in his arms, he carried her back to the house kicking and screaming. "That just might very well be if you keep this up."

***

Cole pressed on as the icy snow pelted his face. He pulled his collar up high and his hat down low over his ears. He was beginning to feel the onset of frostbite, but he courageously plunged on. He had to save Grace.

Lord, I know You're in control, and that You know where she is. Please spare her. Keep her safe and warm, and help me to find her quickly. In Your name I pray, Amen.

A little while later, Cole started to feel disoriented as his mount danced around anxiously.

Out of nowhere, a wolf jumped out in front of him, baring his sharp teeth, as a deep growl rumbled from his throat. Lucky backed up and reared his head as Cole hung onto the saddle horn. Swiveling in his seat, he reached back and grabbed his rifle just as another menacing wolf joined the first. He bared his fangs as Cole took aim. Before he knew what happened, the other wolf had jumped towards him. Startling Lucky and jolting his rider, the gun went off, totally missing his mark.

Caught off guard, one of the angered wolves tore at Cole's right leg. The pain took his breath away as the sharp teeth seared through his nerves. Quickly, feeling faint, he cocked his rifle and shot off another round as the wolf closed in again. The shot rang out loudly, echoing in the frigid cold air as the wolf yelped and fell at Lucky's feet.

Just as Cole was ready to reload, an anonymous shot rang out and the second wolf collapsed, blood flowing heavily on the newly fallen snow. Startled with relief, Cole searched the white wilderness as he helplessly slipped off his horse into the cold darkness.

Sometime later Cole awoke with a start, bundled up in front of a roaring fire.

"Thought ya might not wake up," said a grizzly but kind voice. "Ya lost a lot of blood. I'm just fixin' ya some soup. It's a day or so old but still worth eatin'."

Cole surveyed his surroundings as he tried to sit up, but the pain in his lower leg shot up like wild fire. "Ahh," he gasped.

The old man brought over some soup and knelt beside him. "Looks to me like thet wolf got ya pretty good, but it should mend in time; might have a nasty scar, though."

The kind old man sat the bowl of soup aside and helped Cole sit up, positioning an old raggedy blanket behind him for comfort. "How's thet?"

Cole smiled his thanks as the older man handed him the steaming bowl of soup and a couple pieces of stale bread. "Sorry, but this is all I got to give ya. Might not be the best, but it'll warm ya right up."

"Thank you, I'm much obliged." Cole raised the worn, cracked bowl to his lips and drank in the hot liquid. The soup, which must have been watered down many times, was bland, but it did fill and warm him.

His rescuer sat and watched him as he ate.

"Haven't had anyone here 'bouts in a few months; gets a little lonesome." The old man scratched his long scraggly beard in thought. "I'm just wonderin' what yer doin' out here in the middle of a blizzard, though."

After introducing himself, Cole filled his host in on what he was doing and whom he had been following. The old man, named Silas, sat and listened, nodding his head with an occasional 'I see'. After Cole finished his story, Silas pulled himself up to pour them both some more watered down coffee.

Silas handed Cole his coffee cup as he sat back down in his rickety chair. "So, yer sayin' this man ain't her husband?"

Cole shook his head. "We really don't know for sure. He ran off this past summer and she followed after him." Cole set his cup aside and inched his way down to lay on the floor, pulling the animal skins and blankets more closely around him. "When this guy showed up, there were too many holes in his story. Grace didn't remember him or anything he told her, which we found strange…and now this…"

"Hmmm," Silas scratched his balding head in thought, his eyes focused on the ceiling. "I'm kinda wondering if the young man who happened to stumble upon my cabin months ago could be the one yer talkin' 'bout."

At the look of question on Cole's face, Silas went on. "Yeah, he was about your age. Came bangin' at my door one day, his leg paralyzed. Had been dragging it for almost a mile he said when he happened upon my cabin. He had been bit by a rattler and I brought him in to take care of him, but he died the next day." Silas shook his head at the bad memory, "poor guy, he was so young."

Cole looked at him directly, unsure if he really wanted to know the answer to the question he was about to ask. "Did he say what his name was?"

Silas thought a moment and nodded, "Yes, his name was Clay I think, or somethin' like thet."

Cole's eyes grew wide with astonishment, "Was it Clayton by chance? Clayton Beeson?"

Silas pondered the question as he drank from his cup, "Hmm, might be," he said with a nod, "name does sound familiar. Well I'll be, if that don't beat all."

The sound of a chair scraping against the wooden floor burst through his thoughts. "How 'bout we say a prayer fer her? She's gonna need it."

Cole looked up, really seeing the old man for the first time. He was old and bent over, had rags for clothes, and smelled as if he had not bathed in months. He had teeth missing and matted hair, but there was a beauty about him that Cole had not seen until that very moment. He was a child of God. Cole felt a warmth seep through his body as he grasped the outstretched gnarled hand in his and bent his head in prayer.

"Lord, ya see this young lady and ya know where she is. We ask thet ya keep her and the little ones safe. We ask thet Cole mends soon and finds them and the truth would be known once and fer all. We pray fer peace for her as she

learns the truth and light thy way Lord. We know we can count on you. In Jesus name, Amen."

Cole smiled, humbled by the old man's simple prayer. This man was old, low on supplies and all alone, but he cared and prayed for a stranger, not asking anything in return. Cole sent up a silent prayer to ask God to bless this kind man.

"Thank you, Silas. I don't know how I can ever repay you for taking such good care of me."

Silas waved his hand in the air as if to dismiss his gratitude. "Aww, nothin' much to thank me fer, just doin' what I can."

Cole reached again for the man's hand and squeezed it in friendship. "I will always keep you in prayer, my friend."

Silas quickly got up and said goodnight but not before Cole caught the evidence of unshed tears in his new friend's eyes.

"God bless you, Silas. Goodnight."

Chapter Thirty

"Brrr...I think it's colder out there than it is in my ice box," Amelia said between chattering teeth as her and Adam came stomping though the door, trying to dislodge the snow from their boots.

Ms. Millie met them at the door, pulling her shawl more tightly around her as the swirling wind carried in a barrage of heavy snowflakes. "Wouldn't surprise me a bit," she agreed as she shivered and closed the door behind them. "Here, let me have that little one and warm him up by the stove," Ms. Millie offered as she reached for the bundle Amelia pulled out from beneath her coat. "Y'all make yourselves comfortable; dinner will be ready in a jiffy."

Amelia and Adam hung their coats on the coat rack next to the door and made their way into the warm parlor.

"Good evening, Pa," Adam smiled as Amelia reached out to hug her father-in-law.

"Good evening," he replied with a wink. "Glad to see you made it. It's looking pretty bad out there."

"Sure is," Adam replied as he stretched his hands out towards the fire. "It has to let up soon, or we won't be able to cross the street."

"You can say that again," Ms. Millie exclaimed as she entered the parlor to announce that dinner was ready. "Maybe I'll get more of a chance to hold that youngun' if ya get snowed in here."

"Where is Nathaniel?" Amelia wanted to know as she followed Ms. Millie.

"Do ya really need to ask?" she chuckled, pointing to Myra who was already sitting at the dinner table cooing to her attentive grandson.

Myra Cornwell looked up with a twinkle in her eye. "I just can't seem to get enough of him," she confessed as she kissed his chubby little cheek. Nathaniel was cooing happily as his little fists tried to bat at the stuffed puppy Myra was waving in front of him.

"He sure loves that puppy," Amelia replied sadly, thinking of Grace. "Grace made it for him. She did a wonderful job, didn't she?"

As the men walked into the dining room, all grew silent at the mention of their missing loved ones.

As everyone took their seats, Jed cleared his throat and reached out to those beside him. "Let's pray."

Our dear gracious Father, we thank Thee for Thy bountiful gifts. Bless this food to our bodies, and help us to stay strong so we can be of service to Thee. Please be with Ms. Grace and Cole. Keep them safe and warm, and bring them home to us soon. In Your name we pray, Amen.

There was a round of solemn amen's as the food was quietly passed around the table, each deep in their own thoughts.

As Amelia filled her plate, the silence was shattered as baby Nathaniel cried out for attention. "If you'll excuse me," she smiled, placing her napkin next to her plate. "I believe someone else is hungry as well."

With the silence broken, Nate cleared his throat and looked at Myra for silent approval before he spoke. "If I may have your attention for a moment, there's something Myra and I would like to share with you."

All eyes shifted from Amelia's departure with the baby to Myra and Nate.

"Myra and I have been talking, and we have decided to stay on in Garden City."

Excited questions started all at once. "If you'll have us that is," he laughed in spite of himself, gazing towards his smiling wife.

Adam grinned with a tinge of worry etched in his brow. "What made you decide this?"

"Well, it was several things. One, of course, is that you, Amelia, and Nathaniel are here. We've missed seeing you, and we don't want to miss Nathaniel growing up. Two, we *are* getting up in years, and have decided that we're too old to continue managing such a large house. And, three, we were hoping," he drawled out, eyeing Ms. Millie and Jed with a grin, "that maybe we might be able to stay on here and help out until we can find a small place of our own."

Ms. Millie's eyes lit up in child-like excitement, "Oh, how wonderful, of course you can stay here! We would love to have you!"

After dinner, the group retired to the parlor and stood hand in hand, as they lifted Grace and Cole in prayer. Ms. Millie and Amelia dabbed at their eyes as they petitioned the Lord for their Christmas miracle.

As the evening ended, Adam and Amelia braved the cold, grateful that the snow had finally stopped blowing. The silence was a blessed welcome compared to days on end of the cold whistling wind and blowing snow.

***

Grace fought to control her nausea as well as the continuous torrent of tears as she lay in the corner of the run-down shack. The air was thick with stale liquor and filthy bodies, not to mention filthy language. The violent wind outside screeched and whistled causing Grace to tremble in body and spirit; she was terrified.

After she and Luke had returned to the cabin, at Luke's request, one of the men threw together a crude bed made out of smelly old hides. The men had ogled her and teased her until Luke had finally had enough and challenged them to a card game. Satisfied with the offer, the men pulled another jug of whiskey out from under the dilapidated cabinet as Grace sighed with mixed emotions. She was relieved that Luke turned their attention elsewhere, but worried that the extra liquor would only make their disturbing attitudes worse.

She sent up a silent prayer pleading with God that they will all just pass out so she would not have to worry about them the rest of the evening.

Turning her back against the unsightly scene before her, Grace found herself facing the cold, mud-chipped wall as she wrapped her arms around her for added warmth. Her body ached from the long and uncomfortable ride. Her heart ached at being torn from the ones she loved. The filthy language of the men behind her made her nauseas. Tears slid down her face; is this what her future was going to be like? She tried to focus her mind on more pleasant thoughts, and instantly she thought of Cole. *What was he doing now? Was he worried about her? Was he looking for her?*

Oh, Lord, please get me out of here. Please let someone find me and take me home. I'm grateful that we're not out in the freezing blizzard, but these men scare me, and this smell is making me sick. Help me, Lord, give me Your comfort and peace, and please...please protect my babies. Amen.

Later that night Grace awoke with a start, anxiously searching the darkness as the wind howled ferociously outside. Grace's heart pricked with fear as the hair on the back of her neck stiffened. Suddenly, she felt a hand clench her arm as hot foul breath blew in her face.

With her heart pounding, a scream escaped her lips. "Let me go!" Without thought, she balled her fist and punched at the silhouetted figure with all her might. The loud yell confirmed that she had made contact with her target.

The man released her as his hand went instinctively to his nose. "Why you…" He cursed and backhanded her in the face; the force of the blow threw her head against the wooden wall.

Grace's head began to spin as bile rose up in the back of her throat. The pain from her head, along with the constant nausea, made her vomit.

Someone lit a lamp.

"Leave her alone!" Luke demanded as he threw a punch at the staggering figure.

In the grogginess of her mind, she could see two figures fighting. She forced her eyes to focus. "Clayton, watch out!"

Luke turned in time to see the reflection of a knife bearing down on him. As the knife made contact with his chest, an excruciating moan escaped Luke's lips.

Grace quickly scrambled over to Luke's coat that was lying on a nearby chair and grabbed his pistol with shaking hands. Luke caught her eye as he fell to the ground in a motionless heap. Frightened, she pointed the gun at the man holding the knife and pulled the trigger. God must have directed the bullet, as her target landed with a heavy thud on the floor next to Luke.

The second man pivoted and jumped towards her. She fired, with a prayer on her lips, and once again, her target went down.

Scared senseless, Grace stood in shock, surveying the bodies before her. *Were they all dead?*

Her heart fluttered as she heard a soft moan.

"Grace…" It was a faint whisper, but she knew it was Clayton.

Grace was heaving and shaking. She knew she had to step over the man she had just shot to get to Clayton, but fear kept her motionless.

Silently, a still, small voice spoke to her. *Go to him.*

Reluctantly she jabbed the gun into the still form and when he didn't move, she quickly stepped over him, a sob catching in her throat.

"Clayton, where are you hurt?"

He winced with pain. "Here, in my chest."

Grace cringed as she realized how much blood he had lost. With a prayer on her lips, she quickly ripped opened his shirt to expose the wound. After failing to find any clean cloths, she ripped her petticoat off, ripped it into strips and stuffed the gaping wound. *Tell me what else I need to do Lord.*

As she was administering aid to Luke, she heard another moan as the man next to Luke was beginning to stir.

Grace looked towards Luke for an answer as to what to do, but his eyes were closed. He was unconscious. Grace didn't know what to do. Should she help the man who had just tried to kill Clayton?

Again, the still small voice spoke to her, *help him.*

Frightened, she reached over to see where the other man was injured and found a bullet hole in his upper abdomen. By the grace of God, he too, became unconscious.

Thank you Lord, now I don't have to deal with them while I am attending to them. As Grace worked on the two men, she continued to pray for them both. *Lord, I know you have a reason for these two living, so please give me your peace and a steady hand so I can help them. Amen.*

Grace, petrified of the whole situation, tended to the men the best she knew how. Sighing with sheer exhaustion, she pulled herself up off the floor to make her way back to the makeshift bed.

Her heart flipped in her chest as she realized she had forgotten about the other man. He had not moved. Praying for courage, she walked over to see if he was still alive. After finding no pulse, she said a quick prayer for his soul, and pushing her fear aside; she grabbed his ankles and dragged him out into the swirling snow.

The heaviness in her spirit overwhelmed her. She didn't know what else to do with him, but she knew she didn't want him in the house. *Forgive me Father.*

Closing the door behind her, she slowly made her way to the pile of hides that made up her bed. Carelessly throwing off the soiled hides, she curled up in a ball and cried herself to sleep.

Grace awoke early the following morning to the sound of more moaning. Reluctantly, she pulled her aching body off her makeshift bed to see to the needs of the men. She had hoped that it all was just a bad dream, however her senses told her otherwise.

Slowly, holding her belly as the babies moved within her, she made her way over to Clayton to see how he was faring first.

"How're you doing?" She asked somberly as she felt his forehead for fever. He was burning up, just as she had feared. Infection had set in.

Feeling the need to use the necessary, she hurried outside, squinting as the bright morning sun reflected off the pristine white wilderness.

Gratefully, she inhaled deeply of the fresh air and stole a few moments to talk to the Lord. It was very difficult for her to believe that something so beautiful could be just inches away from something so horrible. *Are you there God?*

As she made her way back to the cabin, she came upon the dead man, right where she had left him, covered with snow. As a shiver ran up her spine, Grace quickly skirted around him and hurried back inside, stomping off her boots as she entered.

Just then, the other man awoke hollering for his whiskey.

"You won't get any whiskey until you have something warm in your stomach first," Grace replied sternly. Hastily, Grace searched through a few cabinets and found some cornmeal along with an almost empty bag of coffee grounds.

It wasn't much, but it would do. She quickly whipped up some breakfast as her stomach growled. She was famished!

As she sat next to Luke, who was lying on the cold floor covered in hides, she reached over him to check his wound. Absently she pushed the wayward locks of hair behind her ear showing the darkened bruise she had sustained hours earlier. Slowly, he reached up and gently touched her bruised face. Grace flinched and pulled away, sensitive from the swelling that had formed from the night before. "I'm so sorry, Grace, can you ever forgive me? I never should have…"

Grace remained silent with unrelenting tears glistening in her eyes. She glanced at Luke to see if she could read real regret in his eyes, but she saw something else…tenderness?

Averting her gaze, she carefully removed his bloody bandage and poured more whiskey on the wound as he flinched in pain, not taking his eyes off her.

"I'm sorry," she said softly, seeing the pain in his eyes, "this is the only thing I can use to keep down the infection."

"I know," he held tightly onto Grace's hand. "I don't know if I'm going to make it, Grace--there's something I need to tell you…"

Chapter Thirty-One

During the days that followed, Grace spent all of her waking moments tending to the two men. Even though it was a tiresome job, she found herself praying for these men and getting to know them.

Clem, the cousin of the deceased man named Red, found it easy after a few days to open up to Grace. He told her that they had been living together since Clem's wife passed away six years prior. Red had never married. Both men had led a very hard life with abusive fathers, and left home at an early age.

Grace, only by the grace of God, quickly began to care for Clem. He was a little rough around the edges, but she could sense a softer side, especially when it came to his late wife.

As the days passed, Grace gave the men as little whiskey as possible, just enough to dull the pain and to keep them satisfied. In the meantime, she hummed to herself and recited scripture verses to get her through the trying bitter cold days. She found it amazing how she can have amnesia and still remember her Bible verses, which was the only thing that kept her going.

Clayton had been drifting in and out of consciousness for days. His fever had spiked to the point that she thought he would surely die. During those horrific episodes of high fever, he would talk out of his head about someone named Ruth. Was he thinking of the baby he had saved, a past girlfriend maybe? Who was this Ruth? Questions tumbled through her mind like the swirling snow outside.

One night Luke awoke in a cold sweat. The fever had finally broken. He was yelling for Ruth. "No Ruth, don't leave me…It's alright Ruthie daddy has you…"

Luke thrashed wildly as Grace knelt beside him and laid a cold cloth on his forehead. She stayed by his side and talked to him softly, shushing him when he became agitated in his delirium.

"It's alright, Clayton. You're safe."

"Ruth...I-I thought I had lost you..." His eyes were closed. He must be dreaming. His shirt was damp with sweat and his breathing labored.

"Clayton, it's me, Grace," she told him, wiping his face with the cool cloth as she spoke.

His hand abruptly reached up and stopped her. "Clayton? I'm Luke."

"W-what are you talking about? I don't understand..."

Luke's eyes popped open instantly. *Did he really say that aloud?* He searched her eyes, pleading for her understanding. "I-I'm sorry Grace...I was wanting to tell you..."

Her dark eyes anxiously sought for answers in his, "Y-you're not Clayton?"

He shook his head in shame.

Grace's face fell. "How could you do such a thing?" she demanded, scrambling to her feet to get away from him.

"I'm sorry, Grace. I know what I did was wrong, but I only did it for my daughter..."

"Your daughter...what daughter?" She hissed at him, whirling around in anger.

"Ruthie, *my* daughter. My wife, Ruth, died after giving birth to her on the trail," he winced in pain as he tried to reposition himself to see her more clearly. "After losing her, I couldn't handle Ruthie. I-I mean, I didn't know anything about babies, but after seeing you with her...well I...," he let the sentence slip from his lips with a sigh.

"Anyway, after the Indian attack, I finally realized that you were no longer with us, and I heard from the wagon master that you came up missing in the Indian raid. Later, we found out that you were in Garden City with amnesia and that's when I came up with the plan to convince you that I was your husband. I was thinking of you and Ruthie both. I wanted her to have a mother and you to have a home."

"Why me?" She asked, barely a whisper.

"I saw you with her; you were as natural to her as a mother could be. You loved her, and you were so good to me..."

Grace turned to him, tears streaming down her cheeks. "I'm sure I did love her. Who wouldn't love a baby?" She rubbed her growing belly, her pale face displaying the painful effects of his actions.

"You were so caring, so loving...I knew I just had to find you."

Grace walked over to a nearby rickety chair and plopped down, emotionally, and physically spent. "Why are you telling me all of this now?"

"I-I might not make it out of here, Grace, and I wanted you to know the truth." He gazed at her tenderly. "I know I haven't been very pleasant to be around, and I'm sorry, but I have grown to care for you, and I want you to be happy."

Grace sat in silence, sniffling and wiping her tears as the little ones in side of her protested at her hunched over position. She sat back with her hand on her belly and looked at him questioningly. Hundreds of thoughts running through her mind.

"Ruthie is in Rock Springs, Wyoming, at the home of Lewis Covington." His mind drifted off for a moment obviously thinking of his baby girl. "She should be about seven months old by now. She's probably crawling..." His voice cracked at the thought of never seeing his child again.

"Don't talk as if you'll never see her again. You will." Grace's heart began to soften.

"You seem pretty sure of yourself." He tried to laugh, regretting it instantly as his chest sparked a lightning bolt of pain through his shoulder.

"No, I'm not sure of myself, but I am sure of God."

Luke shook his head as he stared at the ceiling. "God don't want anything to do with me. I've done too many bad things, and now this…"

"Don't underestimate God," she replied boldly pushing herself to the edge of the chair. "He died on the cross for you, as well as for me. He did that because he *loves* us with an all-consuming, unconditional love. All we have to do is ask Him to forgive us, believe that Jesus died for our sins, and ask him to come into our hearts. He does the rest! He's offering us this amazing free gift of salvation, but it's up to us as to whether we choose to take it or not."

The passion in Grace's voice was almost awe-inspiring. Even in the bare wilderness, in the middle of a blizzard, the Lord was showing Himself, and she was bathing in the warmth of his love.

"God loves you very much and longs for you to come to Him. He will help you with all your troubles. He will lead you in every step you take. He will bless you and prosper you…"

"Whoa," he chuckled half-heartedly waving his hand in the air, "were you once a preacher?"

Grace stopped, a smile playing on her lips. For the first time in months, she felt as though her parched spirit had finally received some much needed nourishment, and she felt the joy of the Holy Spirit.

Grace laughed lightly, "No, but my Papa was."

Luke's brows curved in question.

"What's wrong?" she asked.

"You *remember* that your Pa was a preacher?" He said incredulously.

Grace smiled. Was her memory finally starting to come back?

***

Cole's heart sunk at the realization of how much time he had been laid up while his leg healed.

The blizzard had finally stopped, although the wind continued to blow the snow, covering any possible tracks. He knew it would be almost impossible to pick up their trail, but he also knew that with God anything was possible.

As the two men shared a light breakfast of the usual bland corn meal and watered down coffee, Silas drew Cole a rough map of the closest farms along his way heading west in case he needed shelter from the cold. After Cole rolled up the small map, he quickly finished his breakfast as Silas joined him in prayer for success in his journey.

"I don't know how to thank you, Silas. You've been a God-send." The two men hugged and said their goodbyes as Cole wrapped himself tightly against the bitter cold.

"You too, have been a God-send to me, my friend." Silas handed him a pouch of bread and a can of beans to carry him to his next destination. "If yer ever in this neck of the woods again, stop in, will ya?"

"I'll be sure to do that," Cole replied with a parting smile. "Thanks again for everything. God bless ya, Silas."

Wearing Silas's old snow shoes, Cole made his way to the small lean-to that housed his stallion. As he walked in, he sighed with relief after realizing that Silas had taken care of him as well. Lucky nickered happily and reared his head in welcome. "Good to see you too, Lucky," he replied, rubbing the horse's velvety nose.

Lord, please let me pick up their trail quickly. I hope that the blizzard slowed them down as well. As always, please protect Grace and see her home safely. Amen.

After traveling for what seemed like hours, Cole passed the first farm on the map Silas had drawn. It sat far back in the trees, smoke rising from the chimney in the distance. His aching body wanted to head straight for the welcoming cabin, but a soft whisper told him to keep going. Halfheartedly he obeyed, urging the stallion on.

Sometime later, the snow stopped blowing and the wind died down to almost an eerie calmness. Even though Cole was grateful for the change in weather, he knew that he was fighting the onset of frostbite and needed shelter fast. With a prayer on his lips, he decided to stop and eat. Just as he turned to unbuckle his saddlebag, he noticed what looked like a small cabin a few hundred yards away. Although it did not appear inhabited, as there was no smoke rising from the chimney, he said a quick prayer of thanks as he turned Lucky towards the small building. Any shelter is better than no shelter at all at this point.

***

Grace stole a moment from her nursing duties to relax on her makeshift bed and spend some time with the Lord. The conversations she had with the men over the past few days floated through her mind.

She was grateful that the Lord saw fit for her to witness to these two men, but continued her earnest prayers of returning home, especially since the babies were due in only a month. She stayed in prayer for the men and their salvation until the urgency of the outhouse was too great to bear. The babies were moving around so much lately and pushing on her bladder that going to the outhouse was a constant chore.

As she bundled up once again to make her way to the privy, she noticed that the fire had almost burned out. Grace sighed...another chore. She was exhausted. She hadn't slept well in weeks, and she was cold and hungry.

Grace made her way outside, squinting against the glare of the beautiful white wilderness. She drew in a deep breath and gently rubbed her round belly as two very special blessings rolled around inside of her. As she went about her business, her thoughts traveled to the conversation she had with Luke earlier.

Luke told her that she had watched over Ruthie on the wagon train. Thinking back, she remembered reading about the woman who had died just after giving birth. She tried to imagine what she might have been like knowing now that Luke was her husband.

On her way back to the cabin, she stopped at the depleting woodpile to grab a few logs to add to the fire. As she rounded the corner of the cabin with the logs tucked in her apron, she stopped mid-stride at what she saw before her.

Stifling a scream that threatened to erupt, she hurried back to the other side of the cabin, shaking with fear.

Lord, give me strength.

Chapter Thirty-Two

"I wish Grace and Cole would walk through that front door right now," Ms. Millie exclaimed in discouragement as she passed the washed dishes to Jed.

"I know what'cha mean." Jed dried each dish, placing them in their appropriate place with a slight clink of the porcelain. "It's not gonna seem like Christmas without 'em here, that's fer sure."

Ms. Millie turned to wipe up the puddles of water off the wood counter. "Well, with Christmas Eve bein' tomorrow, it'll definitely take a Christmas miracle."

Jed nodded, placing the last cup on the shelf. "Miracles still happen, Millie."

Myra overheard their conversation as she walked into the kitchen, her crinoline swooshing under her skirt. "Amen to that!"

Ms. Millie turned with a sad smile. "I sure hope so. Can I get you anything, dear?" she asked as she wiped her hands and spread the thin dishtowel on the wooden towel rack.

Myra shook her head as her eyes surveyed the tidy kitchen, "No thanks, just wanted to tell Jed that Nate is waiting on him for their Checkers game."

Jed smiled his almost toothless smile as he walked past her, tossing her the hand towel. "I'm ready. Wish me luck. I'll need it."

The two women chuckled for the first time in days as Ms. Millie playfully waved her hand towards Jed's retreating figure. "Have a seat, Myra. We'll have some tea while we discuss our Christmas plans."

***

Grace quietly dropped the logs and picked up a smaller one, holding it over her head for protection. The hair on the back of her neck rose with fear as she made her way towards the door. Hearing angry voices inside, she held her breath and kicked open the door. Shaking, she stood in the shadow of the doorway, holding the small log up over her head, ready to faint at any moment.

"Grace!" It was a deep, urgent whisper.

Suddenly she felt the adrenaline spiral through her body just as swiftly as the darkness from the room faded. Her eyes slowly adjusted to the dim interior, and her heart felt like it was going to beat out of her chest. Her eyes searched for the soft, deep voice that called her name.

"Grace, it's alright. Put the log down." That voice.... Dare she hope?

She softly whispered, feeling as though she was hallucinating. "Cole?"

Grace cautiously lowered the log with trembling hands.

In two giant steps, Cole was in front of her as she fell into his strong familiar arms.

Hours later as the fire crackled in the stove, Grace awoke to the smell of something almost heavenly. Her stomach rumbled with anticipation as her eyelids fluttered open. Was she dreaming?

All too sudden, her eyes focused on the crude shelter, her prison. Her heart collapsed. It was all a dream. She was still here…still trapped…and felt all alone. The days of travel and bitter temperatures, of fighting off her captors and then nursing them back to health had totally zapped her of all energy and emotion. As the babies rolled inside of her, she prayed for this nightmare to be over. *How much longer Lord?*

An all too familiar tear trickled down her cheek as a hand gently wiped her brow with a cool cloth.

"Shhh…It's alright. I'm here now; everything's going to be alright."

Grace's eyes popped open. It wasn't a dream!

"Cole, is that really you?"

Cole leaned over and whispered in her ear. "Expecting someone else?"

His light chuckle broke the dam of emotions as she threw herself in his arms. Sobbing, she clung to him, never wanting to let go.

After the torrent of tears subsided, she gently pushed him away, "I-I have to check on Luke and Clem," she said, starting to stand. Her head started to swim as Cole gently pulled her back down.

"I've already seen to them, they're fine. I made some beans. Are ya hungry?"

Grace nodded, embarrassed by her actions.

"Good, you stay here, and I'll get you a bowl."

Grace watched Cole closely as he carefully walked to the stove to dip her some beans. Something about the way he walked worried her.

"What's wrong with your leg?" She wanted to know as he plopped down beside her.

"It's just a small cut, but it's healing." Cole handed her the bowl of steaming beans. "I'm sorry, I know this isn't much, but it's all I had."

Grace smiled her thanks, but she wasn't convinced about his leg having 'just a cut.' "You came just in time. We ran out of food this morning." Grace spooned a bite to her mouth and blew on it. After she chewed and swallowed the much-needed but bland food, she absently poked her spoon toward his leg. "I want to take a look at your leg after we eat."

Cole shook his head as he shoved a spoonful of beans in his mouth and swallowed. "I'm fine, Grace, really. I'm more concerned about you. How are you? D-did they hurt you?"

The look of concern on Cole's face touched Grace's heart to the very core. She stopped, resting the spoon in the bowl as she gazed into Cole's eyes. "I'm fine, now that you're here."

Cole's heart flip-flopped at the way she was looking at him. "You finish your food," he urged, setting his bowl aside. "I have something important I need to tell you."

Grace peered at him from under the canopy of her lashes, worry creasing her brow. *What now?*

Grace finished her beans and sipped her weak, but hot coffee as Cole helped himself to another cup. The only sound was the crackle of the fire and the intermittent snoring of their two charges.

"First," he said as he shifted himself in front of her, "I want to thank God." He searched Grace's eyes as he continued. "I really had lost all hope of finding you, but God knew exactly where you were, and for that, I'm so thankful." Taking her hand in his, he bowed his head in prayer. His nearness calmed and comforted her. She finally felt safe.

Dear Gracious Heavenly Father, We come to You with grateful hearts to thank You for protecting us and for leading me here to find Grace. You are always with us, no matter what. Even when we feel like giving up, we know that You never will. Thank You for Your provisions and Your many blessings. Amen.

Grace reluctantly pulled her thin hand from his, averting her red-rimmed eyes. Cole understood her feelings all too well, but hoped that what he had to tell her would change everything.

***

Millie Ramsey, with a heavy heart, listlessly climbed out of bed and forced herself to prepare for the day. As she made her way into the kitchen, a wave of warmth surrounded her.

"Mornin' Millie," Jed greeted her with a fresh cup of coffee.

"Good morning, Jed." His kindness brought a smile to her lips.

"Looks to be a fair day for all the festivities, don't ya think?"

Jed scooted the kitchen chair out for Ms. Millie and took a seat opposite her.

"Mmmm...hit's the spot," Ms. Millie remarked, tasting the coffee. "I was hoping it would be a decent day. I thought I'd get up early to get a good start on everything, but it looks like you beat me to it." Her eyes smiled their thank you for the early morning fire and fresh coffee.

As the two old friends sat and talked, Myra and Nate came down to join them.

"Good morning, you two," Myra greeted.

Nate took a seat while Myra poured them both a cup of coffee.

"We were just talking about past Christmases," Ms. Millie told them as they settled at the table.

"Oh?" Nate questioned, looking over his coffee cup as he took a sip of the steaming brew.

"We were talking about my daughter and her lively Christmas spirit," Ms. Millie chuckled as she remembered how excited her daughter, Lenore, had always been at Christmas time.

"Oh, I didn't realize you had a daughter. Did she move away?" Nate settled back in his chair with a creak, and rested his arms on his ample belly.

Ms. Millie's eyes pooled as she told them how a small pox epidemic took the life of her daughter. "She had just turned 18 and had been engaged to be married when she passed."

Emotions played across her face as she smiled in remembrance of her life. "She was always so giddy, sometimes a little too much, wouldn't you say, Jed?" She asked, absently wrapping her hands around the warm mug.

Jed nodded, unable to trust his voice. He had watched the child grow up and felt as if she had been his own. Carl, Ms. Millie's husband, passed away from a massive heart attack when Lenore was six. After that, Jed became more of a father figure than just a friendly handyman.

After a brief stroll down memory lane, Ms. Millie changed the subject. Even though it had been several years now, it was still too fresh to visit for too long.

"Well, I guess we had better get breakfast started, Myra," Ms. Millie sighed as she wiped a tear from her eye with the corner of her apron, "we got a lot to do today."

The two women rose to prepare breakfast as the men bundled up to venture out in the cold to find the 'finest Christmas tree around' as Myra had called it.

As the two women worked side by side preparing a breakfast feast, they talked about family, friends, and the coming festivities.

As the women were placing the dinnerware on the table, they were startled by the sudden sound of the front door slamming up against the wall, shaking the whole house.

"What in the world?" Myra looked questioningly at Millie.

Ms. Millie moved quickly toward the door.

"Hey, watch out for my lamp you two…," she hollered as she hurried to steady the little table they were about to knock to the floor.

Myra turned, silverware still in hand, as her mouth dropped in surprise, "Well, will ya look at that!"

The men were trying to maneuver a very large pine tree through the front door almost knocking over the small end table in the foyer until Ms. Millie caught it. Then the branches flipped against the wall as Ms. Millie stretched out her hand to steady the mirror which was surely next to go.

"Here, let me grab this end," she hollered as she took hold of the snow-covered branches. "Ya could've at least knocked off the snow before you shoved this thing in my nice clean house," she lightly scolded the men.

Jed poked his red face around the end of the tree trunk that had been hiding him from view with a mischievous smile. "Sorry Millie."

Nate could be heard chuckling from behind the tree. "I'm sorry too, Millie. It was my idea to get such a big one."

After they finally managed to wiggle the large pine into the parlor, they all sat breathless due to the struggle of such a large tree. Everyone stood, hands on hips, staring at one of the largest pine trees ever to be wrangled into a parlor.

"It's a biggin', but it sure is pretty," Ms. Millie said, surveying the tree. "Nice and full."

Nate sauntered over, playfully placing his cold hands on the back of his wife's neck.

"Oh!" she squealed as she lightly smacked him on the arm. "What was that for?"

"That, my dear wife," he said as he kissed the tip of her nose, "was for sending me out in the cold in the first place."

Everyone laughed at his amusing smirk as Ms. Millie ushered everyone into the dining room for their Christmas Eve breakfast.

Chapter Thirty-Three

"Whelp," Cole stated as he pulled himself up, "we had better get dinner on and after that I'll go chop some wood. Looks like we're pretty low out there."

"Uh, you said you had something to tell me?" Grace asked disconcertingly, her eyes barely meeting his.

Cole reached for another can of beans out of his knapsack and nodded. "Yes, I do, but first I want to eat."

"Oh okay," she agreed. Her nerves were on edge just thinking about what he needed to tell her. Must he keep her waiting like this? It must be a doozy if he has to wait until after dinner.

Grace accepted the small bowl of beans with a smile and shivered against the cold, pulling her coat more tightly around. Cole finished his beans in record time just as the men were starting to stir. Cole quickly checked their wounds as Grace spoon-fed them, and then they quickly fell back to sleep.

"I'll be back in shortly, you just rest now."

Grace replaced the bowls in the broken washbasin on the wood counter and made her way back over to the table. Rest? How can she rest when her mind was going haywire, swimming with the possibilities of what he had to tell her. Her heart suddenly sank into her gut. Whatever it was, it was serious, she could tell by his tone. Was it Ms. Millie? Was she ill? Jed or Amelia? She tried to focus on tidying up the small room as she finally heard the door creak open.

"Looks like the snow's starting to melt some," Cole stated with a relieved smile, stomping the snow from his boots. "Just in time, too."

Grace raised her brows. She knew it was good news, but what would she do now that her husband was dead? Only God knew. After everything she has been through, she was choosing to trust God with whatever her future might hold.

I am Yours, Lord. I will go where You want me to go and do what You want me to do because I know You have only good planned for my life.

Cole tossed the logs into the stove as the small embers flew out like fireworks. He shifted out of his coat and pulled off his heavy leather gloves. After running his hand through his hair, a nervous trait Grace had come to adore, he pulled out one of the rickety kitchen chairs for Grace and poured them another cup of coffee.

Cole watched the light from the fire dance across Grace's thin pale face. The dark purple bruise on her cheek concerned him almost as much as how thin she was. Worry for her and the babies filled his heart.

Pulling up a chair for Grace, he sat down beside her. Swallowing hard, he plunged ahead. "Grace, when I had my accident," he said, referring to his injured leg, "God led an old man to me in the wilderness to care for me. He told me about a man who had traveled this way this past summer who he had taken in and cared for after a rattlesnake bite. The hours before his death, he was able to witness to this man, and he accepted Christ as his Savior."

Grace smiled, her lips slightly curved. "That's wonderful, but what does this have to do with me?"

Cole squeezed her hand gently. "Grace, I don't know how to say this, so I'll just come out with it...."

That statement alone made Grace's heart somersault. Immediately Grace felt her stomach knot as the pieces were finally coming together.

In her heart, she knew. As her eyes searched his, she could see resignation, sympathy, and concern.

Cole took a deep breath and told her what she had already feared. "That man was your husband."

Even though Grace knew what he was going to say, she could not help the torrent of tears that demanded to fall. Cole scooted closer to her and took her in his arms.

"I-I just need a little time," she said between bouts of emotion.

"Take all the time you need," he reassured her. "I'm going to go out and chop that wood now. You rest."

Grace was grateful for the much-needed time with the Lord as she allowed herself to cry out all of her emotions. It was sad but therapeutic cry.

Starting to feel better, she stole a few moments to wipe her face with a wet cloth and run her fingers though her tangled hair. *Oh what a mess I must be!*

A while later, cheeks and nose red from the cold, Cole walked triumphantly through the door sporting a whole armload of freshly chopped wood and plopped it on the floor next to the stove.

Grace smiled, releasing a weary sigh. "Can I talk to you a minute?"

"Of course."

Grace sighed as she gazed up into those wonderful dark blue eyes, "I don't know what the future holds for me, but I know that God does. I believe He wants me to go back to Garden City, at least for now," she hurried on, "I was hoping that after these men are able to care for themselves, that we could leave, if that's okay with you."

Nothing could have pleased Cole more, and he told her so.

"I agree."

Both pairs of eyes shot towards the raspy voice.

"I-I think we'll be alright. You two need to go home."

Grace was shocked. Luke was telling her to go home. This trip and injury had really changed him. During their many talks, he had told her everything and apologized repeatedly. She agreed not to press charges. She was just grateful that she had a chance to witness to him.

Grace was uncertain. "Are you sure? We can stay another couple days to make sure you're up to it."

Luke shook his head, carefully pulling himself up, leaning on his elbow, "I've hurt you enough, Grace. The last thing I want right now is to ruin your Christmas. Please go…we'll be alright."

"I agree," Cole replied. "We do need to go if we're going to make it home in time, but first I'll cook up that rabbit I got earlier so you both will have somethin' to eat until you're up to cooking for yourself."

Luke reached out his hand to Cole. "I-I don't know what to say, except please accept my apology, and thank you."

***

Later that evening, Ms. Millie and Myra plopped wearily onto the plush couch in the parlor and sighed as they propped their aching feet upon the padded stool.

"Whew," Ms. Millie exhaled, pushing back a stray strand of gray hair, "I feel like we've been working non-stop all day long."

Myra's tired eyes gazed over towards her new friend, "We *have* been working all day Millie."

The two women shared an exhausted laugh.

"It does look beautiful though, doesn't it?" Ms. Millie exclaimed as she gazed around the parlor in appreciation of all of their hard work. They had spent extra time decorating the large Christmas tree with twinkling candles and shiny red and gold ornamental balls. They had adorned the tables and hearth with extra greenery, which added more warmth to the beautiful and serene atmosphere.

"Yes, it does. It makes me feel more festive…how about you?"

Ms. Millie sighed, her smile slipping from her wrinkled face. "It does makes me feel better, but I just can't seem to get into the Christmas spirit with Grace and Cole missing. I worry about them so."

Myra reached over and patted her friend's hand. "I know, Honey. I know."

A little while later, the two women reluctantly pulled themselves from the luxury of the velour sofa to prepare for the Christmas Eve service.

***

As the small group entered the little church, everyone greeted with wishes of a Merry Christmas as Pastor Barton summoned everyone to take a seat as the service began.

After the service was opened in prayer, Julia Barton led the smaller children to the front of the church to lead them in singing a few Christmas carols much to everyone's delight. Applause rang out as the children had finished and quickly took their seats with their parents as Mrs. Barton reached for her Bible and prepared to read the Christmas Story. The only sounds were the occasional cooing of little Nathaniel and the whisperings of the younger children which just added to the delight of the story. It was a nice service, but still did not seem like Christmas.

***

"I heard Mrs. Brewster say tonight that that Mr. Hollister's gonna propose to Maryanne tomorrow," Ms. Millie commented wearily as she stared at the candle-lit tree, cradling a warm cup of tea in her arthritic hands. A warm fire roared in the fireplace as Ms. Millie and Jed rested in the parlor after everyone had retired for the evening, enjoying a little quite time.

"Really?" Jed's eyebrows rose as he repositioned his slippered feet upon the footstool. "I guess it don't really surprise me none, they both seem to want the same thing…money."

Ms. Millie tossed a quick glance at Jed. "Jed, we don't really know that. I just wish they'd both give God a chance, and then maybe they wouldn't feel the need for all those material things. He's all anyone really needs."

Jed bobbed his balding head. "Yep, that's the truth, but a little money doesn't hurt."

Ms. Millie yawned and stretched as she sat her teacup on a nearby tray. "Well, yes, but the Good Lord always gets us by. Anyway, I'd better get to bed…and you need to too Jed, it's gonna be morning before we know it, and Amelia and Adam are coming over first thing."

"Yes'm, jest need to finish my tea."

"Alright then, have a good night, and I'll see you in the morning." Millie lit a small lamp to light the way to her room as Jed stopped her.

"Millie?"

"Yes?" She turned, exhaustion edging her wrinkled eyes.

"Merry Christmas."

Ms. Millie smiled in turn, "Merry Christmas, Jed."

Chapter Thirty-Four

Christmas morning dawned bright and clear as Amelia, Adam, baby Nathaniel, Sandra, Joel, and the guests at the boarding house came together to celebrate Christ's birth.

"Merry Christmas everyone!" Amelia exclaimed, passing little Nathaniel off to his grandmothers awaiting arms. Adam whirled in after her carrying two pumpkin pies, followed by a burst of cold air. Sandra and Joel entered shortly after with rice pudding and cranberry sauce to add to the delicious array of food.

"Come in and take a seat everyone," Ms. Millie urged after a quick hug all around. "We just got breakfast on the table, hope yer all hungry."

The table was adorned with a beautiful new crocheted tablecloth that Ms. Millie had made special for Christmas Day, as well as her best china, and a beautiful ornate centerpiece of a hurricane lamp filled with cranberries, cinnamon sticks and pine.

"It's so good to see everybody. Merry Christmas everyone!" she exclaimed with a big smile. "Shall we pray?"

After the prayer, Sandra leaned over to ask Ms. Millie about the empty chairs at the end of the table.

"Well," she stated matter of factly. "We've all been prayin' for a Christmas miracle, and I'm expectin' it today."

Sandra's eyes misted with tears as she gazed around the table. "You're so right, Millie. We asked the good Lord for a miracle, and we should keep the faith."

After a wonderful breakfast and renewed hope, everyone piled into the parlor around the Christmas tree to exchange their gifts of love.

"Everything's so lovely Millie," Sandra exclaimed as she took the proffered little Nathaniel from Myra. "You both did a beautiful job with the decorations, and the tree...my, how lovely."

At the mention of the tree, Nate chuckled and gave his comical rendition of the story from the day before when they had wrangled the large pine into the parlor almost knocking over everything in the process. There was a round of laughter as everyone to their seat and settled in for the Christmas gift exchange.

The gifts were passed to each person, and as tradition, they all took turns opening their gifts one by one.

Ms. Millie was first as she opened her gift of a wooden breadbox from Jed, Myra, and Nate.

"Oh, it's beautiful," Ms. Millie cried, turning it around to view the sunflowers painted on each side of the box. "Jed, you did a beautiful job, and Myra and Nate, what beautiful painting!"

Jed blushed. "Yer always complainin' of pests gettin' on the bread; this way, ya won't hafta worry about it."

Ms. Millie smiled her thanks as she set the treasured breadbox aside. "Jed, you're next."

Jed squirmed in his seat, not wanting to be the center of attention. He quickly tore open the brown paper wrapping, revealing two new chambray shirts and held them up with a grateful smile.

"I was thinking that ya might need some new church clothes," Ms. Millie explained with a slight wink.

"That's true, Millie. Thought I'd wore this one almost clean through," he replied, lifting up his worn sleeve, which had been patched several times already. "Thank ya."

"Amelia, I believe you're next," Ms. Millie pointed out as they made their way around the circle.

Amelia smiled as she lifted the lid with child-like excitement and let out a squeal of delight.

"What is it?"

Amelia gently pulled out a light fluffy gray kitten.

"Oh, she's beautiful...," she smiled her pleasure as she placed the tiny kitten on her lap and stroked its soft fur. The kitten meowed and nuzzled her hand in greeting.

"She was just weaned, but I heard she comes from a good line of mousers," Adam explained, "Got her from Mr. Mandry, just outside of town."

"What'cha gonna name 'im?" Jed wanted to know as he watched Amelia carefully place the kitten on the floor as it started to explore the room.

"Hmm..." Amelia paused a moment in thought. "I think Smokey suits him."

"Ahh, good name," Adam commented with a smile, cutting the string that was keeping his gift box together with his pocketknife. He looked down and pulled out his gift.

"Wow, these are nice and thick," Adam commented on the heavy dark wool gloves, hat and scarf he pulled from the box. "I can get a lot of good out of these on those cold afternoons delivering mail."

Amelia smiled, her eyes twinkling. "That's why I made them for you. You always seem chilled to the bone when you come back from your rounds."

Adam reached over to give his wife a kiss, noticing little Nathaniel as he squealed in delight at the antics of the kitten playing with a ball of yarn he had batted out of Ms. Millie's knitting basket.

"Joel, your turn." Ms. Millie urged.

Joel squirmed with uneasiness, ran his hand through his blond curls, and reached for his gift.

"Whoee," he whistled aloud as he lifted a new fishing pole up for everyone to see. "Looks expensive, Ma, ya shouldn't have."

Sandra played with the tuff of dark hair on the baby, not knowing if she could trust her voice, "It was your brother's idea. He knows how much you like fishin' in your spare time, so him and some of the boys went in on it together for ya."

Joel wiped his eyes with the back of his sleeve, missing his brother more than he would like to admit.

As they finished opening their gifts, Ms. Millie, Myra, and Sandra excused themselves to the kitchen to finish the preparations their Christmas feast.

Several hours later, the women announced that dinner was ready as they paraded into the dining room with bowls heaping with potatoes, green beans, and ham.

Baby Nathaniel was sound asleep in the cradle as the group made their way to the beautifully set table. Once again, everything looked and smelled delicious; the table was overflowing with bowls and platters of steaming food.

Everyone took their seat and bowed their heads as Ms. Millie said grace.

Dear Gracious Heavenly Father, We come to You today to not only thank Ya for this bountiful feast that You have blessed us with, and friends and loved ones to share it with, but most importantly for Your blessed birth. Please bless those that are hungry and cold, and, please Lord, Ms. Millie's voice cracked with emotion, *"be with Cole and Grace and bring them home soon. We're waitin' expectantly and graciously for our Christmas miracle. Amen.*

Just as the food was to be passed around the table, there was a commotion at the front door.

Ms. Millie, assuming it was William and Maryanne coming over to share their good news, opened the door to come face to face with their Christmas miracle.

Grace could not hold back the tears as she rushed into her arms.

"Oh, my precious Jesus, we got out Christmas miracle!" Everyone spoke at once as the other joined in. All around were hugs and tears as everyone welcomed them home, questions flying.

"Whoa, we'll tell you all about it at dinner," Cole chuckled with a happy heart, eyes dancing. "We traveled a long way for this Christmas dinner, and we're starved!"

Everyone laughed in joy as Grace stole a moment to wipe her face with an offered hanky from Ms. Millie. "First," she said through a veil of tear, "I think we'd better go wash up, we're a mess."

"Here, let me help you dear," Ms. Millie cooed as she ushered Grace to the washbasin. The whole house was bursting with excitement.

Grace patted at her hair. "I must look dreadful…"

"Nonsense sweetheart, you're the prettiest thing I've seen in a long time," Ms. Millie replied softly, pushing a stray piece of hair behind Grace's ear.

Sandra was all smiles as she walked beside her son with her arm wrapped lovingly around his waist. "I'm so proud of you, Cole, and so grateful that you two are back safe and sound."

Cole squeezed his mother and kissed her on the top of the head as he waited for his turn to wash up.

Ms. Millie smiled, wiping joyous tears from her eyes, and reached over to hug Cole.

As they made their way back to the dining room, Cole and Grace both questioned the two empty seats at the end of the table.

"Those are for you two. We've been praying non-stop for your return and you both are our Christmas miracle."

"Amen to that!"

Grace and Cole gazed appreciatively at everyone around the table and smiled their gratitude for the love that surrounded them. During dinner, they filled everyone in on their long and tedious journey.

After many questions, many tears shed, and full bellies, they all retired to the parlor with their coffee to give Grace and Cole their Christmas gifts.

Grace held little Nathaniel, planting a light kiss on his head as a strange noise stole her attention. Looking up, she noticed Jed, with the help of Nate, pulling something rather large out from behind the Christmas tree.

Grace gazed toward Ms. Millie, surprised. "I-I wasn't expecting…"

"Shhh…open it, Honey," Ms. Millie urged softly as she patted the wrapped gift.

Grace carefully unwrapped the beautifully packaged gift, drawing in a deep breath as her eyes surveyed the elegant hand-carved chest.

"Oh, it's exquisite!" Grace lovingly ran her fingers over the detailed carpentry. "Who?"

Ms. Millie smiled. "Jed made it for ya," she said, grinning at the red-faced man beside her. "Look inside, Dear."

Grace smiled at Jed, her eyes filling with tears as she lifted the lid. "Oh, my," she cried, her hand flying to her mouth in surprise after spying several new dresses. Ms. Millie explained that they had belonged to her daughter, and pointed out the baby outfits and baby blankets made by all three women. She picked up every item, individually, exclaiming her joy over each precious item.

Grace was speechless. "I-I don't know what to say…they're all so lovely. I never dreamed…" She reached over and gave Ms. Millie a long hug, followed by Jed, Sandra, Amelia, and Myra, realizing once again that you do not have to be blood-related to be a family.

"Thank you all so much. You've made me feel so blessed," she cried, wiping the tears that were unashamedly falling from her tired, hollowed eyes. *It's good to be home.*

"Cole, it's your turn," Sandra pointed out as she handed him a small gift. All smiles, as he pulled his eyes away from Grace and her beautiful smile, he slowly opened the box as his breath caught in his throat.

"Pa's pocket watch." Cole breathed, choking back the tears that were threatening to spill. He gently turned the watch over in his large hands and read the well-known inscription, *To the man who has already captured my heart.*

He opened the watch and checked the time. "It still works great...5:36," he leaned over and kissed his mother's tear stained cheek and snapped the watch closed. "Thanks, Ma."

"I knew he'd want you to have it. Joel has his pocket knife; now you both have something special of your pa's."

Cole looked over at Joel as a silent message of mutual respect spoke volumes between the two brothers.

The stated time finally registered. "It's after 5:30? Oh my, where has the time gone? If ya both want to join us for service tonight, ya might want to get cleaned up...unless, of course, you're too tired, then we understand." She could see the weariness etched deeply upon their faces.

"Oh, could we?" Grace asked excitedly, looking towards Cole. "It wouldn't seem like Christmas without it."

"Sure, honey, sure," Ms. Millie replied. "Joel, would you mind getting a warm bath ready for Grace?"

Joel turned beet red at the simple request and left to do her bidding.

"Cole, I have an extra tub," she offered.

"No thanks Ms. Millie. I'd like to run home and get ready."

Grace sighed with disappointment. She did not want him to leave, not now, not ever.

Chapter Thirty-Five

Grace leaned back in the large galvanized tub, allowing the warm water to soothe her aching muscles. The moment she relaxed, the babies started to roll around in her belly. She laid there for what seemed like hours just watching them twist and turn within her. Her life had been so topsy-turvy lately that she had not had the time to enjoy her first experience of becoming a mother. She laid her hand upon her bare belly that was poking out of the water wondering what her future held.

All too soon, there was a light tapping on the door. "Grace, are you alright, dear?" Ms. Millie sounded concerned. "It's getting close to 6:30, we need to leave shortly."

"I'm fine, Ms. Millie...I'll be right out."

Hurrying to dry and dress, Grace found herself standing in front of the mirror marveling over the figure she saw before her. Her body was thin, too thin, but her belly was huge and poked out to almost a peak, stretching her skin as far as it would go. She could not believe how much she had changed in just a few months. Her body was tired, but her spirit was soaring. She quickly fixed her hair to the best of her ability, pinched her cheeks, dabbed on a bit of lavender perfume, and hurried out the door.

"You look lovely, my dear," Ms. Millie complimented as she slipped on her heavy wool coat.

"I don't know about that, but I certainly feel better," Grace swiped her freshly washed curls out from under her collar. "Where's everyone else?" Grace questioned, gazing around the empty parlor.

"They went ahead, dear. Come now," she urged, pulling the front door shut, "or we'll be late."

***

As they hurried to join the others in the pew, everyone quickly gathered around Cole and Grace as they welcomed them back before the service began. Grace was flushed with excitement at just being home, however she would have to admit that some of the excitement was due to the very handsome and freshly clean-shaven man standing behind her. Cole and his family occupied the pew behind them, which made Grace just a little bit uncomfortable. She found it hard to control the fluttering of butterflies in her stomach every time he was near; sometimes she wondered if it was the butterflies or the babies that fluttered more. She gently cradled her growing belly with her hands as the piano began to play.

"You look beautiful," came a deep masculine voice from behind.

Her heart fluttered again. "Thank you," she whispered, lowering her lashes. Her heart felt as though it would beat out of her chest.

Grace fought hard to keep her attention on the Christmas service as her mind traveled a dozen different directions.

After the worship service, well-wishers with a torrent of questions surrounded Grace and Cole. As the group started to disperse, her smile quickly faded as she noticed Maryanne talking with Cole. Grace's heart plummeted as she saw them embrace, Cole smiling from ear to ear.

Tears blurred her vision as she quickly excused herself and rushed out of the Church. Cole caught sight of her out of the corner of his eye and hurried after her.

"Grace!"

She kept running as fast as her large belly would allow, holding it for support, ignoring him as he called out to her.

Before she knew it, he grabbed her shoulders and turned her to face him. "What happened? Why are you crying?" Cole tried to pull her towards him so he could comfort her, but she angrily pushed him away.

"Don't do that," she cried as a sob escaped her throat.

"I'm sorry. Can you at least tell me what's wrong?"

"I just want to be alone," Grace turned to hurry back to the boarding house, shrugging off his hands.

Cole followed. "Grace, it's too cold out here. At least let me drive you home."

Suddenly, beautiful intricate snowflakes drifted all around them. The streetlights cast a hazy glow making it look almost like someone had shaken a snow globe and they were the small people inside.

"I can make it. It's not that far. You can go back to Maryanne now," she sniffed. "I'll be ok."

Cole was confused, "Maryanne? Why would I want to go back to her?"

Grace stopped walking and turned around, holding her belly as a pain shot through her. Ignoring it, she went on.

"I saw you, Cole. You two were hugging and whispering." A fresh stream of tears started all over again. "I thought…"

Cole closed the distance between them and took her gloved hands in his, unaware of the contractions taking hold of her body.

"You thought what?" he asked softly, his eyes searching hers.

Grace was frustrated. How was she to tell a man that she has only known a short time, after becoming a widow and being pregnant with her late husband's children, that she was falling in love with him?

Cole could see her wavering. "You want to know what I think."

"What?" she sniffed.

"I think you misunderstood why I was talking to Maryanne."

Grace's eyes dropped, suddenly realizing that she could no longer see her feet due to her expanding belly. It almost made her laugh until another contraction seized her.

Cole gently lifted her chin so she would see the truth in his eyes. "I congratulated her on her engagement to Hollister."

Grace's eyes widened as big as saucers, "Really?"

Cole smiled, lightly brushing away a tiny snowflake from her eyelash. "Really. Now if you don't mind, I have something I'd like to discuss with you."

As they ascended the steps of the boarding house, Cole led her to the porch swing and brushed off the snow.

"Grace, I know you've been through a lot lately."

Grace tried to speak, but she could only gasp as the pain came again shooting a stronger contraction throughout her body. Unable to ignore it anymore, she grabbed her belly and moaned.

"What's wrong?" Cole became alarmed at the pained look clouded her delicate features. "Is it the babies?"

Grace nodded as Cole quickly scooped her up and carried her to her room.

Moments later, everyone came bustling through the door with festive excitement as a panicky Cole raced out, pushing everyone aside.

Alarmed, Ms. Millie and Amelia ran upstairs to where Grace was doubled over, crying out in pain.

"Oh, Grace," Ms. Millie cried, rushing to her side. "I'm here, Sweetheart; you just lay back and try to take it easy. Cole went to get Doc."

Amelia hastily went for the supplies as Ms. Millie prepared Grace for the upcoming birth.

Moments later the doc came rushing up the stairs, black bag in hand, as another contraction seized Grace's thin body. The doctor was shocked at how thin and pale Grace was, but went quickly to work.

Ms. Millie was gravely worried and prayed earnestly for Grace and the unborn babies.

Amelia snuck silently out of the room and hurried downstairs to ask everyone to pray.

Cole was white as a sheet as he made his way over to one of the chairs and plopped down. Everyone followed him into the parlor and joined hands in prayer.

Nate, after realizing that he was the only one not overcome with great emotion, cleared his throat and bowed his head in prayer.

Our Heavenly Father, We come to you again, to ask you to be with Grace and the babies. She's very weak Lord and we pray that your Holy Spirit will give her the strength that she needs to deliver these little ones safely, and be with Doc and Ms. Millie as they care for her. We thank Thee again for bringing them safely home to us. Now we lift them to you once again. In Jesus's name we pray, Amen.

Cole sat with his head in his hands as the soft murmur of voices faded around him, pleading with the Lord to protect Grace and the babies.

Finally, after all these years of searching for someone to spend the rest of his life with, in a matter of minutes it could all vanish. Cole remained in prayer until his mother came over and knelt in front of him.

"Cole, are ya alright son?" Sandra gently rubbed her sons trembling hands in comfort.

"Ma, I can't lose her." The anguish in his voice broke Sandra's heart.

"I know honey." She grabbed him by the arms, forcing him to look at her. "She will be alright sweetheart, you'll see."

Cole did not look too convinced. He knew how frail she was. Fear ripped through his heart as he thought of his future without her.

Upstairs, as Grace lay withering in pain, Ms. Millie held her hand with each contraction, gently wiping her brow. She looked expectantly at Doc, waiting for his permission for her to push.

"It's alright honey, the contractions are coming closer now. If ya feel the urge to push, go ahead, Doc said yer ready."

Grace grunted and groaned, pushing several times with all her might until a tiny pink body plunged right into the doctors waiting hands.

"It's a boy," Doc hollered from the foot of the bed as he quickly wiped out the baby's nose and mouth.

Within minutes, Grace moaned again as the next contraction immediately brought forth the second baby. Doc was swift in his maneuverings as he handed the first child to

Ms. Millie before the second one made its entrance, which shot out as quickly as the first. The doc laughed with relief. "It's a girl…two healthy babies and all in record time!"

Ms. Millie cried out in joy, "Praise God!"

Grace was silent as Doc and Ms. Millie cleaned up the protesting infants and walked over to show her the babies.

"Here's your babies, little mama," Ms. Millie cooed as she tucked the blanket more securely around her thin body. "Grace? Don't ya want to hold your babies?" Ms. Millie asked softly as she laid one child in the crook of her arm. Almost immediately, before Ms. Millie was to let go of the baby, Grace's arm became limp, falling to the floor. Ms. Millie snatched up the baby quickly. "Doc, what's wrong with her?"

Doc Miller quickly laid the second baby down on the bed and hurried to Grace's side. Her breathing was labored and her heartbeat was slow. Doc looked up, stethoscope still in his ears. "It doesn't look good, Millie."

"Frank!" A pool of blood was soaking slowly through Grace's sheets. "What's happening?"

Doc Miller quickly administered the needed medication to help stop the bleeding, checked her vitals and treated her the best he knew how. Ms. Millie fell on her knees in tears, both babies still crying, as she petitioned the God Almighty to save her precious Grace.

Downstairs, as time slowly crept by, everyone had rejoiced at hearing the crying babies, but worry set in as no one came downstairs.

Concerned, Amelia offered to go up to see what was happening. As she made her way up the steps, her heart quickened at the heart-wrenching cry escaping from Grace's room.

Terrified, Amelia tapped lightly on the door, her heart beating a mile a minute. After a few silent moments, Ms. Millie opened the door and peeked out, face drawn and eyes red.

Amelia just stared in shock. *What was happening?* Ms. Millie slowly and silently opened the door a little farther as Amelia slipped in.

As her eyes fell upon Grace's bed, she gasped and cried out. Grace was thin, pale, bleeding, motionless…lifeless.

"I-Is she…?"

Doc laid a comforting hand upon her shoulder, his head hanging low. "No, she's holding her own, but it doesn't look good. She's lost a lot of blood…"

Amelia knelt down by Grace's bed and reached for her friend's thin cold hand. She sat there sobbing, tears falling softly upon her bed. "Grace, don't leave us. Your babies need you…we need you." The babies continued to cry, still, Grace did not move.

Amelia, unable to control her emotions, gently took the crying infants and silently left the room.

As Amelia reached the bottom of the stairs, arms cradling the infants, everyone knew instantly that something was horribly wrong.

"Grace!" Cole quickly ran up the steps two at a time and burst through the bedroom door. His face crumpled at the sight of her.

"Talk to her Cole, she needs you." Silently, Ms. Millie and Doc, after doing everything they could, left Cole alone to say goodbye to the love of his life.

Cole sat at her bedside for what seemed like hours crying and praying. He recited scripture verses and anointed her with oil.

"I'm not giving up on you Grace," he whispered stubbornly in her ear. "You hear me?"

Suddenly, he heard a sudden intake of breath as she moved her thin hand under his. Gently and softly, he ran his fingers down her sallow cheek, "Grace I love you and I need you…"

He searched her pale face for any signs of acknowledgement as she mouthed the words, with barely a whisper, that he had been waiting so long to hear.

"I love you, too."

Had he imagined it? Ever so gently, she squeezed his hand as a tear slid down her cheek.

Immediately he hollered for the doctor, not wanting to leave her side. Doc Miller came running up the stairs. He checked her heartbeat; it was stronger. He checked her breathing; it was easier. He checked her bleeding: it had stopped.

The doc shook his head in amazement. "I've never seen anything like it."

She had been on the brink of death and had lost so much blood. There was only one explanation the doctor could give them…it was a miracle.

***

Days later, Cole was sitting in the chair next to Grace holding the infant baby boy, a smile playing about his lips

"Ya know we can't keep calling the babies him and her forever. Have ya thought of any names yet?"

After seeing the babies for the first time, Cole fell instantly in love with them.

"I really hadn't had much time to think of any," Grace whispered, snuggling her sleeping baby girl closer to her. "What do you think?"

Cole gazed at her with such tender love, "Well, how about you come up with the first names and I'll come up with the last name?"

Grace laughed lightly. "And, what do you have in mind for their last name?" she asked weakly, playing along.

Cole leaned over, gently placing a tender kiss on Grace's pale lips. "Well, I thought Matthews sounded just as good as any."

Grace anxiously searched Cole's dark blue eyes.

"Are you sure? I…."

Cole gently lifted his finger to her lips, never taking his eyes off hers. "I've never been more sure of anything in my life."

Cole reached into his pocket with the baby still in his arms, maneuvered himself on one knee beside her bed, and extracted a thin gold band. "My dear sweet Grace, will you marry me?"

Grace's eyes sparkled with unshed tears as her heart swelled with pure joy. "Oh yes, my love, for you had already captured my heart long ago."

Made in the USA
Middletown, DE
10 March 2022